The
Navvyman

Nicky Brennan

The Navvyman
Nicky Brennan

Paperback Edition First Publishing in Great Britain
in 2015 by aSys Publishing

eBook Edition First Publishing in Great Britain
in 2015 by aSys Publishing

ISBN: 978-1-910757-06-2

aSys Publishing
http://www.asys-publishing.co.uk

Contents

Chapter 1

I was walking through the town that I had come from in Ireland, on a visit to see my father, who at ninety-one was failing, when someone hailed me: "John Willie Harn, yes it's you isn't it"; I turned towards the person and failed to recognise them, possibly because the moniker John Willie meant the person had to date from my school days; I had been called John Willie after my father, my second name was actually Thomas; "you have the advantage of me" I said to my addressee, a man about my own age of fifty-eight, "I fear I don't recognise you". The man came nearer and hesitated, as he took in more of my appearance. " I'm John Quigley, we were called the two Johns at school, don't you remember?

"Of course, of course, just old age taking its toll", I replied.

I hadn't seen him since just after, I left school almost exactly forty years ago. I asked how he was getting on, for want of a better enquiry to cover forty years," fine yourself", "getting there": my usual response, and it was true, I still had to get anywhere worth going.

"This meeting is particularly fortunate: the old class is getting together for a fortieth year reunion tonight, and you were one of the very few we couldn't contact, and here you are", "do you know my father the real John Willie", I replied cautiously, "he's not doing so well: not too surprising at his age, thus I'm not too sure of my movements at the moment". He hesitated as much I am sure due to my appearance as the mention of my father: though I was well turned out, the life I had lived, had no doubt imprinted itself somewhat upon my features: therefore, those features would be grim; "well I'm sorry to hear your father's failing, and such considerations must come first of course, but if it were possible it would be great, and it's only one night, never to be repeated". It was a good argument. "Well it is certainly tempting, tell me what the arrangements are, and without making any promises I can't keep, I'll do my best to attend" I replied. "It's in Jimmy Burke's place, you remember Jimmy"; I could just, "eight-thirty onwards, do your best, as I say there will be fewer of us around for the eighty year reunion ", "I will certainly do that" I replied. He turned away then back" oh wives and family welcome, we'll accommodate them": that will be easy in my case I thought.

I upped my pace: not wishing for any more unexpected reunions, to my sister's house where I was staying, or rather being allowed to stay, given the family situation.

I told her of the meeting, she asked if I was going, I said, I didn't know, "probably best not, it's hardly as if, you'll have more to boast about than any of the others": never one to mince words old sis. "Well there is nothing all that likely to occur in dad's condition in the immediate future, so just for your sakes, I'm thinking my staying away may look a little strange". "Leave any concern of our affairs entirely up to us," my sister responded abruptly. I decided not to go, but as luck would have it, as we visited my father, another member of the class of, 73, a neighbour of my father's and the one person in the class with whom I had kept even fleeting contact, popped in to see him at the nursing home; my father was spritely, she brought up the reunion: thus I had no excuse not to go. Talking it over with my sister I decided a brief visit, passing between people without going into too much detail of my life, would be the best measure; not wishing the family to appear in any way strange or perhaps I should say stranger, my sister agreed with this.

I had a suit, so I dolled myself up, and my sister left me at the pub: Jimmy's, at ten saying she'd return at half eleven sharp; the excuse for the brief appearance: our father. I'd appear, do the rounds, have no in depth conversations, and convention satisfied: leave.

I entered, in a hesitant manner, into a crowded pub. Faces turned, middle aged, complacent, generally fairly plump: people who were used to the better things of life.

Though many faces, rang faint notes of familiarity, I couldn't really grant names to the faces. I looked for the one or two faces, that I should know, keeping what I thought was a convivial expression on my face. I located John Quigley fairly quickly. He came over to me," I decided I had to make a quick call, but I don't have too much time on my hands, with how things are" I said," of course that's understood, the main thing is you came. There are three missing: Joan Chambers, Mc Gowan that was: cancer, God help us, she has little time left I'm told, and of course Frank Gorman and Willie Fox. I could barely remember these three, and had only heard of Willie Fox's death: on a building site years ago. "Terrible" I said "remind me again what happened to Frank Gorman," berating myself for not making better enquiries with my sister: "it was three years ago; he was a property developer you know: Frank had big ideas of himself. Well they say it was suicide but other tellings say he borrowed money from the wrong people you know: the great false boom." "I remember now" I said, feeling some relief that I wouldn't be the least successful of the class: I was at least still alive, "one in ten the time is taking its toll" I said. "It is indeed and that's why I feel tonight is so important: we may not get many more chances to get together like this; and yet it seems such a short time since we were at school". I could hardly agree with that statement. John brought me around: "hello, long time no see, you haven't changed a bit," "I'm afraid that's not true, but you're looking well yourself John Willie, well now that's one for the books: it must be forty years", "well that's just what it is, heh, heh heh" . We moved fairly quickly as I told John Quigley that time was not on my side". What are you at, construction, yourself, manager of a nursing home, Garda inspector, teacher, civil service? well done," no lingering for too many details of one's own career to be given; the most successful were the Mullen twins: Dermott, was an accountant with his own accountancy firm and also a local councillor, Muriel now Mc Cormack, head teacher of the big secondary school in the nearest big town; children of the local gombeen man: old Jack Mullen, auctioneer, publican and fixer, their success was due to their contacts, for if memory served me correctly, they had little in the line of brains: some things held constant in good old Ireland. " Married yourself," "no never, could find a woman hard up enough, heh, heh, "you might be as well off," "I don't know about that, but it's doubtful I will change now," on to the next person. I eventually joined a group including the woman who was visiting my father, and talked about generalities for a time: the state of the country, how things were in England, etc; when the questioning became too localised:," what do you do exactly in the buildings,": I noticed the time, saying I had a short time left, and though my father seemed ok, I had had no plans to come here originally, just could not miss the opportunity; but the purpose of the visit was my father; this was accepted, but as word of my departure spread, the call went up for a group photograph. I stood a bit off the middle of the middle row: as innocuous as possible; but not innocuous enough: "John Willie can you smile"; I thought I had been; I tried harder: "no really, that's more a grimace" after some other failed attempts, I could only revert to looking in the mirror behind the bar: I saw what they were talking about, after a supervising amount of effort I managed; I stood in for the photograph. "Just a matter of adjusting the makeup," I quipped lamely on my way out. On the silent journey home with my sister I thought what a just reflection on my life: I needed the assistance of a mirror to form a smile.

Chapter 2

During that silent journey, I began to reflect on the past. What went so wrong with my life? I was born the fourth of five children, of a small farmer cum postman. In the Ireland of the fifties, sixties and seventies, we were as a family slightly better off than the average having a small wage as well as the farm: we had for instance a car, most did not. Nuala that I was staying with was the oldest: seven years older than me, she had gone to England, qualified as a nurse, married a mechanic from the next county, and had managed to come home when her two sons were young; she worked in a nursing home, her husband in a local garage. They had managed; her two sons were married and gone, one to Dublin the other Australia. The next: my brother Bill had inherited the farm, expanded it somewhat, never married, and was now a crusty tight old man, gone to seed. The next Eamon was the family success, a guard or policeman, he was married with two kids, both now teachers, and had retired with the rank of inspector; though he was once the member of the family I was closest to, he now barely acknowledged me. Then Muriel seven years younger than me; the mistake she sometimes called herself, but that label suited me better in a lot of ways. She had gone to England in the great exodus of the eighties: first a checkout assistant; she attended night school: becoming a sectary then a legal sectary; married a plumber had a daughter, broke up with her husband, made up with him, had another daughter now fourteen; they returned to Ireland in the heady days of the boom, and they were now under financial pressure. Middle of the road for an Irish family; at least until you got to me.

Life started off normal enough: I was born in the middle of fifty five. My childhood was reasonably happy in the unthinking way childhoods are: I went to school, suffered some bullying and some sibling rivalry, but nothing out of hand; I was the first of my family to complete a secondary level education; my elder sister and older brother completing three years; my oldest brother just finished primary school: he was destined for the 'place'; such was the way in Ireland in those days; long after secondary education was 'de rigueur' in every other developed country. These habits lingered: fifty nine joined the class originally; thirty left at the midway point: the inter cert, to farm land or follow trades, which would benefit them, when they went abroad to work, as most expected to and eventually did. I was in general a bit above average academically, but in no way outstanding. In the middle of seventy three, I did the final exam, the leaving cert, and got on alright: two honours but good ones, three honour grades in lower papers or pass subjects, all safely passed; good enough to pursue an arts, commerce or science degree at university and become a teacher if it were possible to pay for it: which it was not. I fell between the stools: not good enough or at least not rich enough for a profession, too good for a trade. Directionless I set off in life on an orientation that I would keep.

Who was that young man, just an adult in seventy three that left that school?

Physically to give an easy start to that answer, I was mister average: five foot eight and a half though I would still grow another inch; shorter than either of my brothers or father, slightly heavier than average build, fairly strong, fairly regular if plain features, blue eyes brown hair: common in every way.

Certain elements of inferiority existed, as could be expected from the youngest and smallest of three brothers; having had a slightly better education, this inferiority was probably compensated for by having a somewhat more intellectual bearing: ye're bigger but I'm smarter. Socially I was not particularly popular or unpopular. There had been girlfriends but they moved on fairly quickly as was the way with teens. Sports: football, a little boxing: neither good nor bad. I had no particularly outstanding qualities or deficiencies;

no strong interests in any particular occupation. Career advice was along the lines that I should get a white collar job, given my "good" education; what job wasn't specified. Will you not go into the civil service, the guards, the bank, the post office, an insurance firm etc: were the suggestions made. I tried them all: the civil service: your Irish isn't good enough; in the past forty years I never heard of a civil servant claim to have once used Irish; the bank: my sporting prowess or rather lack of it seemed to attract interest: I was placed on a panel; in forty years I have never heard of anyone, placed on one of those panels, being called up for service. The post office: two honours in the leaving cert is too good to be wasted on a job like a post office clerk. The insurance companies: "what background have you got in insurance," what background had any school leaver; but therein lay the clue: background meant someone to give you the pull: a relative, a connection, a payoff: money or "services". In Ireland a permanent pensionable job was attractive, more than just being able to do the job was expected, and if that "more" was good enough, well being able to do the job itself wasn't that important. The guards: you're not tall enough: I was five feet eight and a half, the rules stated you had to be five foot nine: at least that rejection contained merit. There was to be no white collar job.

Ireland was at that time going through, the first flush period of the then fifty year old free state: a very belated attempt at industrialisation was showing some results, the largesse of successful returning emigrants, and entry into the European economic community, meant that for the first time in the state's history, more young people could expect a job at home, than would have to leave the country. A job meant in practice, a building site, a factory, warehouse or pub; low pay, poor conditions and certainly nothing permanent, but more than people had before: therefore valued. If one was to complain in public about these jobs, the refrain quickly arrived: "tad and t'was different in our day when we had to borrow the money from the priest, to get a passage on a cattle boat to England, so we could get a job": you were quickly reminded of where you were, and of your good fortune to live in such affluent times.

A building site near my home was tried: "sure you're probably a bollix, you have the look of one any ways. I'm sick of lazy young fucks coming in here expecting a free wage from me"; I didn't trouble that man any further.

I tried the one factory in town: "you're here for a handy shift at the factory are ye", "I never said I expected a handy anything" I replied; he would put me on a panel alright but he was doubtful of me.

The hotel: it was the backend of the year, the slack period, I had hardly much business going into the hotel trade if I didn't know that.

The agricultural cooperative store outside the town: there was ten on the list ahead of me.

November came; I signed on the dole and travelled further afield. Hints at one's lack of progress became strong: "your boots are a long time under the table at this stage", there is supposed to be plenty around: what's wrong with you", "x, y and z have got jobs why not you: you have the best education in the house".

I thought to apply for a trade: "ye did a leaving cert and ye' re going for a trade", yes I didn't realise than having a leaving cert barred you from having a trade"," well the courses have started and you will have to wait until next June to reapply".

A friend of mine equally without "the pull" tried the guard s ; he was a very tall strongly built lad and obviously made an impression: there had to be so many that could actually do the job, for instance: breaking up a pub brawl; the local sergeant did his best for him:, " join the army for a year; go in for as much physical combat training as possible, and then you'll get into the guards,": without the pull it was an uphill pull to get any decent job.

I tried the nearest big town, which had never been a very successful town: the answers were the same: "sure we have enough to do to take care of our own here," I'd be thinking there would be a better chance of a job around your own town. Johnny "X" and young David "y" couldn't get a job here but did in your town," "if you can't get on in your place: that's doing well; I don't know what you're expecting here: that's not doing well," were a few of the variations on the rejection theme. The biggest hotel in town now it was approaching Christmas: not a slack period: "would there ever be anything wrong with you that you can't get work in your own town"; I was trying to get a job as a dishwasher: to get some employment experience under my belt. A brief visit to Dublin the capital: try again after the Christmas.

Uncle Bat (Bartholomew), my mother's brother visited us before Christmas. He was a large florid, aggressively ignorant and proud man. Some years before he had spent eight years in England, and somehow accumulated a sizable sum of money, with which he bought a large farm and pub near his home place some ten miles from us. He relied mainly on his brother to work the farm: he had only small farm and needed the paltry hard earned stipend his brother gave him; the pub he mainly ran himself, which being the only pub in that local area gave a steady income; of late he had added the small local shop to his empire: his wife ran this and helped with the pub and farm as well as rearing four daughters: I never saw the woman seated or in remaining still for any length of time. My mother was clannishly supportive of all her family, but even she voiced doubts about how Bat got his money. Upon this visit Bat decided to wake up his indolent nephew:" young John what is this I hear, that you're dossing and not getting a job: you're turning out to be a right no good", "I'm trying hard, I just can't to get anything". "He is trying," my mother interjected. Bat hooked his thumbs under his lapels," Maryann my sister do you not remember how t' was in our day, or have you forgotten; John Harn I had to borrow ten pounds from the priest to get a passage on the cattle boat to get to England, when I was only eighteen to get a job," "now Bat you got the money from our father and you were twenty two," my mother interjected. Bat greatly insulted at any assault on his proud record of success in life roared," Maryann my dear sister, I'm attempting to help you here: I doubt very strongly that you have a bad rearing on your hands here, and that your effort in rearing him is going for naught and I'm trying to rescue the situation for you. Incidentally I did get money from the priest, I just got the bare passage from the old man". He resumed his assault on me: "its a lot better today than times gone by: there's any amount of work around; every fellow that can be bothered getting off his arse atoll has a job, what's wrong with you? " "It must be a lot better over your way, I'll be over straight after Christmas, to take advantage of this prosperity". "You're a cheeky little bastard, and all; is it lip like that you give the people you're cadging work from: small wonder you're not wanted anywhere" roared Bat. The work of correction continued: "I'm telling you straight now Maryann: that yourself and John Willie need to get the boot and the stick into action upon this boyo's arse: or ye will have disaster on your hands". "It's only been five months since he left school Bat". "Five months Maryann. There is two lads: the Mc Court brothers who are plastering on price in Dublin; and they've made over fifty pounds a week in the last five months that one thousand pounds: the price of a very decent second hand car: that's five months for ya. I repeat that was all right when there was nothing around: like in our day, but not today. A serious awakening is necessary here". "Could you point me in any direction uncle Bat: if you are so anxious to assist me?" "Everyplace, my cheeky young dosser: there's work everyplace: that is of course for them that wants it". My mother motioned me to leave, to allow Bat to cool down. The consensus in the family after Bat left was that he was right in what he said, if a bit over the top.

Christmas was cold that year in every way, except for the weather. I could now legally drink but hadn't the money: I drank more during the past two Christmases, when it was strictly illegal for me to drink. I constantly met class mates that seemed to be doing better than me: Dermott Mullen spoke expansively on the great time he was having in Dublin studying accountancy, and the great hopes he had for the future; he even affected a Dublin accent.

Patricia Whelan told me of the great time she had studying to be a teacher, and commiserated with me on my lack of success:," you could well be there yourself: you were well as good as some of them that are": that was, I reflected only too true. Worse than the collage "elite", which were few in number were the more regular class-mates: all who seemed to have something: civil service, training to be a plant engineer, training to be an insurance agent, a hotel chef, a hotel manager: everyone seemed to have something and the fact I had nothing seemed to take them aback; really, not yet, isn't about time you got something, what's wrong, were some of the comments. I met Paddy O Donaghue, who had left at the midlevel to become a plasterer. Though I never got much trouble from him: he had been the hard man in the class, and I was relieved when he left, and considered by staying on I would do better than him someday. He was returning from England and was full of himself:" I often make over one hundred pounds a week on price. It sounds very good I might try it myself," I replied not facetiously as I once would have, but with some genuine consideration of the option. "Yes but you have to be well fit to handle yourself: it's a though old town: if I remember rightly you weren't that handy with the fists, and there you need to be". "Well I wouldn't be going in for professional boxing if I went there" I replied. "Laugh if you want, but come over and see for yourself if you don't believe me". As the night(s) wore on and the drink went in the commentary and "advice" grew blunter: "surely man you must be able to get something, it's no use restricting yourself to home territory you need to go further afield," and eventually," I wonder if you're all that pushed either: like I mean, there's a fair amount around". In the past I had dreamt of that first adult Christmas: freedom to do as I liked ; I'd be at collage, have a job, possibly a car, a girlfriend; I'd defiantly be going someplace: in short I'd be a young man going progressing in life. The reality was in complete contrast to this longstanding dream. I didn't go out in the New Year.

I pulled myself together: it was only five months; I had been a bit localised and unfocused in my search, a new year should mean new chances; and if that didn't work out, well there was always England or even further afield America, Canada or Australia.

I started in Dublin going back to the places that told me to return after Christmas: "sure this is the slack period after Christmas: what are you expecting we'd have now". "Why did you tell me to come back after Christmas": "attitude like that will hardly get you a job, my man,"" I mustn't been thinking straight at that time," or more honestly: "all we wanted to do, was to get rid of you". After two week's hard sustained effort all I garnered was: an odd 'maybe next month, keep in touch, when the weather improves in the spring".

By February I was wondering if there was anything wrong with me.

There were other changes; our farm was a small mixed dairy farm; originally about forty six acres, but expanded by my father to sixty two: a small poor farm, but with a small postman's wage: sufficient ; it was always known and accepted that my brother Bill would inherit the farm, but that all appeared a long time away, and we all took a hand in helping to run it, even when we were at school we all had our chores, and since leaving school I had done more work about the place; however after that Christmas, Bill started to take over work I was doing: impinging on jobs I had already started; first I accepted this, then queried it: "what's wrong, I could do it: I was at nothing else?"; finally Bill drew me aside in late February, and asked me if I realised that he was the one that was going to inherit the place; I had never thought anything else: another change in my status was taking place: I was becoming surplus to requirements. I never could be said to be the life of the party, but was always one of the gang on any night out in the pub or at a dance, but this changed: I became at best a clinger on, not welcome, but in enough with the crowd not to be spurned the occasional time I did venture out: money constraints and status of a dosser cutting the number of these forays which had the perverse effect of cutting or weakening contacts that could have helped my pursuit of work, also I was dull and withdrawn when out, which worsened the situation. One of the good points of growing up in the society that I did, was that there was a strong practice and tradition of neighbourliness extending particularly to children: people had time for you, were friendly; this changed; it perhaps had something to do with my now adult status, but it also emphasised my unemployed status: my dosser status, and lead to a further diminution of my self-esteem, and made me less likely to seek their assistance in my plight. I had a slight habit of daydreaming, of non-concentration; now this habit increased and tended to compensate for my lack of success: "what I would do eventually despite my present circumstances, and show up those I more and more thought of as against me": this caused me to further isolate myself from others, even my family: which did nothing to help my situation.

There were those also, who would have taken advantage had they been able; John and Pat Moran were two brothers in their late twenties; smallish, fat and distinctly bad looking; they were bullies with that instinctive ability of bullies to recognise vulnerability in others. Both were standing outside a public house in the town one evening, when I crossed over to their side, on my business of buying a few things for the house; they spotted me, and out of no place decided to have a go: "well if it isn't the dosser of the Harns; do you realise that people like us have to work hard to provide dole for lazy cunts like you". "Well, we can't be careerists like you two working on your uncle's pig farm" I responded. They did work for their uncle on his pig farm; a job even their father was heard to say was the only job they were suited for. They took immediate insult at this slur on their hard work: "fuck you, you little dossing bastard, running down hard working men like us: we'll teach you a lesson"; and both started to approach me in an aggressive manner. My brother Eamonn came upon this scene by chance; a newly minted guard, and over six foot tall, he had the reputation of being well able to handle himself. "What's this, two against one; let's do things fairer than that; let's go down that alley way and have a fair fight two brothers against two brothers": this changed things the two Morans were now seriously on the back foot. "Ah its guard Harn" said John the slightly fatter, older and stupider of the two:" well we don't want to go to jail so we just have to back away," I don't have any uniform or warrant card on me, so being a guard doesn't come into it". "Sure we weren't serious atoll, we were only joking, but he took insult at it, there's no call for any aggro," said Pat. "No, well any time you want any aggro, you can have it as long as its man to man with him or me or any other Harn," said Eamonn. They went into the pub from whence shouts of "I told you two to get out" were heard. It was only two drunken bullies: losers with an inferiority complexes acting out: they should have been ignored; but my situation was affecting me: I was oversensitive and lacking judgement;

Eamonn statement as we parted," it is time though, you got some job" was the worst part of the entire episode to me. I stayed away from people because I perceived them as looking down on me: this worsened my position as contacts were the best way to get work ; in turn people who perhaps could have helped me now kept their distance sensing an unfriendliness in me: in short I was becoming something of an oddity.

March: Galway, Athlone, Limerick and Cork: slight variations in the same theme of rejection, but in different accents. In late seventy three there had been a fuel crisis, and early in seventy four this was having an effect in Ireland: firms were not so much not leaving people go, but were reluctant to take people on or expand in any way; this in no way helped me: the reply I often got was "well a year ago, eight months ago, six months ago, we were expanding but things are too uncertain at the moment, we'll put you on a panel".

Paddies day: I stayed at home; even as a child I had gone to some parade or somewhere: I was turning in on myself. No less than twelve smaller towns were canvassed: the same result.

I became more and more concerned with myself: my problems, my lack of progress, how I was viewed by others and my hopes for the future, hopes which started out as fantastical daydreams but rapidly degenerated into epics of self-flagellation and despair: both sides of a scenario that avoided reality which existed in the centre of these two poles of the escapist imagination I frequently dwelt in.

Easter arrived; at this stage even my family encouraged me to go out and socialise; Eamonn offered me a "loan" of twenty pounds: near a week's wages for him; I declined it, with the option of availing of it later. I ventured out, prepped up well and self-counselled to keep a jovial demeanour, I did my best to play the jolly reveller. Initially in any encounter, all went well: " aha John Willie, long time no see, how's she cutting, etc; but after a time the subject always turned to jobs, despite my efforts to steer away from the subject, after the first few times I met people. "What man nothing yet", it's getting on a bit now, nearly a year out of school", "what are you doing wrong", were some of the comments offered; officious advice followed:" try the civil service again", " what about the big building site where they are putting up the oil refinery in Kerry", "C I E: the national transport organisation", "why not give England a go", "you could try the army for a year, in place of nothing better", were some of the more sensible suggestions; after a time my advisors took it upon themselves to give me a boost: "you know man a year missed is a long time out", to" I doubt behind it all your lazy, you just couldn't be that unlucky": that insult would have in time gone by, earned an invite to "come outside", but so beaten down was I, that it was let slide. People revel in the misfortunes of others: and some predate upon the misfortunate, often masquerading as concerned, but the runt of the litter is always picked on. In my sensitized condition, this dampened my mood despite my best efforts, and my social diversion became a burthen. The second and third night: the same. At the end of the last night I went out, Paddy O Donaghue came as far as me and offered me a lift to England in a few days' time. He was one man I didn't expect to offer anything positive to me. Paddy was a hard man and I still wary enough of him to forgo such a badly needed chance; I thanked him and said that I was certainly interested but I was expecting the results from a number of jobs I had applied for and would give things this last chance, seeing I had put so much effort in already; there were no quips about professional boxing this time.

Easter Tuesday brought uncle Bat; he was coming from the house having completed his visit, and failing to find his prey in: he made up for it by pulling up and getting out of his car to come over to where I was helping Willie with some fencing around the sheds:" aha if it isn't hardworking John Harn; no job yet eh. But of course you wouldn't heed poor ould Bat, when he attempted to awaken you last Christmas and here you are still, sitting on your lazy arse". I left for fear I'd do something, and went into the nearby cow house from which you could hear what was being said outside from the small air holes in the walls: this was a well-known spying technique in the country, something that uncle Bat was well aware of. "Willie it's you who will have to go out and get a job despite the fact you were always the one that was in for the place: for that brother of yours is good for nothing else, if indeed he's fit for the

15

place" roared Bat: to be sure he was heard. Willie was quieter but I still could hear what he said; "it's getting desperate now uncle Bat; you wouldn't know of anything going", "tomorrow morning if I thought he was a good man; but if I sent that man to mates of mine that I know have work: I doubt I'd only end up making enemies for myself". "What's to be done uncle Bat"; "I don't know; it's your mother and father spoiling him I doubt; certainly there was no dossers in the Mc Namaras": his side of the family. I left unable to listen to anymore; had I been in a more relaxed and completive mood I would have realised that Bat never put himself out too far in the line of hard work: giving orders to his brother, his wife, and the barmaid in his pub were the most strenuous of Bat's exertions.

In late April I applied for a trade from the state training agency; this was early, but I was determined to get in, in good time this year. About three weeks later I had to do a manual dexterity test: basically fiddling around with washers and bolts, to presumably show your hands were working; I passed this test and was called up for an interview to see if I could get into training for some trade; I was hoping to be a plumber or electrician or failing that a carpenter or mechanic or at worst bricklaying or plastering.

I was interviewed by a small balding bespectacled man who looked at me in a dubious manner from under his eyebrows: he looked like anything, but a tradesman: which I assumed he would be. "Well young Harn is it", he started looking at me in a sideways, shrewd like manner, as though he had something dodgy in mind". You have applied for a number of different trades; we prefer commitment to one chosen trade". "Yes but I'm anxious to get something and I have marked as my first choice plumbing". "No good: plumbing, electrician and motor mechanic courses are long filled and oversubscribed ", he replied scratching his earlobe in an exaggerated manner as though pondering deeply on some matter," carpentry, bricklaying and plastering the same I think; aha painting and decorating: there still places there," he said smiling at me in an exaggerated manner. "I thought I was applying early for these courses," I almost shouted back," and I didn't apply for painting and decorating". "Well a lot of people applied earlier than you, there is very stiff competition for trades" he said in a regretful manner, leaning back in his chair. "I didn't think trades were that attractive, and I got that from a number of sources", I exclaimed. "Aha it's the oil crisis: everything is tightening up: trades are seen as more reliable; no doubt some of the people who applied for these trades have jobs, but unreliable ones: factory jobs, transport etc, and while they're still young enough to do a trade: they're jumping before they they're pushed" he said in a reasonable manner. Every person I asked for a job seemed to be afflicted by this oil crisis, yet I had seen no evidence of it affecting anyone else and the papers claimed the effects were diminishing fast. "Still there are advantages to painting and decorating: it's a two year rather than a four year course" he said brightly taking up his pen to sign me in, or some such action. "Hold on, is painting and decorating even considered a proper trade", I said quickly; "there must be something else". He started scratching his head, and drumming his fingers on the desk and even drumming his fingernails on his teeth, which I noticed were false, and squinting and running his eyes over several papers: acting as though in a state of great perturbation, all of which looked as false as a three pound note. "There just might be " he said looking me with a troubled expression; "you're out a long time, aren't you," he said shaking his head, he mumbled and shook his head again, and took papers from his drawers and rubbed his mouth again and again. Finally he said in a low voice with a sort of wink, "there might just be something that I can do for you. Tell you what, get your father to come and see me, and I'll try and work out something for you: it might, might just be possible to get you on the carpentry or bricklaying course". "What the hell has my father got to do with it; I'm looking for the position not him", I exclaimed: the vague suspicion long forming in the back of my mind now taking definite form. " Look", he said in a low urgent voice leaning over the desk," the courses are officially filled but sometimes we can slip another one or two onto the course, but we would have to be sure that it was a good candidate: usually someone with experience of the trade, but failing that, as in your case: we have to be as sure as we can be, we're choosing a good man: background of family, what work they do, character, etc, etc, or we'll end up in trouble, young man". "My father's a postman and farmer; neither I nor any member of my family have ever been in trouble; what further information can you get from my father", I replied my suspicions crystallising fast. "Listen man, I'm going out on a limb for you here, this is extracurricular; the courses are filled: I'm attempting to do you a fucking favour," he said in a low angry voice, drumming his finger on the desk. "You're angling for a fucking backhander" I blurted out, my suspicions coming to the boil at last. His silence and angry vindictive look gave me all the proof I needed, to know I was right. "Get to fuck out of my office", he shouted at me in a high pitched voice. "I will, and go straight to Mr Mc Govern the manager of this branch, and repeat this conversation to him", I said, standing up. "He's not in," he replied. The offices were divided by half windowed walls hung with net curtains, and I could see Mc Governs profile. "Yes he is" I said and pointed him out. I went to leave; he jumped into my way, "Look I'm risking my job here, we shouldn't be putting more people on the course, than the rules allow: I just felt sorry for you, but if you are not interested fine. I'll get you on the painting and decorating course; sit down". Desperation made me sit down. I was entered on a painting and decorating course starting at the end of September. As I left he was audibly muttering to himself". That's the last one I'm feeling fucking sorry for": overplaying the part, confirming he had tried on a ploy. A younger neighbour tried and succeeded to get on the carpentry course after his intermediate certificate exam, at the end of June; investigations made much later confirmed the passing of a backhanded: two hundred pounds or roughly six weeks workman's wages at that time; what was different: it was McGovern who took the bung; the other fellow was only a front man.

I sought to join the army for six months, possibly leaving when the painting and decorating course came up. The Northern Ireland situation was in full swing and the Irish army was bigger than it had been since the Second World War, but it also attracted more interest: even people with jobs now proffered themselves in this time of "national need". I was put on another waiting list. I again travelled throughout the country: fifteen smaller towns were tried including some remote ones; here I found even if jobs were available, locals would hold them until one of their own neighbours became available, even to the determent of their business: memories' of harder times were still fresh in any backward area: the locals expected jobs to be given to the locals. This particularly affected retail and leisure: hotels and pubs, and these provided the majority of jobs in any small town. The town I was most likely to get a job in was my own town, and there I was getting a "name", thus putting them off hiring me. Dublin again: "are ye back", was the greeting in more than one place: it was depressing in the extreme.

Midyear came and with it my nineteenth birthday; I couldn't but reflect on the saying I had often heard: that school days were the best days of your life, and how false I had thought that was at the time; now I reflected on how true this appeared, if my first year of adulthood was anything to go on. Midyear brought another development: the year after mine left school, and fairly rapidly some got jobs; mainly those that had the contacts, but the contrast was even more disheartening; I still held to some degree, the school frame of mind of those younger than me being my juniors and somewhat lesser than me; when they started to "pass" me it was disheartening in the extreme: I had been the last in my own division now I was last in the division below me. Of course there were people my age out of work, but exact comparisons were hard to come by, they hadn't the same level of education, they were deficient in some way: one lad who got no job from the same class was very small and had problems with asthma; or the circumstances were different: a girl from my class had a poor exam result and got no job, but the old practice of a girl remaining at home until ready for marriage still held some sort of sway: enough to diminish the ignominy of her joblessness.

I was in a dark circle of defeat: I was jobless and seen myself in contrast to others: this caused me to turn in on myself, and away from others: which led them to perceive me as a tad odd and perhaps more deserving of my joblessness than was the case; this in turn caused me in my sensitized state to magnify the affront of their turning from me, and to avoid them: which cut my contacts which were a way of getting a job, thus propagating the circle.

In early August I met a former schoolmate called Jim Farrelly; he was a bit slow and exited our class after the first year, to go to the local vocational school to do the lowest national exam: the group cert; after that he hung around home doing bits of farm work, then joined the council as a council worker: cleaning and maintaining the roads; he told me the council were recruiting and I should talk to his uncle who was a ganger and he would tell me what to do. I did so and was told to fill out an application form, and that they would be taking on some workers in November, but that quite a few would be taken on in January as there were several retirements: twenty two pounds a week for the first three months when I would be classed as temporary, after that I would be taken on permanent and over a year my wages would rise to about thirty pounds a week: there were small rises every year after that. I signed up: it wasn't what planned to do after I left school: council work was generally ill regarded, but I now knew to refuse nothing, if the painting and decorating didn't go to plan, and considering the circumstances surrounding my signing on, such a possibility had to be considered, then at least this was a job.

Late August brought some lift in my spirits: on the horizon there was at least some job and an end to this dearth: this waste of one's best years, this time when one should be making that principal transition in life: into adulthood and self-sufficiency and manhood. One other thing lifted my mood: uncle Bat crashed his car while drunk and was arrested. I even ventured out to a couple of dances: the first since spring. I was now defiantly least welcome in the gang: but the fact I could answer that question: "what are you at nowadays", by at least claiming to have something definite coming up, meant I had some claim to status among my peers; and my better spirits meant I could at least partake in a bit of banter, and to fit in to some degree in the crowd.

My Indian summer was ever so short lived: I had been provisionally signed on to the painting and decorating course in April and final conformation and a start date was to come in the post about two weeks before the beginning of the course in late September; there was no confirmation received by the tenth of September, so I decided to be thorough: I rang the man who had dealt with me, to see if all was in order: " there is some talk of changes", he started; "am I still on the course", I almost roared into the phone," yes as far as I know yes"; "is that for definite or not", I now roared; " as far as I'm concerned yes"; "if it isn't: they're will be a conversation about backhanders" I replied; leaving down the phone before he could answer. I had not been all that happy about doing the course, but it was something, and I was betting on it; yes I was looking for other jobs, but this I thought was in the bag: it's potential loss assumed proportions far beyond it's worth: I was cast down to a level of despair, that even I knew logically, was unwarranted. I suspended all other aspects of my job hunt. I stayed at home awaiting confirmation one way or the other, barely speaking and just going through the motions of life: eating, sleeping and sitting in my room looking at the wall. On the twenty first I received notification that, the numbers taken on to the course were being reduced, and that I no longer had a place on the course; this was due to unforeseen government cutbacks, and I would be placed on a panel etc, etc and etc. I rang the man I had dealt with; the secretary that answered the phone claimed he wasn't there, though I heard him talking in the background: my earlier phone call had primed them to avoid me. I raced home and got the keys of the car to drive into the state training agencies office; I had driven a bit along the quiet country roads near home, but never the twenty miles of relatively busy roads into the main town where the office was located; also I had no licence or insurance to drive: I just didn't care for the consequences. I rushed straight through the waiting areas and into the little balding man's office, without any preliminaries; he stood up and told me that the manager Mr McGovern would see me, he asked me to wait; I said, I wouldn't and seeing through the curtained windows partitioning the offices, that nobody was with McGovern I walked straight in. "Aah young Harn isn't it" he said as I entered: they were well prepared for me. "You've no doubt got our letter and are disappointed by it, and you are not alone: so are we," he said hurriedly. I was unfit to reply: he took this opportunity to continue; "this was imposed on us out of the blue by the government and we had no say whatsoever in it; indeed we are making staunch protests about it, particularly the manner in which it was done: letting so many people down unexpectedly; at least if they had waited and cut next year's intake: so false promises would not be made, it was something", he said shaking his head. "I'm out of work since leaving school fifteen months ago: I was relying on this," I almost gasped. "look I know quite well that this is a major disappointment to you: indeed you are a long time out of work; but you are not alone: not less than forty have been thrown off courses they were set for, from this office alone", he said shaking his head mournfully, and seeing this wasn't placating me: he got up and started rifling through a drawer. "Wait until I show you now: protest letters wrote by ourselves on your behalf"; he took out a large sheaf of papers and spread them on the desk; he selected one and told me to have a look at it, quickly gathering up the other papers, before I could have a look at them. "That one sums it up best, and you will see that your name is especially marked with an asterisk along with a few others to denote the people longest out of work": it was a common letter of complaint listing about forty names, six or seven marked with an asterisk, these were noted underneath as being out of work a long time, made out to the ministry. "That and many other letters like it have been sent to the ministry: but to no avail" he said shaking his head and the sheaf of letters in his hand. I couldn't see my younger neighbour's name, who had got on the carpentry course three months after me anywhere. "How was I picked" I asked: "you were number thirty nine out of forty two and six places were cancelled: you were just unfortunate". He took the paper from me, and put the whole sheaf away. "Why did they do this", I asked. "Well I'm not privy to their thinking, but I strongly doubt it's the oil crisis," again! I thought: "you see people in employment are unsure of their work, and they're going for trades. The government is trying to cut unemployment, and they don't like this, as all too often the position left vacant is not filled, due to caution on behalf of the employers, or filled by a less experienced person: thus possibly weakening the firm at this bad time", he said in a confidential type manner. It was as false as a sheaf of three pound notes: not one word of it did I believe; I was going to bring up backhanders and my neighbour, and demand to see the other letters, but the fight just left me; they were as trustworthy as scalded snakes: but they simply had the power and there was nothing I could do about it. "Is there anything you can do for me", I asked weakly. "Well now, first of all you're a priority: I don't like this any more than you do" he said looking relieved; "the courses are filled: that's the problem, but I will go out on a limb for you: now there is an industrial polisher's course coming up in Tallagh in Dublin in early February, there's a slab laying course coming up in Cork in March; both are three month courses and they should help you get work. I will definitely sign you on next year courses ; your first choices are plumbing or electrician; I'll try my best to get you one of the two"; how if I signed up now should I not get on a course I thought, but the spirit to fight had left me. "In the meantime if I were you, I'd spent a few months in England: get experience of the buildings. So young Harn there is so much we can still do," he said in a paternalistic manner. I just nodded and left his office: I was unfit to do anything else.

The only thing he said worth hearing was about England. I told the family at tea about the cancellation: they were silent, even little Muriel, normally clatteringly self-important now she was going to secondary school: though only twelve, she could sense the impact this blow had on me and the entire household. My father mentioned something about reading about cutbacks in the paper. What was apparent, was that my mood and situation, was affecting the entire household.

What could I do: I went back to the old round of job seeking; now just going through the motions. I was without hope, and therefore not giving the impression I needed to; indeed in one factory I came across an old classmate, working there as a plant fitter, he drew me to one side as I was making my way to the office, he pointed out to me, that my hands were not washed properly and told me to get the defeated look from my face: to look interested, in the bathroom in front of the mirror I saw what he was talking about; I corrected myself as much as I could, and indeed was told that at least a packer's job should be available in February. My general depressed demeanour was now letting me down to add to my problems. I tried to buck myself up, but any rise in spirits were forced and short lived.

November came and the possibility of a council job: at least something; two positions became available, but were filled by the sons of council ganger men, even in the position of council workman: the pull. Jim Farrelly's uncle told me to wait seven weeks when several positions would become available: this was more or less a repeat of what he said when I applied originally, but it was no use: I chalked it up as yet another failure.

Christmas approached again and with it the wondrous news that the drunken driving charges against uncle Bat were dropped: it appeared that Bat's test results had got lost en route to Dublin, the only one of thirty to do so. Bat rushed off to Kildare to buy a new expensive car: a Ford Grenada, big even for Bat's taste; why he went to the other side of the country to buy such a car was not clear, but coincidently the local superintendent was from that town in Kildare, and rumoured to be related to the car dealer Bat dealt with; Bat said he got a good deal and was going to have a good car under him, since the lesser old car had caused his accident in the first place: for some reason this explanation met with almost universal disbelief.

I now failed to attend some of the interviews that were most unlikely to get me a job: trainee manager at a supermarket, legal clerk to a solicitor. I was simply defeated.

Then about a week and a half before Christmas, Eamonn got me a job: cleaning up scraps of meat and sweeping up in a poultry slaughter house: it was about the lowest job you could get and would only last about ten days, but it was a job. It was up on the border where Eamonn was now stationed, and I could stay in a spare room in the house he stayed in. Eamonn would even drive me back to sign the dole as work was from midday to nine in the evening: the job was cash in the hand: four pounds sixty or four and twelve bob as the owner termed it. It wasn't until later in life that the incongruity of a policeman getting someone an illegal job and helping then to sign on the dole struck me: it showed how desperately my plight was viewed by my family, and also how exactly the law was applied in the Irish republic. The job was dirty, smelly and short lived, but it was something. I felt liberated, and my good humour made me popular, even the owner started to take his tea with me and chat to me. The owner was an old protestant man nearing eighty; he mainly hung around; his son managed the place. During one tea break he told me the problem with the economy was the free state government had never got to grips with business: they concentrated elsewhere: national symbolism and pride, the fact they were running their own affairs was enough, not the quality of that running: things like the Irish language, Gaelic games, and other manifestations of differences with Britishness, took precedence over how to provender for their people economically. I could not, but agree. All too soon the job ended, but it was a most welcome break.

The day after was Christmas Eve; I hadn't planned to go out atoll over Christmas; but with the status of worker of some sort, and a few bob in my pocket I ventured out.

Even though I spent most of my time thinking of myself and my predicament, particularly what others thought of me: my contemplation was of poor quality: instead of my brief status as worker enhancing my status with them, it deprived them of their prey: the runt that even the losers could piss on, and no predator likes to be deprived of it's prey.

People acted as if I personally offended them when I told them I had done a few weeks work: from contradicting me: "you were round here two weeks ago", to sarcasm: "there should be a medal struck and presented to you", to belittlement: "so your boasting about a fortnight's work, what about the rest of us, that has done years of work: do we need to come in here and blow about it". Did the people think I was committed to serving an apprenticeship as the village idiot for good? The best statement from what I thought was a good friend was:" well it's some change for the better, but not before time".

I left the pub in a foul mood, and feeling hostile to all; though I had deemed my neighbours as hostile to a degree: the full realisation of that degree still shocked and embittered me. I went into a pub called Scullys that I nor any other sensible person ever went near: it catered for those, no other pub would cater for. For a while no one heeded me and I drank peacefully on my own, thinking that its name was somewhat undeserved: at least no one here was running you down. Then there entered a notorious bully and trouble maker called Paddy Maher: he was a couple of inches over six foot, broad with a wide ignorant face and small light blue eyes, he was forever in trouble but related to enough of people of influence to escape any real sanction, he had inherited well and was an agricultural contractor, so had access to sizable amounts of ready cash, which also helped to keep him in the clear: " here's two hundred pounds, or I'll give it to someone else that will leave your son with a lot more than a broken nose"; that, his relatives and the general situation in Ireland, where the mentalities of the distant past: of a subculture of illicit but potent authority defying an imposed foreign one remained, while the foreign authority had long gone; the "hard man cum rebel" still counted and has kudos which excused him and protected him, meaning Paddy Maher could get away with his bullying . He typically went up to someone without any provocation or reason and started on them: "I'm Maher have you got a problem with that", if the person said no: he continued, if they bought him a drink, he might leave them alone. I noticed him looking at me, and knew well I should have left, but just for once I was in no mood to run anyplace. For a while nothing happened; he was with two cronies of his, Pat Jack Rainey and Brendan Johnston who were just as vicious as him, but without the same capacity for violence: so they latched onto him. Then he came over to me: " you're that bollix of the Harns aren't you: the dosser"; I didn't answer him, and the barman came over and said" take it easy now Paddy, he only a youngster," you take it easy; if he has hair on his face, he's old enough to answer for himself", answered Paddy: the barman backed away. "I'm not afraid of you Maher," I said. Paddy Maher starting laughing," a dosser that's afraid of a day's work but claims not to be afraid of me" he said: he picked the wrong sentence, on the wrong man, on the wrong day: I challenged him to come outside.

Firstly incredulity at the rashness of the challenge and the swiftness with which it was delivered, silenced them; Rainey and Johnston looked at each other with gleeful incredulous looks; Paddy took off his jacket and said, "I'm always prepared to oblige any man who is looking for fight," and out we went. I attacked him with a ferocity I didn't know I had in me: landing three good blows and drawing blood; he rallied: a few inches in height, eighteen stone to thirteen, and vastly more experience, getting him back into the fight; for a time there was little in it, but his advantages told and he started to drive me back, but my fury had reached a peak and I drove wildly into him, scoring several good hits and driving him back, reach and experience told, and he countered with several good blows now driving me back; then unexpectedly he arched his back backwards dropping his guard: I took the opportunity and hit him on the point of the chin with all the force and fury I possessed and he fell backwards, I took this opportunity to boot him as hard between the legs as possible, which had the required effect of finishing him: he made a sound some place between a croak and a scream, and started vomiting: he'd fight no more. Rainey and Johnston approached me; then Rainey turned hurriedly as though struck, and fell back on his arse; Johnston turned and landed on top of Paddy Maher: someone else had entered the fray. Then someone grabbed me. "Get out of here" he said, and I saw my rescuer was Paddy O Donaghue; he brought me as far as his car and got me into it. "I didn't expect you to rescue me", I said when I had recovered myself somewhat. "Well someone needed to: you did well, but he'd have won. Two years ago he picked on me for no reason, and that was why I abandoned the apprenticeship and went to England. He needed his comeuppance," he said. I was torn, cut and bruised, my clothes were ripped; coming back fully to myself, I realised my predicament, how could I go home like this. Paddy hatched a plan: we went to his house and got his bicycle; I would stay on the small rise before you came to our house, and wait for my mother to emerge, then I would cycle down to the house and take a nasty and noisy fall on to a heap of stones, the council had left outside our house; Paddy would follow in the car and seeing this accident stop and lend assistance: this would cover my cuts and bruises with my mother. We proceeded, and my mother met myself and Paddy half way up the drive, me limping along, Paddy helping me. Even after my mother's cleaning, bandaging and ministrations I was still shocked at my appearance: it was as though a tractor ran over me. The next day was Christmas day, and in Ireland at that time, attendance at mass was necessary; it took most of my mother's sparse makeup and the more copious supplies of makeup my sister Nuala left behind when she went to England to make me presentable at even a distance; I stayed in the porch of the church and made off early.

Over the next few days I healed as my mother grew ever more suspicious of what really happened: "how did you suffer so many injuries in a fall off the bicycle", "I don't know, you seen what happened", why did you borrow Paddy O Donaghue's bicycle", "I was on my way home and I stopped to talk to him, and we both thought it was going to rain so I borrowed the bicycle", " why did he not give you a lift: he was right behind you," and so on. Willie found out just before the new year. Knowing the cat was coming out of the bag, I went out New Year 's Day. The reception I got couldn't conceivably be more different than the one I received on Christmas day: a sort of half cheer went up when I entered the pub: "well done John Willie you mastered Maher", "fair play to you boy," " there's a new hardman in town," "Maher badly needed that", "will you have a drink"; on and on it went there was even hints of people knowing of work, and "having a word" on my behalf. An initial sense of pleasure turned to bemusement and when I fully realised what I was witnessing to utter disgust: just over a week ago when I was perceived as a harmless young fellow or fool, badly in need of help to get on the road of life, thus I was the butt of the joke, the runt of the litter, the one all could belittle and insult; now I was a man of serious standing, a man due respect and even acclaim: because I was capable of violence.

I met Paddy O Donaghue and asked him if I could get a lift with him to England, and if he could help get me started: he promised to do both. I made an arrangement to meet him on the fifth of January to get a lift to the boat and hence to London. I walked out of the pub and home, without speaking to or even answering anyone else.

The next day Jim Farrelly's uncle came to the house to tell me I was starting work for definite on the twenty second of January as a council workman. I told him I was going to England on the fifth; the first my family had heard of it. He attempted to argue: he had gone to trouble on my behalf; ungraciously I asked him where had the job been in November; he protested that he only said there was a chance in November, but it was for definite in January. I was determined: even the prospect of getting to drive a council truck, and better wages didn't stir me: I had had enough of Ireland. My family joined in, including my father: who had never commented or criticized me throughout my entire job search, unlike every other member of my family. This gave me some pause: I ended up by saying I might return by the twenty second, but I was broadening my options.

On the forth I cycled into town to buy a few things, and there I met two school mates that I had always got on with; one was working in the civil service the other was a bank clerk. They invited me in for a drink, and as I wouldn't be seeing them for some time, I went in for a couple. The fight was mentioned and why it had happened; I said that they should enquire with the man who started it not me, and wouldn't be drawn further. The conversation turned to work, both were well ensconced in their jobs, and both were thinking about advancement: one was seeking promotion, the other, on the job training; I was able to keep up with the conversation: I knew for instance the various grades in the civil service. The conversation then turned to cars: both had old second hand cars, and were planning improvements: one a new car, the other a good second hand car. I was reasonably able to keep up with the conversation, though I was only allowed limited usage of our family car, and didn't have a licence. Then as is usual with young men the conversation turned to women; both apparently had played the field and had been through several girlfriends: now they were thinking of something steadier; there was even mention of the "m" word. They could have changed the language they spoke to archaic Chinese : I had no input or even decent understanding of some of what was being said, so limited and constricted was my lifestyle, I didn't even think about women: such aspirations were simply above my realm of contemplation. Eventually getting bored, and with England on my mind, I left. I got my few bits and pieces and headed home; it was only on the top of the rise going down to my home, that the thought struck me like a blow in the face: John Harn are you not yourself a young man coming up on twenty: how come you have no thoughts of such a topic as women; I perused the thought; how come it hadn't even struck me as wrong, until I had cycled out of town; how far was my development retarded; how far behind real life had I lagged: I was seriously not with it. The more I thought of it, the more it shocked me; a lot happens in the two years before twenty and two years is still a long time at that stage of life. That evening I cancelled the council job with Jim Farrelly's uncle: after forty years I have to admit, that the biggest career blunder I made, was to turn down a job cleaning the roads for the county council.

Chapter 3

England, America, Australia and more exotic locations were always somewhere in the experience and expectations of Irish people: it was considered normal to emigrate, so I wasn't feeling discriminated against, or disappointed or wronged to end up having to leave: it was just the mind frame that generations of emigration had instilled into us. Logically there was nothing right about it: the country was running it's affairs for a long time, was part of the EEC, had a relatively small population in relation to its size and natural resources, compared to similar European countries; not to mention the fact that any half idiot could get any job they liked if their "pull" was good enough. Emigration had simply become so much the practice: that it was accepted without question.

I hadn't originally wanted or planned to leave home and emigrate: but over eighteen months of failure, stagnation and more than occasionally being made a fool of, changed my preferences. Emigration always in the back of an Irishman's mind, came more and more to the fore over the period I was out of work, and I had given it considerable thought, concentrated on England: the typical destination for an emigrant, that wasn't over sure of the duration or permanency of their period of migration. It was difficult to establish any certainties about the country, and the lot of the Irish emigrants ; to be sure there were successes: some Irish people did well there, even surprising candidates like my dear uncle Bat, but there were also quite a number of failures: worn and wasted men often returned to Ireland to live on their relatives here, unfit for any work or able to participate in life to any great degree; there was also men who apparently died of drink, or in violence, or simply on the streets: their homecoming: their funeral. Stories about life there often conflicted each other: it was the land of opportunity, it was a hard tough land where no value was left on a man, it was up to yourself which you believed. I was wary but hopeful, when I got in that car on the fifth of January nineteen seventy five.

The car belonged to P J Mohan: a forty five year old father of four; he had been a carpenter, and was noted for his skills: he had got work in the local cathedral, in government offices, but he never could get enough work to support his family, so he, like many others went to England, to work on the buildings, and eventually as a bus driver: which he said was more reliable overall, as he had to be sure of a wage to send home to his family. The fare was twenty eight pounds for a car and passengers on the car ferry: I proffered a third share, but this was refused, as P J Mohan said he'd have to pay the same whether he had passengers or not; a lesser contribution was also refused, with the comment, "to take advantage of it, as this was the last thing I was liable to get free concerning England ": something I found out to be only too true. We set off at two o clock in the afternoon to get the night sailing, stopping for a meal; in Dublin; along the way I sought to get as much information as possible about England. P J Mohan drove while Paddy O Donaghue appeared to sleep in the back seat: I didn't know P J all that well, so was circumspect in drawing information from him, and at any rate he appeared to be more interested in Ireland than England, constantly referring to it; but I got some bits: England was no nice or easy place to live; the Irish there were generally a hard drinking, hard living crowd, easily given to violence, especially those in the building trade: I in part garnered that this was why P J no longer worked in it; the authorities were anti Irish or at best couldn't give a dam: this in part entailed that the wrong element flourished, which all too often got the upper hand in the business and general affairs of the Irish community. I had heard these sort of things said about England in one way or another before, but stitched together they did daunt one somewhat; however I thought back on my recent experiences and knew someplace other than Ireland had to be tried. His final piece of advice: start off in the building trade: it was the easiest place to get a job in but think hard about moving out when you got your feet on the ground. We boarded the ship for the night sailing to Holyhead.

I have often heard and read lachrymose tales of the departing Irish watching the land of their birth depart over the horizon with a " tear in their eye", and "sorrow in their hearts", but all I felt when the lights of Dublin faded was relief.

It was my first time at sea and I stood on the deck looking out at the dark ocean; P J and Paddy were stretched out on the front and back seats of the car sleeping; most of the passengers seemed to go to the bar at once, or very soon after sailing, and the sounds issuing from the bar grew, more and more raucous over time. On the dimly lit deck I sought to increase my knowledge of England, if by no other means, by listening in to the conversations of others. I leant back in the shade near the door to the deck from the bar, to spy on, or if possible get into conversation, with people out to get some air. The first was two middle aged women discussing the old cattle and passenger ship the" St Murdoch": which had been in service up to six months before:" well I remember the first time I was on it, in fifty eight: 'twas brutal: there were no toilets on it: 'twas all right for the men, but what could the women do but go down among the cattle pens and try to get some hidden corner, and you know a crossing on that ship could take six hours: well didn't I have go down to go, and as I was at it, didn't this stream of what I first thought was hot water but then realised was piss landed on me; first I thought I was in range of the cattle, but then I realised that it was a man: drunk no doubt pissing down on me from the deck". "Indeed and you were not the only one that happened to Brid: my own sister Anne was caught by at least two bastards pissing down on top of her, and on the train to London, she could only lean out the window to try to hide the smell, and you know what those old steam trains were like: she got plastered with soot: and there she ended up arriving in Euston station stinking of piss and plastered with soot: wasn't that some presentation to make of yourself". Amusing as this was it portrayed a rough and crude mode of life. Next three dodgy looking individuals came out on deck: smallish men with their shoulders up to look bigger, they looked around warily, but probably due to drink, they failed to see me; they stood there unsteadily talking in low voices, after a while their voices rose, and I caught snatches of the conversation: they were from Athlone, they appeared to be running from trouble; odd phrases reached me: "I'm not doing twelve months in Mountjoy," "I had to hit him with the bottle," and worse: "I thought the bitch wanted it, didn't I: alright I was too drunk, but it wasn't meant as rape," and so on. After about two hours I went inside to the bar; the crowd were showing signs of rowdiness: at least one fight was being parted by the participants companions; it was coming near the end of the sailing and I went up on deck to see the spectacle of docking in a more wary mood than the first time I went up on deck. Paddy drove the rest of the way to London with P J Mohan asleep in the back, thus I could make proper enquiries.

I began:" now Paddy don't think I'm not grateful for this effort you are putting in on my behalf, but I understand there may be more to England than I realised, certainly minuses".

"Put it like this much: England is a necessity: it's where you have to go if you want to get on, not where you would like to go, if you had a choice. But I thought that was your case".

"That's correct: I have no prospects of any reasonable job at home, nor am I likely to get any co-operation from anybody to get one; indeed I am little more than the town joke; but England seems to be a fairly dicey spot: so I would like to get clued into what is really going on, and how to avoid any tough scrapes". "Avoid tough scrapes: not easy in England, or at least in London: it is one tough town. Basically you are alone: if something starts, well unless you're mates are on hand and they can't be all the time, there is no fear the neighbours will intervene: like at home. If you get injured on a job or anything like that: no sentiment will be spared upon you. You are a paddy: the authorities aren't interested if a crime is per-petrated against you. If you can't pay your way: no-one will help you". "A lot of that I can understand: it's a big impersonal city, but there appears to be a particular danger in being Irish: is this just the troubles". "You have heard the phrase ducking and diving: well that describes a lot of the Irish people there, or here, as I should now say; a lot of people have dodgy backgrounds from Ireland or have got sucked into some sort of dodgy dealing here, if only mucking around with tax: the building work goes up and down, and people find it hard to even out their spending and therefore fall short with tax and national insurance; other times people have to work cash in hand: it's hard to be legit fulltime; also it's difficult to go to the authorities being Irish, so a subculture has sprung up: hard men or rather gangs have a big say, and they are tied in with the subcontractors: the main employers: so in a lot of ways you are your own justice and enforcer in this town ; throw in the great Irish feature of jealousy and add drink: well its a little like the wild west. " You could say the same thing about Ireland: Paddy Maher shouldn't be walking the streets, for instance". "True and it probably from there such behaviour originated; but there is a restraint to people in Ireland, from neighbourliness or even religion; no such restraints exist here in England". I digested this for a time: not liking what I heard but again remembering what I had gone through in Ireland. "So what would you advise, someone who wished to live a reason-ably peaceful life, and make a bit of money". "Give up the idea of completely avoiding hassle: it cannot be done, not here: so prepare yourself to some degree, there is a sort of "fixed up" boxing club that I sometimes go to; it's not up to much, but you could pick up a bit there and get fitter: it would help. Trust no-one: it's the stock and trade of many of the Irish to live by conning and leaching off their countrymen. You have family over here (I had: a sister and three aunts); make contact with them and get them to provide a refuge for you: just in case things go badly wrong, which they can over here, have a backup plan. Try and save up a few hundred quickly, and if the opportunity presents itself consider leaving the building trade: the money's ok, but it cannot be relied upon". I felt like a soldier going into battle; but the more I thought about it, and my adviser, the more water it held: Paddy was the hard man of the class, but not the bully, quick to fight if challenged, but not a trou-blemaker; also he wasn't stupid: the reason he left after three years was because that was what would be expected from a big strong lad: get a trade, get a job, and get off your parent's hands: but he was no dunce. I had to some degree heard all this before, but put together and imminent: it appeared I had not embarked on an easy road.

The wonders of a motorway and a vast metropolises, appeared and disappeared and we eventually stopped outside a small drab terrace house in a part of London called Stonebridge: my new home. I had a room there until March: a six foot by seven foot room without a bed, but with a mattress and a few blankets. There were four more people in the house, Paddy downstairs, a man described as a rough old man, called "ould navvy", and two brothers who shared the biggest upstairs room, and kept to themselves. I was to go to work in two days' time on a Monday as a general labourer with an uncle of Paddy's: this job would last until March. I had two days to get some grip of London: the transport, buses, underground; shops and knowledge necessary to get by in general.

After a day of enlightenment and some enjoyment: new sights and sounds, I met the first of my fellow tenants "ould navvy": he was a small wizened, obviously toothless old man, by the way he was attempting to eat a greasy pork chop: cut very small and sort of sucked; he had a tar smeared flat cap pulled down over his eyes, out from under which he peered at me in a suspicious manner. I spoke to him twice but got no answer; I looked enquiringly at Paddy: he just gave a shrug; "how are you getting on I almost shouted at him", this elicited the response: "what about yaa". Paddy told this was how he spoke and acted, and there were a lot more like him around. We went to a pub in nearby Willesden to meet Paddy's uncle; the pub was quiet and the beer poor, and the company was rough-hewed: scarred faces and ears with rounded bits gone out them were fairly common: biting your opponent's ear was commonplace during fights, according to Paddy. Paddy's uncle was in groundwork, and after asking me if I could use a jackhammer, appeared to lose all interest in me, asking question after question of Paddy of what was happening at home. The next day, Sunday I got myself as prepared as I could for work: asking questions of Paddy and one of the two brothers who lived upstairs. The three of us went around a few pubs that afternoon, all seemed quiet; our new companion told us that himself and his brother were labourers on shuttering work, that is putting up forms for concrete. I mentioned that all seemed respectable to Paddy, he said this was because nobody had any money after Christmas.

I got up at half five the next morning for work, a bit early, but ould navvy was up, a mug of tea in his hands which were shaking so much he could hardly drink it, as I passed him he pawed me: "you'd not have a drop of whiskey or brandy, just that I could put in me tea, to stop the shakes" he said: "no" I replied; "well double fuck you anyways" he shouted at me. With this blessing ringing in my ears I set off, to catch the van to my first day's work. After an hour sitting uncomfortably on various pieces of building implementia, we arrived at our worksite: my four companions appeared to be in the same state as ould navvy and any attempt at conversation, was met with a dull glare. We set to breaking the tops off concrete foundation piles to expose the reinforcing steel so it could be tied in to steel reinforcing bars in ground beams: it was hard but not very complicated work and I soon got the hang of it. I thought that I did alright certainly as much as anyone else, but the ganger still came as far as me and asked was this my first day: when I said yes, he said that explained my lack of progress. We went home, my workmates to the pub, me to the house to try and do some cooking, and ask Paddy a few questions. I knew as much about pile breaking as Paddy, and all gangers acted like that: they were just not there to be satisfied. The week passed, the crew were every bit as hung over every morning as the first one, they went to the pub every evening. At the end of the week the ganger said he understood the agent: Paddy's uncle, said I was to get a chance, but next week there would have to be improvements despite me clearly out working everybody else, at least on Friday. But I had a week's wages: forty five pounds on me, and I felt good for the first time in ages.

Chapter 4

It was January; the pubs were quiet, the dance halls peaceful. I did a round of the area: three different pubs every weekend, a dance, nothing adventurous, just having a look. I was almost deceived. It all seemed fairly quiet, you could get into a conversation with someone, somewhat like you could at home; the Irish people I met seemed regular enough; indeed they seemed more understanding to the likes of myself, than a lot of my old neighbours : probably because they experienced something similar. It was not unlike being at home.

But there were differences: after a few drinks and people loosened up: the conversation grew darker: fights of great violence with bottles and pick axe handles were mentioned; fights where people were seriously hurt or worse; people not paid wages for work; protection rackets; this scam, that scam. When you entered certain pubs: everybody turned looking at the new arrival in an obvious state of trepidation: expecting trouble. Men constantly scanned the crowd: clearly a developed habit, something they had got used to doing as a matter of course. A certain air of menace was constantly pervasive in these places. I attended the "fixed up" boxing club: it was only a double garage with a heavy bag and a few bits of old training gear: medicine balls, a bit of a roped off ring for some sparring; I didn't do anything to serious: some work with the bag, and medicine balls some exercises, under the instruction of the "trainer", a man who had reputedly fought in some professional fights; I eventually had a limited sparring bout(no head shots), with another attendee and seemed to do ok: he was determined, but was inaccurate. I had a drink with my "sparring partner" later, and gave my opinion that the main benefit of attending the boxing club was for exercise; London wasn't all that rough. In a startling move my sparring partner reached up to his face and took out his eye: it was a glass eye; "see that", he said "I used to think that too". I was too shocked to speak. "Good God" I said" you went into the wrong pub". "In some ways it wouldn't have been as bad if it happened in a pub: drink is some excuse. This happened on a job. I was working for a Donegal setup: Duffy and Conroy: steel fixing, and when I received the pay packet, I noticed it was open and there was money missing. I went to the foreman at once and demanded my money from him, as only he could have taken it: he told me to fuck off, and some shoving started: I giving as good as I got, but behind my back his mates attacked me. I was fairly strong, but no fighting man, yet I gave them a battle; one against three, but then two of them grappled with me and threw me face down on to reinforcing bars, and it was deliberate; one of the bars took my eye out. I'm not sure what happened after that: I was in agony; but it appears they attempted to carry me down to the basement, but there was other trades on the job, and at that stage and they interfered: otherwise I doubt I'd be here. I was brought to hospital and the boys scarpered from the site". "But, didn't the authorities, em, the police, eh get involved", I stuttered. "After I came round at the hospital, I was asked if I wanted to report it: I said I did, but no body arrived for over a day, then a single police officer took a statement. When I got out of hospital I went back to the site; the site agent said it was a matter for the subcontractor: Duffy and Conroy; when I went to their offices, they claimed that a subcontractor of theirs; they gave some bullshit name of a company, was the employer of the men involved, and that they had no communications with them since the "accident", despite strong efforts to contact them: indeed they had lost out thousands from that firm deserting the job. It went on like this: one fob off, to the other: " that company had only a post office box address, and now Duffy and Conroy were in trouble with tax", and ",when they got them they were going to do "x, y, and z", to them", etc, etc. The police took statements but got only vague descriptions and first names: which they doubted were false, and they didn't seemed too pushed to solve the "crime" at any rate.

Eventually Duffy and Conroy offered me a "good will" payment of five hundred pounds: though they were in "no way responsible" for what happened to me. I threatened to go to a lawyer. That Sunday evening I was in my room with the door locked as some of the other tenants were dodgy, especially with drink, when it was unlocked and opened: the boss of Duffy and Conroy and three very large men with their caps pulled down over their faces entered the room: they had gained entry to the house and got my key from the landlord. I was proffered a deal: he'd give me one thousand pounds, and that would be it; they were not responsible, and they had told me who was, but if I continued stirring the shit, I would make trouble for them, then the "boys": his companions would deal with it. I took an axe from under the bed and told him to come on. "Hold it" he said, and took two photographs from his pocket: they were photographs of my mother and father outside our home in Ireland, taken recently as shown by a repainting job on the house that had just been completed. "Are you also going to protect these people with that axe" he asked me, as cool as all that. "I'll make it twelve hundred", he said counting it out "but that is it, twelve hundred pounds will do an awful to these people" he said pointing at the pictures. I could only accept. On his way out he told me, if I had hung on and talked to them: they'd have put it down as an accident and I could have got ten times that amount on insurance. Had I not seen him take the glass eye out of his head, I would have thought I was been fed a pack of lies. I stuttered and stammered and mentioned police, and unions and failed to give a sensible response. I was cold stone sober on the walk home that evening despite, the drink I had consumed.

I just didn't know what to do. I mentioned the story to Paddy and one of the brothers the next evening; ould navvy was also there in the kitchen. Both said it was possible that such things could happen: but they thought it would be a rare occurrence. Ould navvy spoke up: "if it's too hard for you over here, why do you not go home to your mammy, little boy"; I threw my tea over him: he got up and grabbed the blunt butter knife and came at me; the brother just grabbed casually him by the back of the collar and opened the back door and threw him out bodily, he then shut and locked the back door, and returned to the conversation; leaving ould navvy scrabbling at the door, without any attention being paid to him. I was no longer deceived: this England was as hard as it was reputed to be.

I was not for the first time between two stools: I had gone out to work every morning early, on to the grey, grimy, piss stained streets of a wintery London, with a spring in my step: I was going some-place; I had gone out into the glorious summer fields of Ireland with no such enthusiasm, as I was going no place; I slept in a large unheated cupboard on a mattress, without disturbance, unlike in my clean comfortable bed at home: where worry beset me nightly; I ate my amateurishly badly cooked meals with a relish I failed to find in my mother's well-cooked thoughtfully prepared meals: I had a purpose. I was living a life here, not merely existing. I thought about this during the quiet month of February and into March; but I also looked and observed with critical eyes the environment in which I lived; at work I observed the glee with which my workmates reacted to someone getting sacked: someone I could find no fault with; relief that it was him, not them, couldn't explain this glee; I found out with shock that the two oldest men on the gang: men in their early fifties couldn't read or write, at least not properly, and some of the younger men were barely proficient, yet all these men seemed to be of normal intelligence: well able to converse on any average subject; everyone drank heavily and smoked and appeared to have no interest outside the pub, and who was fighting with who; every-body bar myself was broke Monday morning and usually someone was marked; I found out to my amazement that wizened ould navvy was in his late fifties, not at least seventy plus, as I had supposed. These findings, on top of everything else I had learned, led me to conclude England or at least the building trade in England was best as a short lived endeavour.

So what was I going to do? The first idea was to save the price of a house at home: that would take about four years, then pick up some job like the council job or a factory job: if I had my own house, I should manage; against this was my memory of what I had experienced during the twenty months I was out of work: I was a nobody; I simply did not want to go through that again. The second idea: get in on some trade, as this would provide one with more money, and perhaps a house could be bought in London. As an example the two brothers in the house stated that it was their intention to "chance their arm" as shuttering chippies (form workers) later in the year. This idea would mean staying in the building trade in London for a longer period: but maybe one could learn to manoeuvre around the problems one could expect. The third idea as suggested by P J Mohan and Paddy was to move out of the building trade. This appeared a good idea as long as one had some skill: a driver, book keeping skills, a qualification as a machinist, or office skills like a stenographer: otherwise one was facing the prospect of very poor wages. The incongruity of someone whose academic abilities, and results were verging on the professional level twenty two months before, getting job fulfilment out of labouring on a building site and aspiring to be a driver or basic office worker, simply didn't strike me atoll.

Paddy's day, when all was supposed to "liven up, arrived; I went out. The pubs were crowded with a rather raucous crowd: even at seven o clock everybody seemed to be well loaded. I went with Paddy and one of the brothers to the pub I used most. I approached the bar, and a small curly haired man there asked me, "who the fuck are you": Paddy quickly said I was a mate of his. The man looked away quickly but clearly things were livening up. After a while there Paddy departed, we went to a shabby pub nearby, noted for bad, but cheaper beer; we thought it would be less crowded; ould navvy was at the counter, he immediately turned his back to us when we entered: nice to meet your housemates out. We went to the nearby area of Willesden: to see what the pubs there were like. We went into what appeared to be a lively, but not very crowded pub, where a lot of women were present: a subject I was determined to brush up on. I was unadventurous: merely remarking to any woman who came alongside me at the bar:" plenty of people celebrating paddy's day here," or some such innocuous remark: just to get some very basic practice of speaking to a woman. I continued this practice

as well as chatting to the brother: sometimes I got a reply, sometimes a nod of the head: all very banal and harmless. The seventh
or eighth time, I spoke to a woman a little man certainly not over
five foot four interposed himself forcefully between us, he didn't
touch me, but his behaviour was insulting; he faced the woman and
demanded to know what I said: " nothing" she replied and left the
bar with the little man after her: I was going to follow him, but the
brother intercepted me, saying he could well be with a gang. We
moved onto a large pub beside Willesden station, from which a lot
of noise was coming; I opened the door to go in and an ashtray hit
me in the chest; there was, to me at that time, the mother and father
of all melees in progress. I backed out and then noticed a crowd
gathering outside: this event was apparently not unexpected. The
brother motioned me across the road, and we stood observing the
action that was now spilling out onto the street. The police arrived:
three black marias from which over a dozen policemen emerged;
they laid straight into the crowd with batons without any preliminaries', men, women: no difference, were just batoned brutally out
of the way; from the third black maria, two extra policemen with
dogs emerged, which they set on the crowd indiscriminately: it was
no holds barred all the way. We edged up the street anxious not
to get involved. I then seen one man being dragged out by the
police, but he fought then viciously even desperately, beating off
two of them, but four others jumped him and battered him unconscious with their batons. An old Irish man standing near us, said
that would be the last we would hear of him; I agreed saying he'd
get jail; the old man looked at me scathingly and told me to find out
what jail he'd be sent to, adding that this was his last paddy's day.
On the way home the brother told me there was good evidence that
at least some Irishmen that were arrested never surfaced again. He
said that and the general situation was why he and his brother were
going to try form working: there was more money in it and they
might get enough to go home; there was little there, but it was safer.
I participated zealously in my next boxing lesson.

The next morning I got up for work; ould navvy was up and
had two of the finest black eyes I ever seen, he could barely see out

of them, yet managed to glare at me the entire time I was in the kitchen. There was no work: no one else made it.

Easter was early that year and both the room and the job were rescheduled to last until May. A rise in money was asked for the room: six to seven pounds a week by the landlady: a Kerry woman, who wore one of the most bitter expression I had ever seen on a woman: she always observed you, with her head back and at an angle, her chin constantly working back and forth, with a glare, and spoke in a high pitched rapid manner; nearly every sentence she spoke had an acidic twist to it. I told her I'd pay when there was a bed and some form of locker, in the room. "I supposed you came from a palace at home," she responded," "no but we did have beds; it must be different down in Kerry" I replied. "I don't remember you been as smart when you came here" she came back, and walked away quickly without allowing a response. She always managed to leave a bad feeling behind her.

On the job: a man, who was a decent worker and certainly the only one beside myself who was worth anything of a Monday morning was "let go", and a pretty useless individual taken on; when I enquired about this I was told he was "one of the boys", so he got the job over the clearly better man. This man was also a troublemaker: he tried to start an argument with me about why I wouldn't go for a drink with them, and when I replied they lived too far from me: he got insulting, an argument almost broke out, but was halted by the ganger's shout of "enough". This man's employment in place of the other was beyond reason.

Easter came and we had a week off: I decided to come to some conclusion about England: was I going to stay or not, was I fit to hack it or not. I decided to delve into any source of information available: pubs, dancehalls, clubs even churches and to visit my family: this should provide a wider view of the entire issue. To begin with church; I had not gone to mass since I came here: mainly because no one else did, at home it was "de rigueur": done if not taken all that seriously. I went at Easter: for one, thinking I should, and secondly to see what sort of Irish were to be met there. To my surprise I met some people from the pub, and not the quietest people either. I went into the club afterwards, and it was a bit quieter than the pub: not that that was very hard. Conversation seemed to veer towards the sentimental: home being the principal subject. The clientele was older, and as time went on, there appeared to be a lot of cadging going on:" sure don't I know you from the pub; you couldn't just slip me a pound until the next night I meet you in the pub, it's just I forgot me money etc", I did give money to one old man that had seemed friendly in the pub, only for it to be whispered to me by another man from the pub, that this man was the biggest leach around, and a total dosser. Upon closer inspection it was clear there were shortcomings, for instance there was a lot of old threadbare, if clean clothing worn including among the women: underneath a clean ordered patina there was obviously shortcomings in resources: despite all the money there was supposed to be about. You got the idea of a struggling people. I went to meet my sister Nuala in the nurse's home in south Kensington that she lived in. In truth I didn't know her well, as she had left to go training as a nurse when she was sixteen and I was nine, and though she had come home many times since, she wasn't someone I was as familiar with as I was with my other siblings; she had a poor cramped room to herself, she made me tea, and a surprisingly stilted conversation about things at home took place; things I wished to mention: such as could I rely on help from her if I needed it, what was her insights and experiences of London, I felt unable to mention. It was only when I was leaving that I twigged what the problem was: she was ashamed of the circumstances in which she lived; when she came home she was always stylishly dressed, and even rented out a car the past two times she was at home: unusual in those days. She like so many others had projected a brighter picture of England and her life there, than was the case. I then visited my aunt Nuala, my mother's younger sister in her house in Harrow in west London. She was also a nurse, married to a bricklayer with three children. Her house was cosy and well done up, if a bit small. She was as I remembered her, a friendly person: chatty and hospitable. She mainly talked about her family: her oldest daughter had started work as a bank clerk recently, and the next child, her son had begun an apprenticeship as a plumber. She bade me join the family for dinner, thus I got a chance to talk to her husband about work. He told me that he preferred to work for non-Irish people: they were straighter and there was less aggro and bullshit about them. He wasn't over pleased with his son entering the building trade, even with a "good trade" like a plumber: he thought he'd have done better if he stayed on at school and tried for an office job: you got more reliability and respect and indeed in the long run, money from such a job. We talked about the Mc Namara family in general and Ireland and how people were getting on: a general all round discussion. The only strange note entered the conversation, when I asked in what area Bat had operated: looks were exchanged between my aunt and uncle, and my aunt who seemed very well informed on all other subjects, appeared uncertain and gave the hazy answer that she thought it was around Camden town; I remembered the same haziness in my mother answer when I asked about Bat operations. I left with a promise to revisit and was told, if anything ever went wrong to call on them for help: this was what I wanted.

I went into two pubs that evening; the first was a seedy dive where everybody turned and looked at you when you entered: this evening was no different, but in addition an old man at the counter turned to me and asked me with a belligerent stare if I belonged in this pub or what. I didn't answer; a man in his company who I had drank with before, said I was just a young lad going around the pubs: the old man turned away. I drank a pint feeling distinctly uncomfortable, but standing my ground; the old man stood up and moved off; he was smallish and obviously had some impediment to his walk; I couldn't help but wonder what did he think he was going to do with me. I thanked my intercessor saying it would look bad if I had to take action against such an old man. Don't underestimate him he said, he was one rough man in his day, and he has backup: he was apparently in with a subby (subcontractor) called Flannery whose "base" this pub was. I went further looking for a hassle free hour in a pub. I went into a slightly grander pub that rejoiced in the title hotel. On entering there were two sets of doors and a foyer before you got to the bar proper.

A young man was sprawled over a couch, he appeared to be gone completely with drink: he ranted and raved and used the most disgusting sexual terms: "she peeled back the foreskin of my cock, like a banana; now my cock is bigger than a banana," and on and on; a group of what appeared to be his mates were standing near the couch laughing at him, they appeared to be waiting for a cab to get their drink depraved companion home. A well-dressed couple entered the foyer on their way into the bar; the dissolute youth got down on the ground on his hands and knees, and groped up under the woman's skirt, not surprisingly her companion hit him; at that the young man's companions, five in number attacked the man viscously and also assaulted the woman, they drove them out through the double doors on to the street: the man fought back frantically but was overwhelmed by force of numbers, he was knocked to the ground and was kicked in the head a number of times, the woman was also knocked and her knickers ripped off and her skirt pulled up to expose her. I stood in the same place in a state of shock looking at this. Finally the woman's plight elicited some shouts from onlookers and the assault was abandoned. The assailants rushed back into the foyer where they were met by a big heavily built jowly individual who asked them: "did you get the bastard"; when they replied in the affirmative the man said good and " now he'll know who's boss around here": it was some form of setup. The dissolute individual remained on his hands and knees the whole time: it appeared he was also to some degree set up: when one of the assailants pulled him up on the couch, he didn't seem to know him, the assailant said" remember Jimmy we bought you all that drink, and you told us about your girlfriend": the scenario appeared to be, of some drunken fool being led up the garden path. A siren sounded; the jowly man rushed out to his "hit crew" and bade them leave by the back way: which they appeared to do. I simply didn't know what to do; I headed for home, but called into ould navvy's local, out of curiosity to see how rough did things get. There was some old fool squawking and screeching in an effort to sing while his mates cheered him on to make an even bigger fool of himself: if that was possible. I left in disgust; outside the door ould navvy was in some argument with the landlord: I overheard enough to know it was over unpaid bills. That was enough of pubs for one night. The next night I ventured out with Paddy and one of the brothers to a very well-known Irish pub: this was supposed to be a lively place, good for women; I had heard of it even before I left Ireland. There was a lively somewhat raucous crowd, with plenty of women present. Everything looked sociable; there was a dancing area and several couples were dancing there, and people seemed to be having a good time. Paddy declared that there was a "queer one" here that seemed to have an eye for him; the brother also said he was after someone: a lively night seemed in prospect. Paddy met his girlfriend, and the brother met his quarry; we had a chat together at the bar, and met up with a few others that Paddy seemed to know: two girls and a man. We eventually got a free table and sat down together; one of the girls appeared free and I got chatting to her: she was a nurse from Galway and was a few years older than me. The evening went swimmingly: I even got up and danced with the girl a couple of times. The last time I danced with the girl Paddy and his girlfriend went missing; it shows how "au fait" I was with the times and the habits of youth, that I couldn't figure out why he'd left, and now conditioned to think the worst: I asked the brother if he thought Paddy was alright: he replied, looking at me quizzically that, he doubted if he needed any help. The seemingly mandatory racket broke out: a group of five attacking one, however there were bouncers here and they threw the entire group out. The evening drew to a close, and as we left the girl I was with, mentioned that she didn't know how she'd get home, as she couldn't find her purse: gallantly I got her a cab, and as she was living in Holloway the opposite direction to where I lived, didn't get in but paid the taxi fare through the driver's window; as they were about to move off, she wound down the window and handed me the fare, saying she'd found her purse; never in the remotest corner of my mind did I conceive the thought that she might have wanted me to go home with her. The fight was still on outside the pub: the five aggressors were kicking the one man on the ground, one egging the others on," kick him until the shite comes out of him"; the bouncers who had been looking at this, but not intervening as it was outside the pub, finally intervened and stopped it. I went home, thinking there could be no good night in this town.

The next morning I was up early though there was no work that day; ould navvy was up and uniquely seemed friendly: "how are you getting on, sure I have the kettle here boiled so you can have a cup of tea for yourself": at first this shocked me, but then I remembered the row between him and the landlord outside the pub over money, and gigged what he was up to: cadging a loan which wouldn't be returned, so I struck first: "it's good to see you so good natured, I wonder if your good nature would extend to the loan of a couple of pound until Friday when I get paid"; " the curse of fuck be upon you" he roared and threw the kettle into the sink, and stormed out the door.

I started on my quest to move on from the buildings by reading the local paper: I came across an add for a bookkeeping course: three two hour sessions a week for eight weeks priced at thirty pounds; I could well afford this and it stated that this would give the basics for a job as a clerk, or for working in any wages department, or in a bank. I went to a bookshop and bought a book on the basics of bookkeeping, and looked through it for a few hours: deciding that yes, I should be able to pursue such a course. While I was looking through the book ould navvy came into the house, he looked at me like he caught me having sex with the neighbour's cat, and asked in a stunned tone what I was at, I replied that I was reading a book, while wondering if anything was genuinely wrong, seeing ould nav-vy's reaction; his expression turned to horror"; what in the name of fuck are you at that for", he almost gasped; " to find out what is in it" I replied: now perplexed at his reaction; "who the fuck do you take yourself for, some professor; you're only a common navvy like myself"; "yes but I might not always be one" I replied. Ould navvy's reaction to this was one of outrage: you would think I had mortally insulted him, he was shaking and stuttering and seemed barely to be in control of himself. I left the room fearing the fool would try to do something, though he was no match for me. Later I asked Paddy and the brothers about his reaction, fearing he was seriously deranged: " books would play no part in ould navvy's life", "misery loves company: he wants as many people as possible at his level," " his goose is cooked and he'd like to bring as many as possible down with him": someplace in there was the answer; I later found a lot of Irish people in England thought that way: if you cant get on yourself: stop the other fellow from getting on. The following day I went into the local poly technical college, to sign on for the basic bookkeeping course. Behind the admissions desk was a rather heavy young woman who had her hair tied back so tightly so as to stretch the skin of her wide plain face, which was heavily made up, a crimson slash of lipstick on her rather thick lips especially prominent; she was chewing gum, but stopped when I approached, putting on a weak smile. I told her I was interested in doing the bookkeeping course; her smile turned into a scowl; she appeared to consult some papers then told me it was full up; the other receptionist sitting near her said: " no Sharon that course is still open"; Sharon bent down near her colleague as though to pick up something to hide what she was saying, but I could still hear:" it's an oirish": " perhaps I'm mistaken" said her colleague. "But it's in the paper" I said: "no definitely full up, sorry", said Sharon. I left thinking there was poor encouragement for any Irishman to improve his education from any angle you wished to look at it.

Work restarted, the new individual who was always baiting me continued: "are you still here" he'd ask, with his lips curled back and twisted into a sick smile as though finding this fact amazing in its impertinence; then directly: "why are you still here". I spoke to the ganger about this, and the fact that this man did little work: the ganger agreed that it was uncalled for, and that he was useless, but said he was in with the main man and that he couldn't do any-thing about it. Another man told me he was saving his own job by picking on me, to force me out, as I wasn't one of the boys. How I wondered was this business ran. I chose a time the main man was present then clearly outworked him; he appeared to shut up after that, but by his gestures and looks clearly resented me. April and May came and went; I got what I could from the job: I learned to operate a dumper and various types of tools: circular saws, angle grinders and all types of jackhammers; I learnt some woodwork especially some formwork and how to tie reinforcing steel that went in concrete; I got as familiar as I could with every aspect of the work. I also saved more money as my taste for nightlife, had waned somewhat. The job ended in June; the new individual was let go a week before me; he protested strongly:" what you're letting me go and keeping that wanker" he shouted at the ganger: " he does twice as much as you" he was answered; fed up with this unreasoned hostility: I invited him off the site: he didn't come, then the other men intervened and that was it. I had at the end of the job over five hundred pounds saved: there was an upside to England at least financially speaking.

The room continued at least until the year's end.

I didn't know what to do: I saw that indeed there were perils in England: great unforgiving violence, dark undercurrents of criminality and poverty, things be they social or work related seem to follow a different agenda than the one they were conventionally supposed to: to be the best worker didn't seem to matter, as much as being one of the "bouys", and in with the right man. However was Ireland in some respects not as bad: you might not get killed in a fight, but being in with the right man was more important. Five hundred pounds was enough to put a good second hand car on the road in Ireland and to tour the country for a job, but would the results be any different, except this time it would cost me money, and give the impression I'd failed in England: as a sort of compromise I decided to stick it out as long as the room lasted.

Chapter 5

I was out of work: this was expected, and was habitually the lot of the construction worker. I asked the other lads in the house, my few acquaintances, the man I had worked for: nothing, but they'd keep a lookout. I travelled around the sites, not enjoying once again cadging work, but thankful for the chance to see more of London.

Where was I from, in Ireland, where did I stay here, who did I know from there, what pubs did I drink in, why was I not asking for work in the pub like everybody else: were the questions put to me by the men I asked for work from; the actual work itself or my ability to do it, were not queried, or added as though an addendum of little importance: "and like you know the work, aye alright". Again the sense was of an altered reality, of the real script being hidden by people acting in a manner masking or in some effort to conceal what was actually happening. The beggaring question was why: fear of the powers that be, due perhaps to the troubles; that there were a lot of people breaking or skirting the law; that there was some criminal type system utilised by the few to exploit the many. I soldiered on; the plan get a good thousand pounds by year's end then go home, look at my options and make a final decision as to whether to go or stay. I asked in the pubs I went into, the reply: "sure you're not one of the gang atoll": "I'm asking for a job not to join any gang": a look of askance. When I was out of work about a week and a half I called my old employer to check if he knew anything; he told me a ganger on another job of his, might just have a job, and if I went down to a pub in south London where he drank I could ask him. I did this; he was one of the most ignorant men I ever saw: a large almost square head on a smallish fat body, with dull light blue eyes and a contemptuous twist to his lips; he listened to what I had to say and asked if I was prepared to come over with a few pounds every week if he gave me the job; wary at this stage, of what can happen in a strange pub, I just walked outside the door without speaking. I rang the boss the next day with this information; he told me there was nothing he could do: he couldn't get between the men and the ganger hired to be in charge of them; I had to accept this as an answer. I went into a rough site where I could see, even from my brief experience that things were badly managed. The ganger was a tall curly haired Irishman standing with his knees slightly bent, and hands curled into fists on his hips with a flat face and glassy eyes which he directed to one side of me when talking to me, his mouth curled into an incredulous smile, his tongue was protruding slightly: he made a picture of ignorance. He immediately verified this picture when he started talking: "sure you're probably only a bollix, in here trying to fool me"; I invited him off the site to repeat this on neutral territory. He didn't come, but moved off to some of his cronies; they must have been cronies, they weren't working; a gang then rushed at me, led by a small wizened old man that barely seemed fit to walk, in some apparent effort to attack me; I picked up a piece of reinforcing steel and took a stance that showed that I was prepared to swing it at them; they stopped, and I backed off the site, a good twenty or thirty yards. It wasn't just the bad, but the mad that seemed in charge of things, backed up by the completely daft. The two brothers got a job for me, for a week: replacing a man who had to go home to Ireland unexpectedly; it was pouring concrete. I was subjected to various enquires as to " who I was in with", " who did I know", "where did I drink", "how did I know about this job", as though one had to be part of a conspiracy, or some plot to land a job pouring concrete for fifty pounds a week. Finally I got the brother to explain to them that I was replacing a man for a week or so, while he visited his sick mother: at last I got some of peace. The job lasted three weeks, but kept me going, and I got a few new contacts from it. From one of these contacts I got a job with a subcontractor, whom I doubted anyone else wanted anything to do with; he had short term work in very widespread locations, a very rough crew: all drunkards, very bad conditions; you travelled to work in the open back of a pickup truck, exposed to all weathers, the ganger drove the men all morning, shouting and abusing them, he went to the pub and got drunk in the afternoon. I got three days one week, four the next, a full five the next, three the week after; it kept me going, but was no good during the middle of summer: the best time for work. I asked every contact I knew: no good; I even asked ould navvy: he asked, "what's wrong with the job you have": I listed my grievances with it: "Sure you're as soft as the shite you'd make, after a heavy feed of porter: too good any job is for the likes of you": I once again retreated for fear of my reaction. In mid-July I got a job, breaking down piles for twelve hours a day, seven days a week : it was on a job that was behind. I got eighty pounds a week which was great, but as soon as that job ended in early September I was "let go", despite being in terms of time keeping, work rate, quality of work etc: the best worker there; again being good at your work, was no real benefit to you. I got back with the crew the brothers were working with, as a labourer with the form workers: this job lasted a month and I learned a bit about formwork, but by October I was out of work again. I ended up back with the three day a week on the back of an open lorry subcontractor. This job and the subcontractor's career ended when on the way back from a job, one individual decided to relieve himself over the back of the moving lorry and this was spotted by a police car; the truck pulled in, everybody jumped off and ran into the fields, I followed, not knowing what else to do, the subcontractor and ganger were in the cab, both were drunk, and were caught, the pisser fell over the side of the truck and was also caught: that subcontractor was never heard of again. We had to walk back to London, over twelve miles, initially through fields; I had a bus fare in my pocket so could get relief from the outskirts of London, the rest hadn't, thus had walk another four to six miles to the parts of London in which they lived; I lost two day's wages. It was the wrong time of year to be out of work; jobs wouldn't be started or get properly get under way until spring. I was desperate to at least get work until January when the room was to go, and then decide on the basis of a year's work whether to go back, or stay, or maybe try something else. I tried everywhere; in one pub I tried I was followed when I left and accosted by two individuals who accused me of "invading their territory": I claimed I had a right to look for work anywhere I liked; things got heated and an exchange of blows occurred; there was little in it: the poor training I had from the boxing club told; I landed solid blows, and took the stance of a boxer which they perhaps recognised; I could not but wonder how far things would have gone without that training, and all I was doing was looking for a job. Finally after being out of work three weeks, the individual who had put me on to the three day a week in an open backed truck subcontractor, suggested a certain ganger might have work but I probably need to take care of him: give him a backhander. Paddy and the brothers told me I might as well over the Christmas: I had to hand over a fiver a week out of fifty pounds; luckily the job was easy, as the disheartening effect of that fiver mitigated greatly against effort.

I went out regularly over this period, sometimes with Paddy or the brothers, but they didn't seem too anxious for my company, probably thinking I wasn't with it, but mainly on my own; I travelled widely but didn't get too involved with anyone, or in any situation; I played mainly a watching brief: how did other men pick up women, how did they get attached in the first place and how did they progress with the relationship; I went no further than an occasional chat, a rare dance and very rarely buying a drink but I got no further, but I wasn't trying in earnest. I also checked out whether places were best avoided; I ended up being able to caution Paddy and the brothers in this matter; they failed to take my advice about certain venues, only to find out I was right: after that I was listened to. There was the occasional push or shove usually without warning and always without cause; this was generally not responded to: eventually being accepted as "part and parcel" of the London Irish scene. Any venue I went to there was a fight at it, or at least outside it, sometimes these got vicious: I seen men glassed, one I doubt losing an eye, kicked in the head, attacked by mobs; and the authorities were little help: outside a large dance hall in Cricklewood I seen a fight between two men; the police arrived, one fled; the aggressor and at that stage the loser, the other put up his hands; the policeman set his dog on him which fastened onto to his privates, the policeman then hit the man with a baton on both arms preventing him from getting to the dog: he was left curled up on the street in great agony, and there was no attempt made to arrest him. The strategy of the police seemed to be to inflict more hurt on somebody without discriminating between offender and victim; the impression given was, that they were only Irish so they could do what they liked to them. Christmas came Paddy headed home, as the "job" and room was due to end in January I stayed to get what I could until that time and then decide what to do. But, but what was the alternative: a life without work, or in a worthless dead end job, got by brownnosing some crook or near crook, in Ireland: this was in essence, the dilemma. I went out over the Christmas more due to the fact that I was twenty and it was the time of life to go out, than for any other reason; I was not entertained, and wasn't expecting or even looking for romance. The "social scene" was quieter in terms of crowds; people went home for Christmas, but what was left: those that couldn't go home for a variety of reasons, mainly legal or financial, made up in terms of action and excitement and hooliganism for those that had left. I was guarded in any foray I made. Over the Christmas period all went fairly well, aside the occasional push and shove, which I mainly ignored, once I followed a particularly vicious shove by shadowing the man until I could get him on his own: when confronted he claimed to be drunk, though he was fit to enunciate this, I invited him to shove me here on his own, as he was still drunk; he declined protesting strongly that the drink was to blame: this he seemed to think was an "answer all" excuse; I left it, but felt I had done no harm to upbraid him. I continued with my habit of making small talk with any woman I could, to at least make some effort in that that direction, which was going to vaguely end up in having a girlfriend, marriage, or some such of that nature: training for a proper effort after I got everything else sorted out. I was in a dance hall in Kilburn on new year's eve, and got a bit more than I had bargained for; I was propping up the bar, as it was nearing closing time, when a woman of about thirty came up and started talking to me; not bad looking, a little seedily dressed, a little worse for wear. The conversation began about how quiet it was compared with normally, moved onto where we both came from; she got a drink out of me, because she couldn't attract the barman's intention; we went on to talk about our situations here; I got her another drink. About this time I noticed we seemed to be observed by an individual I had noticed earlier in a pub, standing with his back to the bar, his eyes going all over the place: not a good sign; a smallish ill made man, with a receding chin, and a misshapen mouth: wider and thicker lipped on top and sort of pulled to one side; I looked directly at him and he quickly looked away, but continued to keep some surveillance on us by glancing out of the corner of his eye: I didn't know what to make out of it. We continued to chat; she stated she would be glad to get someplace to stay tonight as the plumbing in the house she was staying in was leaking, I thought hard; my room was out of the question but Paddy's room for which I had the key was available, as Paddy was still in Ireland. The music had stopped by this time, our observer was nearer, but had his back to us: he still appeared to be listening, but with his back to us, there seemed to be little one could define as amiss. I went to the toilet to ponder matters; only then did it occur to me she might be interested in more than a spare bed for the night: well my education did need enhancing in that area, I decided to proceed: with a bit of luck we'd both have Paddy's room, and my knowledge would be enhanced and 1976 got off to a good start. On the way back to the bar through the passage way from the toilet, a man that I didn't recognise but seemed to ring some bell, blocked my way, I moved aside he moved as well; this dance continued for an inordinately long time; I asked him what he thought he was doing, he replied that he wanted to get to the toilet, I stood with my back to the wall, He stood as well; I shouted at him to move: finally he moved. I returned to the bar, but the woman I was talking to was gone, also gone was my observer and the people he seemed to be with; " so what" I thought: it was too good to be true. I finished my drink, the mandatory outbreak of a brawl, speeding me along. I left, and as I was walking down the road home a battered old ford prefect pulled alongside me, and blew the horn: in it was the woman and the little man in the back seat: she seemed to be struggling with him, and he appeared to have one of his hands up her skirt, he put up his two fingers to me, and leered at me; as they drove off; I could just make out my dancing partner from the passageway in the front seat. It seemed they had distracted me and forcibly made off with this woman to do who knows what: was I witnessing a rape. I did not know what to do: I thought of the police, but at this stage was conditioned against this approach, of trying to make enquiries in the pub, but dismissed this though as ridiculous, no matter what they did know, officially they would know nothing: this was the universal actions of such people. I went home, torturing myself with recriminations at my own lack of street cred, and the ever more monstrous imaginings of what was happening to that woman. Ould navvy was on all fours outside the house, his key in the lock; there was nothing unusual about that, and I generally helped him, getting abused for my trouble; tonight I took the keys out of the lock and threw them into the hedge bordering the front garden and kicked him out of the way, and locked him outside. I could not sleep, throughout the night, my sense of being wronged and humiliated rose, and by morning I came to the conclusion, I'd not rest until I got my own back. At eight o clock I got up and let ould navvy in; he rushed in with both fists to attack me; I fended him off and threw him outside the door again; I couldn't but remember that all the times I had helped him, and he had abused me, him claiming later to have no memory of it due to drink: obviously his memory was better that he made out. He was shouting and scrabbling outside the door, so after a half hour I let him, fearing complaints from the neighbours; he rushed past me swearing vengeance. I was in the kitchen about ten minutes later when ould navvy returned, he seemed to be dragging his right foot somewhat and kept looking at it;" right me boy I'll have you, I'll give you a beating you'll never forget", he roared at me throwing off his jacket dramatically; he came at me swinging both fists but seemed to veer to the left so as to bring his right boot, which I now saw had some shiny item on it, into play; I fended him off with ease, he came on again this time I moved to my left to give him the opportunity of kicking with his right boot so I could catch it, and see what was "afoot" so to speak; this happened, and I held his foot up high, unbalancing him, so I could see what was special about this foot: he had a razor blade wedged into a grove he had cut in the toe of his boot: nasty enough if it caught you wrong. I took the boot off him and threw him outside the door. Under the sink ould navvy usually kept a couple of black plastic containers of rough scrumpy cider, which he'd loaded up on before he went out, as he was always short of money; these I emptied down the drain: which was about the worst thing I could do on him. This amused and distracted me from my dire contemplation of the night before. I headed out that night to the same dancehall intent on seeing the man from the night before, and teaching him a lesson; I was not an aggressive or vengeful man but mortal man could only take so much. I seen no one; it was a Friday night and everybody seemed jaded and unusually there was no fight that night. I left unsure what to do; as I went to cross the road, I found a tug at my arm, and turned just in time to part evade a blow in the face; I responded with a right cross that landed solidly: the boxing training was kicking in and paying off; I would be incapable of such a fast evasion and quality return before I started boxing. I was faced by three individuals I did not recognise, though one seemed to strike some note of recognition; but I was left little time to ponder this. The first one came on swinging hard; I caught him with a perfect left hook, and with a right cross put him down; the second one joined in: I blocked him fairly and returned well: finally putting him back, meanwhile the third one was getting a few sly kicks at me; the first one got up and came at me, I noticed he dropped his left so I concentrated on the right hand and put him down again; the third one came on; I managed to kick him between the legs and land a solid right: he went down; the first one came on again: game as you like: expecting the advantage of surprise, he had in turn being surprised, but he hadn't come to give up; I blocked him and landed a hard kick to the side of his knee, I then landed a perfect right on the nose he went down and hit his head off the corner of a wall: that finished him; I approached the second one, who now backed off; I followed him;

he ran and when I returned to the other two they had gone; I had however remembered where I had seen no three: he was my dancing partner in the toilet passage way of last night. Had it not being for the boxing training and the zeal I followed it with, certainly after my encounter with the one eyed man, I realised I would have been badly injured or even worse. I could conceive no reason for their enmity, but could only follow things up: I couldn't risk meeting such people by accident. I had one asset: I knew what pub, at least the abductor drank in. Paddy had a weapon: the chain of a chain saw attached to a wooden handle, it was a fearsome weapon and kept because in London you never could be sure what was around the corner, I got that, and taking a leaf from ould navvy's book, fixed the razor blade with some wood glue, in a grove I had cut in my shoe; thus armed the following night I lay in wait in an rubbish filled alleyway across from the pub. The abductor entered the pub before I could intercept him, but I got my dancing partner: I came up behind him, and swung the chain saw chain around one of his lower legs and jerked him off his feet, I pulled him into the alleyway and ripped the chain away, even in the bad light I seen I had cut through the trousers' leg and cut gashes in his leg from which he was bleeding heavily. "What the fuck" he said; I lit a match so he could have a good look at me: "what the fuck was going on last night you" I said. "It was Hughie, he said, you were cheeky when you came back to the dancehall, he decided to get the boys to teach you a lesson: you should have stayed away"; "who is Hughie", "he is the man that took the woman from you that night: we thought that showed you were only a bollix". I wrapped the chain around his arm and pulled it away with all my might: it did even more damage: tearing through his leather jacket and tearing off a layer of flesh underneath; he was bleeding heavily and crying at this stage. "The abductor and rapist" I roared. Why shouldn't Hughie have a go with her as well as you" he blubbered. "Because she didn't want to go with bloody Hughie" I roared. I was now tempted to hit him again, but the blood was pooling under him, and I figured another blow might finish him. I pulled him up and dragged him to the far end of the alleyway, got the names and address of the other two assailants: this effortlessly, he was beaten at this stage, told him to fuck off and tell his mates I would be calling on them. I then went in search of Hughie. After about two hours during which time my mood did not improve, my quarry left the pub; he sauntered off, hands in pocket whistling; not a care in the world. He went up a road which bordered a park; down into which there descended a steep and long set of concrete steps; also this road had less street lights along it: ideal for my purposes. I crept up behind him, the noise of the traffic, and no doubt the drink he had taken, my allies. "Hughie" I said; he turned a sick smile on his misshapen mouth, that resembled a leer; I hit him straight in that mouth as hard as I ever hit anyone in my life: he went down; I booted him with my razor blade enhanced shoe in his private parts: this obviously cut through his trousers and broke the skin as there was blood splashed up on to his clothes'; he grabbed himself there, and gave out a sort of screech. "Hi Hughie I am the man whose girlfriend you abducted and I doubt raped, and then set your thugs on, don't you recognise me?": " eackh, twhy should I not get the "ride" as well as you" he answered confirming my worst fears of how far things went; "Hughie she didn't want anything to do with you, she was with me, wasn't she," I roared; " tad and she was on for it : why should I not get the ride as well as you, am I not as much a man as you" he asked his face contorted into a sick smile as though incredulous at the injustice visited upon him: I was dumbfounded: could he be that thick, or demented through jealousy, even of a stranger, that he genuinely thought he was entitled to do such a thing; "Hughie if she went with you fine, but she didn't: she went with me"; "fuck you why should you be entitled to the ride and not me" I raised up the chain and as he put up his hand to protect himself; I struck and wrapped the chain around his arm, then pulled it away as hard as I could, ripping through his jacket and shirt and taking a round of flesh from his arm; he grabbed his arm with his hand and blood seeped readily through his fingers; I kicked him with all my might between the legs again and apparently did damage, as blood flew up on his face and the new pain diminished that of his arm to irrele-vancy: both hands flew to his crotch and screeching he bent into a foetal type contortion; I grabbed him by the back of his trousers and the hair, and picked him up, and swung and threw him down the concrete steps, which he cart wheeled down still holding this position. I turned to leave: my senses were returning and I was beginning, to fully comprehend what I had done. It was only then I noticed a lone figure standing on the far side of the road looking at what I had done; as I looked at him he quickly turned away pulling his cap down over his face; middle sized with long hair was all I could make out; long hair was not unusual in a young man at that time, but this man had streaks of grey in his hair, so he was not so young. I followed him as he went on to the high street with a swinging gait, following the way I had come after Hughie; I saw more than one person glance at him and move quickly aside, as though wary of him. I then came fully to my senses: I had injured two men possibly seriously and with Hughie conceivably worse; I forgot about the man, and rushed back to the alleyway, cleaned myself up as best I could and made my ways home. From sheer exhaustion I slept well that night; the next day rested and my mind more in balance: I contemplated what had happened; whatever the provocation I had purveyed some serious aggro; the last time I had deliberately set out to fight or hurt someone I was in primary school: at most ten. I could well have done permanent damage. What changes had occurred to me: had all the pushes in pubs and dancehalls and the humiliation and abuse on jobs thwarted my mind, made me in turn vicious, and impaired my conscience. What did this country England, do to Irish people; like so many Irish I neglected to think which country had sent me here in the first place. As I went through the day I became more perturbed: what was I to do: I couldn't live a life like this, but what was the alternative: hanging around the place in Ireland, somewhere further afield that I had no insight into and wouldn't be so easy to come back from. I got no place; I was more confused that night, than in the morning. I got up for work the next day, as I was sitting at the table drinking tea, ould navvy entered, he pointed his shaking finger at me, taking a stance like superman taking off, and glaring out at me from under his ever present cap, he informed me: "you will die by this hand", in a hoarse whisper; I took less heed of this than the rain beating off the window; I would have to go out in the rain. I set out early to the pickup point, to give me more time to gain my equilibrium; it was only when I arrived and was taking shelter from the rain in the nearby bus shelter that the thought struck me; I had never even got the woman's name. The van didn't come, no surprise there; but sitting in that deserted bus shelter I finally reasoned things out: a year ago I came here desperate to get some work to go someplace with my life; though I had been told what things were like here: my plight overrode all logical considerations; now I knew what London was like for the Irish; a vicious uncalled for trick had been played on me, and I had responded with uncalled for violence: did I cripple a man, castrate him, kill him even; was I at this hour wanted for murder and would I next see freedom again when I was an old man, if ever. The cure was worse than the disease.

I got practical: I had just over a thousand pounds saved up; if I stayed indoors and I had little inclination left to go socialising and was very careful I should be able to get about thirteen hundred by Easter, I would go home, get an old jalopy for a couple hundred pounds, and tour Ireland to find work, I had experience of the building trade behind me, and I would get a driving licence while I was here; some job on the buildings or driving would be got somewhere; as an afterthought I decided to have a look at the bookkeeping again.

Paddy returned from Ireland later that week and filled me in on how things were going at home: nothing much had changed; finally he asked me what I had done on ould navvy; I told him I had poured his scrumpy down the drain after he annoyed me too often; he laughed and told me ould navvy had said he'd stab me while I slept; I wondered if I stayed here another forty years would I end up like ould navvy. I started by giving no more backhanders to the ganger: he had failed to turn up for two days and I had lost wages; this didn't please him, but the job was behind and I was the only to come in without a hangover, any morning, or to come in atoll most Mondays. I started taking a few driving lessons and got in some practice in one of the brother's cars. I signed up for the bookkeeping course: Sharon wasn't there. I found the course easy, but I was the only Irish person there; I was not treated with any hostility, but with no friendliness either; a few attempts to talk to my fellow students were met with no response or some inane excuses to avoid talking to me: I just concentrated on the course and ignored them back. The room lasted, apparently no one wanted to live in a large cupboard with only a mattress and a few grubby blankets in it. I had got a locker and found an old chair dumped, I also bought a transistor radio so some improvements were made. The boxing club, the bookkeeping course and the driving lessons were the only time I ventured out. Ould navvy took personal offence with the fact I no longer drank: "so now you're gone too mean to even have a drink", "I didn't know it was mandatory", I replied: "every right Irishman should smoke and drink", he responded: "look what it done to you", I said, " you bastard: if I was a young man again I'd kick you up in the air", he roared," ould navvy: the best day of your life you were never fit to beat the flies off your own shite," I responded: now castigating myself for continuing this conversation," tad and we'll see about that me boy", he roared picking up the chair with some intention of hitting me with it; luckily Paddy entered at that time, grabbed ould navvy and the chair and threw him outside the front door and bolted it; I was glad, with my humour as it was, I might have failed to restrain myself if the old fool did manage to hit me. Indeed during this period of time the only excitement I got was from ould navvy; late in January, and entirely polluted from drink, ould navvy decided to have a piss on a traffic island while crossing a road : he was caught by the police: normally an Irishman behaving in such a way would receive a hard beating, but even the police thought ould navvy too pathetic for this: so he was fined; the upshot of this was letters coming to the house giving his real name James I Ferris: the first I or anyone else in the house had knowledge of it, I standing for Ignatius; probably ashamed of this moniker he refused to tell me what it stood for, answering " mind yer'e own fucking business ye bastard,"; annoyed at this uncalled response to a simple enquiry, I said, it stood for James Ignorance Ferris: which would have been most suitable ; immediate insult was taken, and he rushed up to his room and got a shovel that he kept there for some reason, probably as of now, to hit someone with, I took the shovel off him and dragged him out on to the road, threatening to kill him if he ever came in again; this was witnessed by the brothers who quickly ascertained the cause of the ruckus; they dissolved laughing, and word of ould navvy supposed real name spread to the dive he drank in, when this was brought up, as it was often, ould navvy would issue an immediate challenge, to the man or more usually group who so dared to insult him: eventually he was barred, the only man anyone I knew, or had heard tell of being barred from that particular establishment. This was all held against me, on top of the natural aversion I seemed to induce in ould navvy.

All went swimmingly: in early March I passed my driving test. I also passed the exam for a junior certificate in bookkeeping, getting a high mark; the instructor, unbending a bit at the end of the course advised me to pursue a senior certificate, this would take longer and was harder but was a considerably better qualification to procure a job with, and could even be utilised as a back ways route into the profession of accountancy. I therefore managed to pass two further milestones in life: driving and gaining some sort of qualification extra to a basic education. Paddy's day arrived; even then and despite invitations I did not venture out: I had had my fill of socialising in London and I was heading back for good in a month's time at Easter.

The next morning I got up for work, despite the chances of the van turning up being slight: I might as well get any pound I could, while I was in England. Ould navvy was as always up, one black eye this year, an improvement on last year when he had two; he got up and stared at me as though I had arrived in the nip and declared my intention of buggering him; he backed up until he could reach back and lean on the sink, as though fearful of fainting with shock at the gross scene in front of him. "Well in all me days, in all I ever seen: never did I think to see to see the day when an Irishman was too mean to go out on paddy's day; the meanest cunts in this town were out: what sort of bollix are you any ways" he said in a sort of dramatic whisper, as though should things were unfit to be said aloud. "Ould navvy it's a great loss there isn't a competition for bollixes at Crufts as well as for dogs, you'd get best in show no problem" I replied. "Ye useless bastard, ye're as mean as ye're shite and ye think ye're some fucking professor going to that night school instead of the pub, giving yerself airs and graces, and calling yourself qualified like some gent: ye're a disgrace to the Irish, so ye are". "I should be a drunken sludge, full of bullshit like you James Ignorance to be good Irishman, is that what you are saying". "Ye bastard don't I regret the days of me youth are gone: I'd put you through that wall in me day, with one hand stuck up me own arse"; the conversation continued on this lofty plain until Paddy who had "company" got up and wordlessly threw ould navvy outside the back door and locked it. I headed for the van that didn't come. The job was due to last a couple of weeks more; that and something to fill in until Easter and that would be it; I'd have the price of some old banger and a thousand pounds and some experience; I'd tour Ireland and somehow get something; it had to be better that having some woman, you were getting it on with, abducted and raped, and in turn maybe killing someone; also the likes of ould navvy and the backhanders were no help. P J Tobin who I got the lift over with was going back as one of his kids had had an operation for appendices, and I arranged to take a lift with him; the loss: two possible week's work would be little enough. I told Paddy I was heading home and didn't know if I'd be back, I wouldn't give notice on the room, just in case, but as soon as I was sure, I'd let him know and he could tell the landlady. The last evening I was in the kitchen, unusually with all my housemates, a desultory discussion was going on about work with the occasional interjection from ould navvy: "pile breaking is hard work; I can handle it alright but you earn your money" I said;" yes but formwork is heavier work, you get better paid: but you earn it," answered one of the brothers; " ye'd not break the tip of your own shite, I doubt" interjected ould navvy: this was ignored. The conversation was continuing thus, when the landlady arrived in: she considered it her right to come into the house unannounced and furtively: rent paid notwithstanding. She stood there with her arms folded her head back and at an angle glaring at us, as though suspicious of us, as was her habit; "well" she said," well, "myself Paddy and the brothers answered; "good day to ye ma'am" answered ould navvy standing up and touching the brim of his cap; she condescended to nod to him in response," how is everything here" "alright", we three coursed; " well now ma'am as ye know well, I'm not one to complain, but I fear there is little respect for age in this house" answered ould navvy, his hands on his hips holding back his jacket, giving him a larger aspect and showing a full expanse of his not too clean shirt; he rocked back and forth slightly giving the impression of a bird of ill omen, his beak or cap pecking in my direction; " is that so", said the land-lady"; " yes ma'am all I can say is that standards of behaving yerself in Ireland seems have fallen greatly since my time," said ould navvy; " this one" said the landlady indicating me ; "aye" said ould navvy; "you, what have you got to say for yourself" she shouted at me; " I have respect for those, that respect me" I answered; " this ma'am is the sort of smartarse answer you get, from this one" said ould navvy: "aye I know this one is a smartarse; you: if you don't buck up your behaviour, get out of here to fuck" she shouted and turned smartly to leave so as to ensure she had the last word; ould navvy ran after her; "and God bless ye ma'am if it wasn't for ye I don't what would happen in this house" he said opening the door for her: " if he does anything else I'll have him out" she said. "Now" he said returning and standing in the doorway; Paddy slammed the door hitting him in on his long reddened scarred beak of a nose; I was ready to go for his scrumpy and drink it this time, not pour it down the sink. Ould navvy was deeply ignorant, by inclination as well as naturally, vicious, and bad minded and jealous in the extreme, but he had a certain animal cunning, which allowed him to survive: he was well fit to lick even the most undeserving of arses when he had to: like the landlady's; he paid only five pounds rent for a room worth about ten; the one time he got any money out of me was early on when I wanted to get on with everybody; he stated, he was short for the rent: I agreed to help him but I insisted on paying the landlady knowing if I gave it to him, it would at least in part go on drink: he got two weeks out of me which needless to say I never got back; he had caught Paddy and the brothers out in a similar manner; his very peculiarities were his salvation: he was hired as a day labourer, because of the Irish weakness for a character, even a malevolent one, as he was long past any working abilities.

I got into the car the next day with P J Mohan like I did fourteen months ago: then I had hope that I was moving on to better things, now I had hope I was going back to better things. Once again the events of my life seemed to take the form of a circle. P J drove to the boat, he was untalkative being I suppose preoccupied with his son's health; he had had an appendix operation and P J was unsure all had gone well. The image of the circle again formed itself: on the way over to England I began to have doubts about England over what P J said, now again I was having doubts about my new destination over what P J said: it was a bad country when a good tradesman had to go and work in a foreign land, to keep his family and was left rushing home in a state of apprehension when one of his kids got sick. The bad old memories of Ireland started reappearing, and reasserting themselves, but unlike the last time I travelled this route the memories of where I was coming from: the memories of Hughie and co, overrode them: that sort of thing didn't happen in Ireland.

We got the boat, this time I went up on deck, but to get a place to relax; the last time I wished to garner information about England, now if anything, I knew more than I wanted to know. I drove from the port down: this was at least something beneficial I had learned in England. I left P J at his house, and walked the rest of the way home, about four miles.

Chapter 6

Everybody seemed very welcoming: my family, my neighbours and my friends. The old adage: absence makes the heart grow fonder seemed to be true, but only to a point, the chat we had in the house started well: how had I done, job: good, driving licence: good, bookkeeping qualification: well it certainly could do no harm, and who was to say, it might be come useful some day; you did well out of England, certainly a lot better than you did here. Now it has to be said I did nothing to play down my accomplishments: a dishonesty that has often cost the returning Irish: it raises jealousy and the expectation you won't be around very long, to say nothing about being expected to buy more than you're fair share of drink. The conversation in the house continued: "well you're entitled to a good holiday, when will you be going back", "well I am not sure about going back, it rough enough over there": silence. My family looked at each other, and then back at me," well what's around here for you", " you can hardly go back to hanging round here doing nothing: like you were at that long enough", " work, money, driving licence and bookkeeping, er, thing, in a year: what did you get in the two years before that, around here", " you're just tired: take a bit of a break, and you'll be well up to it again"; "if it's rough" said my mother; "if he was going to get caught out, it'd have happened when he was green, just be more aware of yourself and learn to avoid the pitfalls" said my brother Bill; "yea, you'd know all about it Bill" I answered," I don't want you to spend another two years around here, doing nothing, but putting your life to waste, and doing the rest of us no good either" answered Bill; Eamon nodding in agreement. I went to the pub and got seemingly a warm welcome:" it's great to see you doing so well: you did exactly the right thing, like if you hung around here much longer it's hard to know if you'd ever come to the good"; "there's more could take a leaf from your book: there's too many hanging around doing fuck all": this from Dermott Mullen who got the pull all the way. There followed some frivolous queries, mainly ribald: "what's the women like over there: I hear they're very easy"; "they say every biddy that goes over there, turns from a holy Mary into a right ould whore," and on and on. "They say the money is very good over there", from Dermott Mullen: "anytime you want to try it: you know where it is"; "well you certainly wouldn't do as well here: yourself is proof of that" another of the well informed. Then finally on to the subject: "when will you be going back": I refined my response a bit, " well I'm thinking of considering all my options before I commit to any place"; " you mean to try America"; "no but London is a rough old town : I might give here a last go while I can": silence. "I don't know about that John Willie, you weren't exactly a success when you were around here before", "you were near two years out of work around here: I'd have thought this was the last place you would consider", "you hardly want to go back to that; sure you must know John Harn you were considered little other than a fool around here". From the reaction in the house I was somewhat prepared:" the point is that in a few years' time there are many jobs that one couldn't go for, and I'd like to try these jobs first before I give up completely on them: the guards for instance, why not give them a go while I can, if I get nothing well: back to England". I could see I had not pleased my audience; things got a tad abrasive: " you know there's not all that much around here at the best of times: we can't afford ye coming here taking what there is": "who's ye: am I not an Irishman atoll; did I not come from this town, and go to the same school as ye lot", "look John Willie there is only so much around, and if your set up in England and on good money, you should leave what's here to us, that's stuck it out". Did they see themselves in some sort of heroic light: holding the fort while others deserted, just because they had the pull. "I never said what money I was on, but the point is I consider I have as much right as any of you to a job and life in this country": "if you consider that John Willie you might need to be thought a lesson",: "well you come outside the door right now and teach me a lesson" I replied. There was immediate intervention: "steady on boys", "cool down", "I'm just saying it as I see it": before Paddy Maher, I'd say he'd do more, than say what he seen. "The challenge stands to any man, here that wants to teach me a lesson": "cool down John Willie," "cool down": I walked out. It was a dank, drizzly, dreary evening that reflected my mood as I walked home; the question was where did I stand now?. I stood on top of the rise leading down to the house; I was drenched, cold and totally dispirited, even at the bleakest period of my unemployment, I never felt this way: someplace in the back of my mind there had been hope: England, America someplace, now I was after finding out, in the most glaring terms the truth of the old saying "far away hills are green": if England in some ways gave you advantages over Ireland, there were deficits and dangers in other ways that levelled the score. I stood there in the drizzle for close on half an hour before I entered the house, far earlier, soberer to say nothing of wetter than I had intended.

That finished the town for me; I hung around the house doing little; I offered Bill a hand with the work:" don't heed about me: take it easy for yourself": words that now had a double meaning: you're on your holidays, and that's the only reason, you're welcome to be here any longer. How fast can a change of mind come about; I came back to Ireland determined that at a minimum, a very hard long effort to secure employment would take place; I had short of thirteen hundred pounds with me, as a rough plan I was thinking of spending about one thousand plus, totally in an effort to get work; if that failed well, I might look at America but I'd probably return to England, now I had to consider the question: what I was spending this thousand pounds on.

I started up the old familiar sorry regime again: cadging for work; I took the car, it wasn't being used during the day, and covered the locality quickly: " are you back again: I haven't seen you in a while": this where it was not known I had been in England; I went into a factory in the nearest big town, directed there by my another man I had canvassed for work: there seemed to be interest,

I was asked to come back the next day to see the boss as there could well be some jobs going, I returned, to be told abruptly there was nothing going, I queried this asking why I had been told to come back yesterday: it had been a mistake, I pushed further, stating that this abrupt change of mind seemed strange: "it was a mistake, but any ways I hear you have a job in England to go back to": this got to the nub of the matter: someone had been talking; I continued a fruitless argument a while longer: "didn't I have a right to look for a job around here the same as anyone else even if I had been in England": "What would the locals without work think of that" : locals, where did he think I came from, the moon: there was no avail. Dublin for a day: I was placed on a number of panels; Cork: more panels or did maybe I know someone. Saturday, I was in the town, Dermott Mullen and two others that had been in the pub the other night came up, to me and started talking; things went a bit over the top the other night, what they were saying was right, but they pressed matters too far, they had felt sorry for me when I was around here before and they'd hate to see me repeating that sort of mistake again; would I not come in and have a drink: "no". Another course was tried: "sure even if you got a job around here, what sort of money would you be on: forty pounds a week if you were lucky", " your own mate Paddy O Donaghue was telling us that he was getting one hundred and twenty pounds a week," " yes and had the payslip to prove it", chimed in another with an emphatic nod of the head; this continued," a mate of mine a fully qualified accountant, started work last September: what was his pay?, "how much", "fifty pounds, a fully qualified accountant", "yes". It was a conversation I shouldn't have entered: what defence or explanation did I owe them, for trying to get a job in my own country, the money in England or in Timbuktu notwithstanding; "will the accountant's pay always stay at fifty pounds; did Paddy O Donaghue say he was getting such a wage fifty two weeks a year, if so, he's the only con-struction man in England that can make such a boast: wages don't rise, if you miss time for holidays etc you don't get paid, you get no expenses, but that's not the point, do I not have the same right as any of you to get a job here". John Quigley who was training to be a teacher and had some intelligence unlike the rest, had joined the crowd, he'd been briefed by the others, and he now joined the debate," John Wille, er sorry John Thomas, I and I'm sure the boys here are happy to say yes": no agreement from the boys, " but there is limited resources and opportunities here, if you have the option to have a job in England: well it's only fair to ask you to go back to it, if not someone else will have to go: someone who will have to get a job, get used to the ways things are, learn about all the pitfalls: things you already know, it's not that we want to get rid of you or anything": vigorous nods of agreement from the boys, " but you have the knowledge and experience to make the most of it"; "that's right, sure maybe if we were doing the right thing ourselves we be over there with you": " if that is so you know where it is, and no matter how you put it, I know what I'm listening too" I replied and walked off displeased with my answer. Only later did it occurred to me that those arguments had been rehearsed and not just among each other, there was more experienced input: input from more senior people.

The following week started with a repetition of the same; they were putting a concrete retaining wall and foundations in for a school that was relatively local, utilising a lot of the skills I'd grew familiar with in England; when I entered the site I could see they were struggling and I asked for a job, claiming experience: the foreman was interested and asked a number of questions, which I answered; he asked where I had obtained such knowledge, I told him: he hummed and hawed and asked me to come back tomorrow. I returned the next day he was still clearly interested, and obviously the work was not progressing, but what seemed to be the clincher was: would I move away from my home which was about four miles away to say the nearest town where I wouldn't be known, for a time at least: "to like let the local lads come to terms with someone from England getting a job and not them", I replied fiercely: "you pig ignorant bollix you, where the fuck do you think I come from": "cool down, you know the people around here resent anyone that's been to England getting a job before them": " if they're better than me, then give them the job; but if not give it to me"; I turned and started to leave fearing my own possible reaction, he shouted after me, "hold on we might be able to sort something out"; this after the insults I had lathered on him: the fellow clearly needed me on the job, but was willing to jeopardise the job rather than hire an "untouchable". This knocked me for six: how could one prevail against such an attitude. I didn't know what to do: I had been the village idiot, now I was the public pariah. Images of England started to soften: Hughie and co might be only a one off, ould navvy was only a joke, backhanders still left you with most of your wages and weren't universal, at least one wasn't feeling betrayed as well as abused. Other thoughts emerged to counter these: how badly hurt was Hughie, what was the long term plan in England: did I ever envision rearing a family there, could you ever be sure of anyone you met there. I decided I would at least try some of the higher value jobs, police and civil service, and leave the likes of construction for now. I decided to apply to join the guards, it was a permanent pensionable job, with decent enough of wages, fringe benefits like low car insurance and mortgages, and early retirement; of course, there were dangers and risks but legality and the entire police force were behind you; in England there were risks and you were on your own. I went into the guards barracks that Thursday, the sergeant Peader Mulvey was there, he peered at me quizzically as though trying to recall me, " um young Harn is it not," " yes sergeant Mulvey I was thinking of having another go at joining the guards while I'm still under the cut off age of twenty six,"; he looked at me as though I'd just confessed to being a serial killer; "sure aren't you in England"; "yes I was but I'm back now and like to try to join the guards while I can": " ya can fuck right off John Harn" he replied. I was taken aback at this response, for one thing I knew from Eamonn that they were required to act in a courteous manner, but mainly I could see no reason for it. "What sort of answer is that" I asked; "you're in England: how would expect a job in the guards", "what the hell are you on about man; I'm from up the road, and my brother is a guard, as you well know" I replied. "If there is a position going in the guards it's going to someone who is out of work here, not someone with a good job in England. Oh

I also remember you were too short; so if you don't mind wasting any more of my time Mr Harn, goodbye": it was clear he remembered me and my details well, for all his put on confusion, when I came in. "I am now over the height, else I wouldn't have wasted your time, and I deeply resent you telling me I'm not allowed to even apply for this or any other job in this country", "get out to fuck outside that door, before I come around this desk and batter the living shite out of you" he roared. I went around the desk to him, and noticed I was actually taller than him, and as I was only three quarters of an inch over the bottom regulation height, what height was he: you wouldn't notice such a small difference, and he was only in his mid-thirties; this brought the suspicion of the pull into my mind. " Sergeant Mulvey", I said " I have as much right of a job in this country as you or any other member of the fucking guards, and I resent being excluded, because I got up off my arse and went to England, I went there to avoid being idle and to get some experience of work, so I'd be better qualified to get a job here", "you fucking bastard," he sort of shrieked at me, and grabbed his baton and came at me: I struck him in the mouth and drove him over a chair so he ended up with is head under the desk and his legs leaning on the chair pointing up in the air. This was an imprison able offence; to go into a police station and hit a police officer causing him at least some injury would entail about six to twelve months in jail; so maybe I'll stay in Ireland after all I thought. I was still enraged; I walked out of the barracks slowly and sat into the car and drove home; at least when I got to court I could testify under oath to what was said to me by sergeant Mulvey. Nothing happened, not that day or Friday, on Saturday I was in the town and I walked past the clearly marked sergeant Mulvey and he didn't even look at me. It wasn't too hard to figure out that the reason why he did nothing, was that his reaction to an emigrant looking for a job would not stand public scrutiny: public and actual policy being two different things again. Sunday evening came and I found he managed another way: Emanon. Emanon was supposed to be on duty and therefore not expected back that weekend; but Sunday evening he rushed up to the house a jacket over his uniform shirt and confronted me in front of everyone else in the house; "what in holy hell were you up to with sergeant Mulvey" he roared; this elicited enquiries from the rest of the family, "he attacked sergeant Mulvey, when sergeant Mulvey queried why he was asking to join the guards when he had a job in England, apparently there are a lot of local lads interested, lads that are out of work and sergeant Mulvey eventually had to use force to remove him from the station. He said that only for my sake he would have arrested him". I stated this was lies and gave the true version of events which elicited even more horror from my family, I invited them to look at his face for proof : I'd left my mark; my little sister Muriel confirmed sergeant Mulvey was marked. Muriel was sent out of the room, the rest confronted me: "did you go mad in England? what got into your head? do you want to disgrace the house", "did you think you would do Emanon any good". I told them what happened and told them that I thought I was as entitled as anyone to get a job here; I also said that I didn't want Emanon to in any way defend or intercede for me, I was pushing twenty one and would take sole responsibility for my own affairs. People didn't think that way; if you went they, assumed you stayed gone, or brought something back: the price of a house; set up your own business or at least not compete with the locals for jobs; I might disagree with this, but that was the way people thought. What did you think I asked them. "Well you seemed to do a lot better in England than here", "you're attitude seemed to have changed: is it any longer suitable to here", "you have to consider what the neighbours think around here", "the way you are going you will get yourself jailed around here": it was clear I was no longer welcome. To finalise matters P J Mohan called to say he be returning on Tuesday and would I like a lift: I could see no option but to accept it.

It wasn't as though I was expecting much, I had envisioned seeking work for a long time; perhaps returning to England after four or five fruitless months, but to be apparently rejected by all and sundry even my own family. I spent the next day wandering about the house and farm aimlessly, thinking of this stratagem, that stratagem: rejecting all. Bill tried talking to me about the neighbours; I told him I didn't consider them neighbours any longer. I just didn't know where I stood: there wasn't even much point in even coming home for a holiday any longer, to what or whom was I coming home to.

On the last day there was one strange note struck: I was coming around the far side of the house when who should arrive in his big fancy car, but uncle Bat; good I thought, here is an expert who will be well fit and willing to tell me how to succeed in London; but surprisingly he only stayed a very short time, driving past me looking out the opposite side I was on, as though something very interesting was taking place in the field: if it was anyone else, I'd have thought they were avoiding me. I enquired with Muriel who was at home for the Easter holidays, she said it was strange, he sat down and took a glass of whiskey from my mother, but when my mother mentioned that I was at home, he swallowed the glass of whiskey and rushed off, saying he forgot something, and he surveyed the back of the house where his car was parked as though afraid of something; it appeared uncle Bat wasn't anxious to see me after all, which was totally out of character.

I gained some sense of peace that evening: if you were careful and perhaps changed out of the buildings a reasonable life could be lived; around here it appeared even if you did get a job, you'd be resented forever. As for socialising: hang in with Paddy and the brothers and be watchful and wary at all times. P J arrived the next day; my mother asked when I'd be back I reminded her, that she always told me, never to stay anyplace you are unwelcome, so I didn't know when I'd be back. There were protests at this, and old arguments were regurgitated as to why they acted as they did: my good, how I done before, what the neighbours thought; I replied I wasn't thick or daft and I knew how to read the situation for what it was. I got into the car and headed off once again to England.

P J told me his son had had a burst appendix and for a while it didn't look good; he was still rattled over the entire affair. He told me he was glad to have me along so he could get some rest as he needed to work the next day: some way to have to rear a family. I went up again on deck on the way over to assay the crowd; again it was obvious there were men fleeing the law. I drove from Holyhead to London, P J sleeping in the back. I entered the house early in the morning and as always ould navvy was up; "well fuck and blast it and here is me hoping you were dead and buried" said ould navvy to me in welcome: same old, same old. I met no one else and got a few hours' sleep, but was awakened by the landlady banging on the door demanding rent; I had been prepared to pay up to date, but this abrupt demand incited me to argue that I shouldn't have to pay for when I was on holidays; I ended up paying for one of the two weeks; as she left ould navvy approached her saying, "do you know what now ma'am, and I doubt that I could get someone right for that room," " I already tried ould navvy; but if things take up a bit, I'll clear him out regardless"; she left, ould navvy opening the door for her. Ould navvy was beginning to rib me. I met the others later; Paddy had got into a fright with a local Irish hard man and though it was a close thing he had managed to win, but he was well marked: he figured the boxing saved him. The brothers though I could get a couple weeks with them after the Easter, this would get me back into the scene. Finally I asked them if they knew what was up with ould navvy: I was afraid that I'd forget myself and do something. Various ideas were mentioned: natural stupidity, drink induced brain damage, lack of said organ, finally one of the brothers suggested that the reason he was so jealous and vindictive was that, he'd never got the ride: that he was a virgin, and the germ of an evil plan formed in my mind. I ventured again to the pubs but in a very conservative and restrained manner, generally with Paddy or the brothers, drinking little, keeping very aware of myself and leaving early; I found I had acquired the habit of scanning the company regularly like so many others. I in the main limited myself to seeking knowledge about work.

My plan to scupper ould navvy came to fruition: I thought of a way in which he could show himself up badly in front of the landlady. On Easter Saturday I was positioned in the brothers' room which overlooked the road and about five o clock I noticed the landlady walking up the road: this was the only time of the week you could predict her movements. I went down into the kitchen where ould navvy was loading up on the scrumpy preparatory to going out: this was the time at which he was at his most insulting and easy to set off. As expected he set off up the stairs muttering "bollix" or some such; I ran past him up the stairs shoving him, this stopped him exactly where I wanted him,"fuck you ya bastard, I'll do you in yer sleep if that woman doesn't throw you out". I could see the shadow of the said woman approaching the door. "The problem with you ould navvy is you never got the ride": "twhat are ya saying ya cunt I was riding women while ye were ateing shite out of yer nappy". I could see the landlady put her key in the door, I started laughing at ould navvy; "you ride a woman: look at the cut of ya" I said, moving out of sight of anyone at the door. Ould navvy was now enraged: "titn'd I ride women up and down Cricklewood high road, Kilburn high road, and in every dancehall and pub in London", he paused for breath; "I rode every landlady I ever had, and the barmaids in nearly every pub I went into"; "ould navvy" I heard the landlady shout; I rushed into my room, to one, contain my mirth so as to not give away my presence, and two to carry out the rest of my plan: I had freed the painted fast little window in my room, I squeezed out of in on to the ladder I had left there previously, it was so small I had to take my jacket out afterwards; I climbed down the ladder, ran into the overgrown little alleyway at the back of the house, went around to the shop, and bought the newspaper and a few things, and headed back to the house; I entered as the landlady was taking ould navvy to task in no uncertain manner: "what in the living fuck do you mean James ignorance by saying this man ruse you into talking the shite you did"; I stood there stunned; ould navvy's toothless mouth was forming into various contortations and emitting unhuman like sounds; "what's up" I asked: "ould James ignorance was roaring the wildest most immoral dirty minded rubbish, at the top of his voice when I came in here, and he claimed you ruse him to it" she answered ; "Mrs Walsh if you go out and check under the sink, you'll find what was rising ould navvy" I replied: she carried out an immediate inspection and found the scrumpy. The upshot of it was the scrumpy went down the drain; ould navvy had to pay five weeks back rent, and his rent increased from five to eight pounds; as ould navvy was only a day labourer and was hired more for entertainment that work value he spent a sober month afterwards: something the other lads elicited from ould navvy's mutterings, that hadn't happened for well in excess of forty years; he even looked better: his usual red facial colouring fading and lightening, except when he was around me, then he went a deep purple. Silence; except for the odd ejaculation of bastard under his breath, reigned. I started work with the brothers' employer on Easter Wednesday: back to square one.

Chapter 7

I then began to get the picture, at least in the large, of what life for the Irish in London was like: bare, scruffy and constrained and it also came with risks. You worked in jobs locals disliked or disdained; you lived in rough accommodation with rough and ready manual workers many of dodgy character: either natural or acquired; you socialised in the pub: there were no other social outlets or amenities to make use of spare time; your work and social associates contained a fair proportion of criminal and sometimes dangerous people, whom critically you would not know, unlike at home, where such people were widely known and notorious. Outside those territories the Irish were not welcome. We came from the wrong side of the bog road, to live on the wrong side of the tracks.

It was little enough wonder that so many went to hell on the drink, especially men who found the conditions harsh: the unneighbourlyness, the ruthlessness, who failed to find fulfilment from the rough monotonous work that was the majority of the building work: most probably the more intelligent men, by extension the men who could have made a difference to the whole Irish community, could have branched out into other fields: widening the scope and opportunity of the Irish in London. It probably was at least some mitigation for the unscrupulous greedy behaviour of many who got positions of power: at least if you got money you had some compensation; but this gave rise to excessive greed and ruthless efforts to control men, which in an Irish setting manifested itself, as coercive cliquish behaviour, which bound men to a particular role, job, pub and place to stay: usually ordained by home neighbourhoods, and gave rise to separate, small and antagonistic fiefdoms controlled by bullying unscrupulous individuals, that were almost always inadequate opportunists: men limited and incapable themselves, who by force and chicanery usurped the abilities and production of others; their allies, drink and the authorities: that were just apathetic at best, or at worst regarded the Irish as lesser or enemies. I had the general picture alright, but the devil lay in the details, and these I hadn't got.

Back to work: six weeks with the brothers' employer, three months on the pile breaking and that was the summer; careful ventures out, scan the crowd before you go in, scan them while inside, great care with any contact with women: Hughie went to every pub and dance with me. Initially I sought to go as much as I could in company with Paddy or the brothers; initially this was well accepted, but the wary behaviour, the lack of perusal or sometimes even response to women, caused this acceptance to become bare, I was once again the "hanger on" in the gang: again a circle formed in my life.

I became interested in pursuing the bookkeeping once again: a November start of eight months course for a senior certificate was pencilled in. I saved money. Ould navvy was quieter but resentful. I got to drive the van for two weeks: longer days but experience of driving and taking care of a van. I didn't respond to letters from home.

September came and I was once again seeking work: the usual round of altered reality: who did I know, where did I drink, where was I from, was I in with "x" or was it "y"?: Machiavelli himself would have trouble besting the scheming that appeared necessary to get a job digging a hole. I got a job breaking piles and produced near double what anyone else did for no other reason than to avoid the nonsense job hunting entailed listening to; but when the bulk of the work was done I was let go: the "lads" were kept; the foreman probably feeling a bit sorry for me, gave me the whispered tip that I should get "in" with someone.

In late October I sought to sign up for the bookkeeping course: again I was told there were no places available: this time I made a complaint; I was signed on a course and an apology was forced out of the receptionist. I got a job pouring concrete in late October, and this was resented by two lads on the site who apparently wanted to get their brother into the job: what value there was to a job pouring concrete. It appeared the memory of need, plain resentment and the desire to form a clique, or have some sort of hold on a job over-rode all reason and balance: it was a job pouring concrete: a hard and dirty job. My assiduous attending of the boxing classes again came in handy: I only exchanged a few blows with them, but the fact I could handle myself, clearly staved off more trouble, and they got the sack. The boxing came in handy again one night I was out with one of the brothers and someone picked a fight with him for no apparent reason, when he began to get the upper hand another intervened, I had to step in then, I owed the brothers too much: it was a short but vicious encounter which we won, but we were both marked; the brother didn't know them, or what it was about: same old, same old. I started my course, again the sole Irishman, again there was no interaction with others; I did as before: done my work and kept to myself. Women: the odd dance or drink; no more.

Christmas came, the brothers and Paddy headed home, myself and ould navvy had the house to ourselves, in which a total lack of any communications reigned. I sent a card home: "merry Christmas to all; from John T". Try as I might I could not get work over Christmas: I was left with too much spare time on my hands. I went out hesitantly: boredom and a feeling I should be partaking in a youth, which I had always been out sync with, the forces impelling me. The first couple of days I crept about, very hesitant on my own. But after a few days I reacted against this; I was here, I was young, if necessary I could defend myself: if this was where I had to live, then I could hardly be afraid of it. I ventured into the more "exciting" venues: push, shove, "it was the drink", etc. On New Year's Eve I ventured out to the same pub and dancehall I had the year before when I met Hughie; I had scrupulously avoided them until now. I again found tribulation, but of a different sort. I seen neither Hughie or any of his mates, and the single enquiry I was able to make to the only person I knew there, also drew a complete blank. This person was a sleazy individual whom I met on a job; he never worked hard but slimed his way in with everybody he could;

I had been told never to trust him. The conversation turned to women, he pointed out there was few here tonight: this was true; he said him and his mate, an individual like himself were going to a brothel nearby and would I come. Drink fuelled daring, and the burthen of one's "virginity" drove me to investigate further. After a journey through a back alley and a backyard we were let into a darkened house; inside the house was a pleasant comfortable lounge, hung with dirty pictures, around which clients sat smoking and talking in a relaxed manner, waiting for their turn: it was not unalike a hotel foyer. My mates turn came, then mine: I balked, but got the opening times to leave open the possibility of another foray. I didn't go the next day as it was new year's day and likely to be busy, but I did the day after. What drove me? Lust, an inferior complex towards those so experienced, jealousy, a feeling that one wasn't whole, and that one was not one of the crowd, most of all, the feeling that I had missed out on enough of the things other people my age had done during their life. I followed the route of the night before, and was met by the "day madam": one bitter looking woman; "looking for fun" she said in a curt businesslike manner. She nodded to one "lady": a tall blonde in an ultra-short skirt; they consulted and I heard snatches of the conversation: " no oirish... above that... who... well, Cherie always needs business": I knew I should've run. "Cherie's the only 'lady' available I'm afraid: she's not the best but is very experienced"; how experienced I was, is shown by the fact that I acquiesced to such a recommendation. Cherie was small, distinctly on the heavy side, and not good looking atoll; a smallish scrunched up face under a mop of curly brown and black hair painted and powdered heavily to cover up what seemed to be eruptions of some sort. She was smoking a rolled up fag, and smiling at me with her mouth but not her eyes, asked what I wanted, and prompted: straight up, blow job or back scuttle. "Straight up " I replied and was told to take my clothes off. She finished her fag and took off her clothes, the discernible odour of piss becoming evident. I was highly inexperienced and had only the knowledge gained from a couple dirty magazines, and numerous unreliable recountings around canteen tables and in work vans to guide me. I started to fondle her breasts: "stop pulling at me tits, me twat is down there" shouted Cherie, the last pretence of any even, put on amiability gone. I came to the fore, so to speak and was fumbling around to position myself; "what the fuck are you at or have you got anything down there" shouted Cherie; I finally got myself in the correct position and started the job; "stick the fucking thing in to fuck: I haven't got all day" roared Cherie: this was enough for me, even in my clearly disordered state of mind: I withdrew and put my clothes on rapidly and gave Cherie her fifteen pound fee to prevent more shouting, and left. I don't believe I ever felt a bigger fool in all the days of my life: I could barely hold my composure on the way home. "Well" I thought when I arrived home and calmed down a bit, "new year is John Thomas Harn's time for romance: Hughie and Cherie": it was almost laughable.

I spent the next few days analysing my stupidity, as I did exactly one year ago: again a circle in my life; but this time there was no correction, no assuaging hurt pride: I had been a prize fool plain and simple.

I ended up figuring that women might well have no part in my life: I was a late starter if my shapes could be considered a start; I had two very bad experiences which seemed to point to a naivety or ineptitude in my dealings with the opposite sex; and finally I was uncomfortable with my present existence. I thought of my uncle George for the first time in many years. He had never married and lived in the local town after spending most of his life in England; I was only one of the family to go near him, and in time found him quiet interesting; I ended up spending a fair amount of time with him often doing some chores or running messages for him; he had died when I was fifteen; he seemed to manage quiet well without a woman. So the bottom line: women were not an absolute necessity.

Paddy and the brothers returned from Ireland, one of the brothers had a black eye for failing to repeatedly buy drink for his "mates" in Ireland: former schoolmates and "neighbours". So nothing much had changed there.

I went to meet the van which didn't come, and with a clearer mind accessed things. I had a job, in six months I should have a qualification which would be capable of providing me with better work, I had a few pounds saved and had a fair idea of my surroundings; the rest I would have to leave to the future.

The job concrete pouring ended in March, I was out two weeks, the usual canvas: a descent in status to the lowest rung: an out of work Irish navvy; a descent in reality to the near surreal: who you knew, where you drank, where you came from in Ireland, who were you in with, and so on, and no questions about the actual work; a descent to the corrupt: "would you take care of one if they gave you a job", "a fiver or more off the wages to me"; a descent into depression at one's lot. I got a job pile braking again; with experience I could pick which piles were easy to break: ones where the digger had knocked pieces out of when digging out the soil around them: I chose these and ripped into them nearly doubling what the next best man was capable off: this done me no favours with my workmates, but I was desperate to avoid another round of work cadging. One or two were let go before me, but I went in June: one of my workmates informing me I would have being better if I took my time and the lads would have had me along for a drink to "their pub", and I could have got "in with them".

I got my senior certificate in bookkeeping: third out of forty. I, decided I'd get the summer out of the buildings then away for good. Another subcontractor: I decided I'd make some attempt to get "in with the boys ": first night's drinking: alright, second night a wild scrimmage of a fight in which it took all the skills I learnt in the boxing club to get out of the pub without serious injury, if not unmarked. I was let go the next day: I had being perceived as deserting, and three of the boys had got hurt. The cause of the fight: our subcontractor has a dispute with another subcontractor, and such was their sway, that they got most of their men to fight for them, and such was their duplicity that they duped others into taking part; like yours truly. Neither subcontractor took part personably: they were both small, physically inferior men, but seemed to think that they became big men by having bigger men fight at their behest. How one wondered did the Irish survive atoll, and how when discordant, demeaning episodes like this, could be sown by such inferior men, could they conceivably act, or certainly thrive as a body. Getting in with, where you were from, what pub you drank in, who you knew: it was all an issue of control. Then "who" was the control exercised by. What then were the effects in Irish society in England in general: it is the common reaction of the bullied to bully in turn, of the abused to in turn abuse; how was Hughie made; what was at the base of the casual push, shove and dig one received in nearly any Irish pub or dancehall; how far from the truth was the old saw about the Irish as wife beaters.

Thankfully this time I did have an option: I had a senior certificate in bookkeeping: a qualification that could get me a job; I also had about two and a half thousand pounds saved enough to give me a fair bit of time to access some job. I got a suit, I got a briefcase and told ould navvy, when he saw me dressed up and enquired if I thought I was a "fecking lord", that I was getting married. I read a book or two on applying for such jobs: interviews etc, to the accompaniment of hissing and drawn out sighing from ould navvy: books really seemed to exasperate him. I set forth and after a stumbling start, seemed to be making an impression, but I found it depressing: memories of the long vain job quest I had undergone in Ireland came back to me; I was also in an alien environment, even if I worked in England it was always in an wholly Irish or Irish dominated environment; also the spectacle of an Irishman looking for an office job was unusual and it's fair to say in some quarters unwelcome. On top of all this it was midsummer the high point for construction work; after three weeks I suspended my job hunt and returned to the buildings. I went working as a form worker: it paid better, as one of the brothers said it was an unreliable rough job at high rather than low wages, and I would have another occupation to fall back on. Why did I need so many need so many ways of making a living: to begin with the long futile job hunt I had carried in Ireland and its attendant humiliations and to end with the same futile job hunt which failed to obtain for me a job in any ways commiserate with my abilities or preferences. Some things you never overcome.

With a few hitches I managed, and by late autumn I was earning over one hundred pounds a week. It was my intention to try the bookkeeping again, and after that job and I did make a brief try, but there was word going around of a job with long hours and good money: about one hundred and forty pounds a week; I had about three grand saved, and the idea was to get another two and then have a go at the bookkeeping. That is at least what I told myself; how when I had a chance, could I not separate myself from the scrabbling, scheming, violent and overall harsh and uncertain world of the buildings in which the lowest rank of people intellectually, morally and ethnically: the Irish, toiled to exist, is a hard question to answer. It was probably down to fear of the unknown, the crossing of boundaries totally into a foreign world. It's basis originated in what we were: emigrants; we didn't want to travel, to change our culture; and reinforcing this characteristic was the circumstances of our exile: we didn't leave because we were unable or lazy or crim-inal: in the vast majority of cases; indeed many that could be better so described stayed at home to get good and responsible jobs via the "pull": our exile was unjust, and being that it came from our own people unlike in times gone by from an alien source, was diffi-cult to react to: where could or should your loyalties lie.

The job started in November: the same codswallop: who do you know, are in with, were from, but slightly more subtly: there was some evidence of slightly more intelligence among chippies than labourers. I got on with work; the challenge of new work and the fact one was earning good money buffering the more noxious aspects of the job.

I went out regularly enough during the year to the safer places; tried my hand at courting: even got a woman to come home with me, but she sobered up when she met ould navvy lurking in the kitchen, and demanded a cab home.

Christmas came again surprisingly fast: the boys went home, I sent a card home: "best wishes John T". I didn't go out that new year: I was superstiously afraid to; neither did ould navvy : he had no money. This lack led him to speak to me for the first time in a month to sub money from me: "in the name of fuck and all decency will you not sub me a fiver, so I may go out this new year's eve": the burst of laughter that I responded with, elicited a stream of swearing and cursing extravagant even for ould navvy. It was nineteen seventy eight.

The job continued and was relatively stable. There was the odd bit of baloney: two brothers decided to pick on my mate: a peaceable older man, probably for that sole reason: to let out their vitriol on someone who they could bully; I got involved: again my boxing skills became the most valuable asset I had. The job was in two stages and towards the end of the job men were hired by the main company from the subcontractor to work on the first stage on a short term basis: a practice called day work, to do the snagging and accommodate last minute changes of mind: pipes going a different way etc. One morning in April two vans disgorged twenty new workers to apparently work on this basis; these included no less an individual than ould navvy and several others of his type: past any value as workers. This it transpired was because there was to be an inspection of the entire project by the main contractor's head office and this included a headcount of the number of men working on site; ould navvy and co were picked up at short notice to represent "dead men": men who were on the books, but didn't in fact exist, their wages going to the subcontractor, out of which a cut would be paid to the contractor's management staff. The inspection couldn't have been too through: they passed despite the calibre of worker like ould navvy, being evident. The next day the entire new "workforce" was gone. Where did the corruption end, one wondered; and by what means could one hope for stability of employment never mind advancement in this game. Gear was stolen from the subcontractor; the evidence: the fence was knocked and a container broken into, the lock cut; the same gear which I was very familiar with: marks, numbers etc, was later seen by me on another site this subcontractor worked on, when I was sent there, to help collect some gear. Towards the end of the job a new arrival who had been a foreman on another job sought to make life difficult for me. He started off by comments like "there was not much work on this job", to questioning my work, to attempts to give me orders:

eventually he gave orders in front of the real foreman allowing, me to ask who the real foreman was: this stopped him; this was indicative of the low level hassle and animosity that seemed to be a part of any Irish run job. I didn't however, through the activities of this new arrival, get transferred onto a new job this subcontractor had. This turned out to be a good thing: about one quarter way through the new job, the subcontractor asked for, and by means of threatening to stop the job midway through: making it expensive and difficult for another subcontractor to take up, got most of the payments for the job; to get a full payment he had to complete a further six weeks; he went "sick" and a small part of the wages were paid in cash as he was "unfit to get to the bank" and was relying on a sub from the local pub landlord: this amounted to about a quarter of the wages; in real terms less as it was paid in the pub, which necessitated the buying of drink. After he got the money he disappeared; this behaviour was from a subcontractor who had carried many high quality relatively complex jobs over a ten year period, had good workmen and was ran his business in a viable manner, but when he got the chance to "pull the stroke": he scuppered the lot. Like so many other Irish subcontractors he was merely a common crook, and despite having decent qualities as a builder when the chance presented itself, his criminal nature asserted itself, subverting these qualities.

My social life continued in its own dismal manner: I managed to "pull" a woman in February only to have a man confront me and identify himself as her husband: a fight would have ensured, but for the intervention of Paddy O Donaghue who confirmed his claim: how could one win. I went out to a major Irish pub in Cricklewood on paddy's day; the fight that broke out was so bad I had to crawl out under the benchs that lined a wall for part of the way to get out unscathed; I seen a woman glassed and the police released their dogs into the pub, to bite and maul without restraint. Ould navvy had once again two black eyes the next day: some things just didn't change.

Easter followed rapidly that year; I spent a day around Madame Tausauds and a day in the British museum and enjoyed myself. The job ended in early May; I found I had over five and a half grand saved; in the final analysis, there was money to be made on the buildings in England. I decided it was time to turn seriously to bookkeeping: I had half the price of a house in Ireland; get experience of bookkeeping; buy a house in Ireland, get a bookkeeping job at home and all would be sound. I turned to the night school I had attended and they sent me to a number of agencies that let out bookkeepers on a temporary basis to firm. The most seedy one of these agencies, sent me to a rag and bone concern in the docklands: there over two days I began my new career, and managed to do the job; another rag and bone concern, a wedding dress shop, a minicab firm ran by Indians that could speak only very poor English; it was varied and badly paid: full time, forty pounds a week, but I had an alternative to the buildings. Ould navvys comment "was I now a fecking Englishman, thinking that I was too good for the buildings" was easily answered: I said he wasn't good enough for the buildings as all the other replacement dead men that came on to our site were there the next day but him, this wound him up no end, and made our relationship even worse, if that was possible.

The source of an insult, as much as it's ferocity can have effect. I was sent out the beginning of my forth week with the agency to a travel agency to do the books. I was met by a tall willowy blonde woman, she had classical if slightly severe features, and a cut glass accent. I found myself attracted to her, and maybe by showing it a bit, I set her off.

As she was showing me about the place of work, she pointed out the toilets and asked me if I had any problem with them; I didn't understand this and enquired if she was asking if I could use them; "well you know with some oirishs" she said: "no I don't: are you suggesting some Irish people don't know how to use the toilet" I replied: "well we've had problems before" she said, "what sort of problems" I replied more bemused at this stage than anything else, "oh don't mind" she replied and continued with her induction. It was only when I settled into work that it dawned on me that she had deliberately insulted me, for no other reason than being Irish. A thousand times I had being far more roughly insulted, but it didn't sting as much: perhaps my view was again skewed by past experiences: my relief at leaving the buildings and finding a job I could do, had presupposed me to thinking my new surrounds were perfection, and the shock when finding they were not was severe; my inexperience with women also contributed to the hurt: I just didn't expect an attractive sophisticated woman to act in such a way. I finished the job in four days not the at least five expected; the boss was pleased and hinted at a full time position coming available in the near future: I ignored this indeed was in such a state of dudgeon that I wouldn't shake hands with him as I left. I seethed all weekend and I didn't go back to the agency the following week. Instead I heard tell of a formwork job going nearby so I went into the appropriate pub, claimed I was from a different county than I was, bought a fellow I knew from there a couple of drinks, and was hired from that Wednesday. I lied to myself: saying it was only to get the best out of the summer.

Why? We were not tourists or travellers or explorers: we were exiles: we didn't come, we were sent: thus we lacked the ambition to immerse ourselves in another culture. Resentment against our exile, our belief that elsewhere was our true home, made us seek some element of the place from where we originated, however unsatisfactory that element we ended up with: occupation in my case. To copper fasten my self-delusion: I was informed about and invited to my sister Nuala's wedding in late September; this invitation was accompanied by a letter from my mother which nearly begged me to go home. I visited Nuala, met her intended: a diesel mechanic working for a muck away firm: they were buying a small house in South Norwood and the long term plans were to move home. After the wedding I'd go back to the bookkeeping.

The job lasted until mid-September: the usual high level of bullshit, but I didn't have to display my boxing skills; so there was some advance there. I attended the boxing club assiduously: being afraid not to; myself and Paddy with whom I could now easily spar attended a proper boxing club and I found I could spar with proper amateur boxers. I may have being becoming known for my boxing skills: I was in a pub one night and I started to chat with a woman over some mundane subject and a little man pushed himself between us: I caught him and shoved him back a good distance: his mates caught him as he attempted to come forward and I heard the word boxing mentioned; the woman cleared off. The social life was still the same: boring or dodgy. I listened to the little transistor radio in the evenings, or read up a bit more about bookkeeping and accountancy: which I now thought of as my true calling, despite my reluctance to practice it; I made the odd visit to the pub; and with women I was totally unambitious.

I went home to the wedding: my parents seemed pathetically grateful to see me, both Bill and Emanon seemed angry that I had stayed away so long: " ah it's the return of the exile, we were wondering if you ever coming back": I didn't bite, but when Emanon brought up the affair with sergeant Mulvey saying it caused him into trouble, I bit: I proffered to go and see Sergeant Mulvey there and then and inform him that as an adult man I was well fit to take responsibility for my actions; my parents intervened on my side which left Emanon fuming. I went to the wedding and stayed as much as I could in the background. Uncle Bat was there but didn't seem anxious to impart his wisdom on how to get on in England to me: which was just not like him; even when Emanon still prickly from our row the day before tried to set him on me: "do you have any advice to give this man about England uncle Bat, so he might get on like you did" he didn't rise to the bait: "the way it is, I'm just thankful that that man is holding down any job, considering the way he was going on: we have to be thankful for small mercies" and with that he walked away. It struck me then, that Bat could be hiding something; deliberating avoiding the chance to have a go at me just wasn't his style: it was as though by doing so he'd be navigating in dangerous waters.

I returned to England two days later; I promised my mother that I'd probably return sometime next year.

Back again I tried the old bookkeeping agency: no go, the frequent strikes were to blame: maybe, but my dropping them without warning probably didn't help; other agencies the same answer. I got a job form working with the brother's firm for a fortnight, then back to the weary old ritual of the job hunt once again. It was a time of industrial unrest and uncertainty therefore building work in general declined, as indeed did office work.

I got a week form working after two weeks, then a further two weeks break and a week pile braking; this job was stopped by the client: apparently unsure of the economic conditions. The subcontractor's response to demands for pay: "I'll pay you when I get paid".

Two more weeks out of work, a week sweeping floors: pay twenty five pounds. I tried the pubs, varied what county I was from, bought the undeserving drink, contacted every old employer, retried the agencies: every stratagem I knew: nothing. I spent a couple of days labouring for Paddy. December came; no work: it was now likely that if one was out of work much longer, it would be into the new year before they got work: I was desperate. England with work and money had purpose, to compensate for all the deficits: without this purpose it was scarcely bearable. It entered the second week of December: I didn't know what to do.

Late in that week I was in Sutton and I entered a large site which was in its early stages; I approached a man described as a "gaffer" to ask him for a job; he was a large powerfully built man with dark red hair, his two eyes when he turned to me seemed to have no expression atoll, that and his total stillness seemed to give off, what I can only describe as malignant vibes; he answered "no": that single word to my request for work; I was often more roughly refused: "fuck off", "no bollixes here" etc, but that one word was enough; I left that site feeling sort of relieved, despite my desperation for work, when I heard a summons behind me, " here you; the foreman wants to see you": it was the man who I was beginning to label the soulless one. Though I had only my intuition of this man to go on, had I not being desperate, I wouldn't have gone with him. The foreman was sitting behind a desk in an office, he was a bony, middle sized man with long dark greying hair, he had a heavily lined face, but lines that seemed to originate in bitterness rather than age, as he was only about forty, large deep set eyes which seemed to flicker, over a wide slightly open mouth, the lips curled back like a dog about to attack: the thought that entered my mind unbidden was "evil". I told him I was looking for a job as a chippie; he responded that it was not a good time of year to be out of work, but he might give me a chance; was I able to drive," yes", "good": I was hired. I left the office with a distinct feeling of unease at the people and the appointment, but could put no logical argument behind this feeling. I started the next day and there seemed to be little amiss: the people were noticeably quieter but everybody was busy and all attended Monday morning even if some were obviously not in the liveliest of form. I began to doubt my misgivings; the foreman was a bit harsh and drily critical, but how unusual was that; but then as I seen him walking about the site I seemed to think that I'd seen him before, but I couldn't say where. However I was earning one hundred and fifty pounds a week, when even Paddy and the brothers had trouble holding onto work. That the men were clearly afraid of the foreman, and the red haired man who was apparently a sort of ill-defined ganger man, I put down to the fact that work was scarce, and the times were uncertain. Signs however were appearing that my intuition was not that far out; the second week I was there I chanced upon an attack upon the foreman: I was coming up a temporary passageway when I saw two men rush in from outside the site and lay into the foreman in as viscous a manner as I had seen; as much from a sense of unfairness at two against one as to gain credit or advantage I entered the fray: I hit one with a sheet of plywood I was carrying and punched the other out of the way, I then grabbed the sheet of ply and jammed it in the passage way effectively, sealing then off from myself and the foreman; it was then I noticed than one of had been was using a hammer; attacks on foremen were not all that unusual, but using a weapon was: they seemed really put out about something. The foreman though bloodied seemed remarkably unshaken by this, as though well used of it; he told me to come up to a certain pub on the Harrow road and there "I would get in with them": knowing what that meant, I was reluctant: I didn't want to become a vassal of some quasi crooks quasi fiefdom, but I was sick, sore and tired of cadging work, and above that failing to get credit for my work because I wasn't one of the "buoys". I went for a drink in "their pub" on the harrow road; if I ever seen hard battle scarred men, it was there, but nothing untoward occurred; however when I was leaving I met a man who I knew from other work on the street outside; he mentioned to me that I was now going to the hard men's pub, when I pressed him to explain, he would only say to watch my back real careful with that crowd and that the main men were dangerous; I didn't know him that well so I had to leave it at that . Then on the last day before the Christmas closedown I was told by the foreman who I learned had the nickname "Sid viscous", that I was wanted to drive the van that evening as "someone had to be seen". I picked up "Sid viscous" and the red haired man and another individual a large wiry curly black haired individual with a glassy stare who I'd seen in the pub. I was told to park outside a particular pub, and after a time the "wanted man" was spotted, the two boys jumped out and accosted him, they then hit him a few times: roughed him up, no more; the foreman then jumped out and appeared to give the clearly frightened man a lecture. They then returned to the van and told me to drive off. The foreman chatted away to me in a friendly manner; he told me that the man was bad-mouthing the subcontractor and they had to warn him off, he also apparently knew that I did some boxing and seemed interested in this; I down played it, growing ever more wary of my new firm. I dropped them at the pub, and he handed me an envelope, as I went off to park the van at the yard, I found there was a hundred pounds in the envelope. I simply didn't know what to do: if I gave up that job I was unlikely to get another job until March when both the bookkeeping and buildings took up; if I stayed on that job I was clearly moving into dodgy territory. I left the question, for consideration over the Christmas period.

There was the usual departures of Paddy and the brothers this Christmas as the others, with myself and ould navvy remaining in mutual totally silent hostility. A departure from the usual form: I pulled a woman on boxing night and we returned to the house; however the police were at the house arresting ould navvy for being drunk and disorderly and then attempting to fight with them: end of romance, back to the usual form. I didn't go out New Year's night: superstitious fear; neither did ould navvy: no money. It was nineteen seventy nine.

Chapter 8

For a forth new year in a row I was in deep contemplation and perturbation about the events of my life. This new outfit was clearly dodgy and violent; well beyond any others I had encountered. I had been co-opted into participating in a criminal act; what else could be asked of me? There had to be dangers associated with this sort of activity; and if there was one thing I didn't want: it was hassle. I could afford to stay out of work for a while. I might get another job. What was I to do?

Not for the first time: I lied to myself. I'd hang on until March then back to the bookkeeping, when things would be getting busy for the April tax deadline. I'd not stay idle, losing money. Why did I take this clearly risky unnecessary step? Why did so many other Irish do likewise? At its base was what we were: forced exiles. This induced the ambition to show them up at home: "the stone the builder rejected turned out to be the corner stone" and such like. It also induced an element of self-pity: we were unfairly put upon; it was not right; and self-pity tends to be self-procreating: the more we dwell in it the more we enjoy it, which leads us to seek further reason for it: to magnify the insult wrongly done to us, even to the extent of seeking a harder environment. Therefore one accepted conditions one would not ordinarily accept. There was also a shade of machismo: we were the ones who struck out on our own; we took upon ourselves the veneer of the venturer, when we were the exact opposite: the banished. I started back, and was helped for the first time on site: I was put with a very experienced chippie, from whom I could and did learn: good. I was called to drive on two further missions in January to "see to men": nothing too drastic: a bit of roughing up, a lecture; I got one hundred pounds each time, even so: not good.

In February Paddy moved out to live with his girlfriend. The brothers offered to rent the room, but the landlady gave it to some distant relative of hers. Somehow his intellect was probably below that of ould navvy's. At first I thought he was pulling our legs, but with time realised he was genuinely as stupid and as awkward as he acted. He had no clue how to take care of himself; he couldn't cook, I tried to help him, but after five demonstrations on how to boil potatoes, and absolutely no progress made, after showing him the laundry and what to do there a number of times, and still have him come into the kitchen and shove his shit stained underpants almost under my nose asking, "And twhat am I ta do with them" and various other's aspects of total stupidity: I gave up. He was also ignorantly contrary and would attempt to spit at or hit someone, if they didn't accede to his demands. In company with the two brothers I went to the landlady to complain: "yearra 'tisn't he my cousin's young lad, so he'll be there when ye're gone". He was a lad that was too thick, and awkward, to do anything with; someone that properly speaking needed some sort of remedial care; a bur-then and cause of ignominy to his family; they followed the Irish habit of divesting themselves of the "black sheep" by sending him to England: letting their own people there shoulder such unjust encumbrances. I had to go: one ould navvy was enough. I asked around to see if I could get any place to stay. I got a room in one place: the other two lads staying there who were both barmen seemed friendly enough and reasonably intelligent. I didn't give notice where I was just in case things didn't go right; this rapidly turned out to be a good thing: I returned late one night quietly so as not to disturb anyone, when I heard strange noises coming from one of their rooms, the door of which was slightly open, I looked in more out of a sense of the wariness that my experiences had led me to develops than nosiness, and found my housemates involved in full homosexual sex; I had never even seen this in some of the dodgy books found around the sites: I left that house in that hour. This was another example of Irish banishments. Back in the old house the two brothers told me they were leaving, they had two rooms rented with a mate of theirs in Dagenham, unfortunately they had nothing for me. I regretted their loss more than that of Paddy: they were two quiet decent working men, who often helped me. I got another place near hand, but the second night I was there a fierce fight broke out between the other three lads that was there. Though it didn't involve me: eventually the sounds I was hearing drove me to investigate; one of them had an injured eye, and needed to go to a hospital the other two were trying to stop him: boxing skills again and a cab to the hospital, back, pack, back to ould navvy and co. Ould navvy designed to speak to me for the first time in weeks: "I'm beginning to doubt that the new lad is a bit thick" he confided to me in a low confidential voice; when ould navvy found you thick: you were thick. Shop window and local newspaper advertisements, were followed up: somehow there was always something up: it's just gone, I've just spotted "x", "y", "z" wrong with the plumbing, the electrics: basically no Irish; the resentment this caused was tempered by my own experience of living with some of the Irish. Eventually I asked around the job; an excellent room was offered: twelve pounds a week, front room upstairs, upstairs and downstairs toilet, good kitchen: I demurred wary of the source. That night I was in bed a bit early about ten when there was banging on the door: it was the new man, half holding his trousers up, barely covering his modesty but not his arse: "do ye have any shite paper" he shouted a couple of times. I locked the door got dressed, went up to the pub on the Harrow road and "signed up" for the room.

I was entangled further: and I soon found out what that entailed. In early March "Sid viscous" informed me a man had to be dealt with; I was to transport the two boys to a certain address and they would deal with him. What was different this time was Sid Viscous wasn't coming with us, and I had to put false number plates on the van. I went to where I was directed, and a thin, medium sized, fair haired man, in his mid-thirty's was attacked as he left his house: he was beaten harshly, his pullover and shirt ripped off, he was knocked to the ground and kicked, he crawled into the garden, and he seemed to be crying; the door of his house opened and a woman rushed out and attempted to intervene; she was slung roughly into the house, the man got his head and shoulders inside the door where a small girl screeching shrilly, attempted to cradle the now clearly distraught man's head, his wife tried to comfort the man and also tried to protect him from the kicks the two boys drove unrelentingly into his body: it was too much for me I got out, and got a hammer that was lying in the van to intervene I then found my arm grabbed: it was Sid viscous the foreman, he shouted at the boys and they left the man alone, with his screaming wife and daughter; we got in the van and somehow I drove away without crashing, dropped the boys at the pub, drove to the yard and removed the false plates. What in the name of fuck had I got myself involved with? I was just told the next day when I questioned the action that sometimes these things have to be done; I got four hundred pounds.

I didn't know what to do: they had me every which I turned: job, residence, they even knew I did a bit of boxing. The only thing that I could think of there and then, was to make a record of the events places times etc, and get it notarised: then if something did happen to me: there might be some comeback. I had no faith whatsoever in the authorities; I could think of no Irish organisation, or even well positioned and resourced person that I could turn to; even Paddy and the brothers the only good mates I had, were not as accessible any more, and I seriously doubted they could do anything. I knew that leaving an average subcontractor against their will, was a risky move: this was part of the purpose behind the "fiefdoms": they gave the leader of a clique the power to coerce men to do work that was dangerous, to live under conditions that were harsh, to impose on men, unfair burdens, all too often to make for their own inadequacies': to make up for in control, what they lacked as bosses in ability. But this crowd seemed to be a thing apart. I could only come up with the idea of hanging on, until I somehow came up with a better idea or maybe until I had saved enough money to buy a house in Ireland.

When I least expected or indeed wanted it, I acquired a girl-friend. I had to get a bus to the pickup point, and back in the evenings from my new residence; on the way back there was always this girl, also waiting for the bus; and one evening when we were sheltering under an awning waiting for a bus, we got talking, she asked me for as light, which I hadn't got as I didn't smoke, but this started us conversing on a regular basis: she was fairly good looking, was a bit older than me, a typist, and from about forty miles from me at home. We started going for the occasional drink. I found that no more than me, she was tired of England. My idea of getting the price of a house in Ireland, now began to assume other dimensions. I had by late March the sum of almost nine thousand pounds included in this was the proceeds of two other roughing up missions; a house in Ireland could be got for about twelve thousand upwards. As we got closer I started to tell her about this idea but was purposely non-committal. This got the response that she always had the ambition of moving back to Ireland. This swayed me against all reason, to stay with the outfit I was with, until I did have the price of a house in Ireland.

The truth: I was a coward: afraid to leave; I was callous: not really that worried about what I was involved in doing to people; I was greedy : I was making the best money I ever made; also: was I resentful of my presence here, of all the insults, shoves and general downgrades I received: did I wished to hurt someone back, however ill directed or at a remove that was; above all I was prideful: I wouldn't go back to Ireland until I had some evidence of my success such as my own house: that would show all who rejected me up.

I was the square peg in the round hole, forced there by circumstances, and developing a malevolent conformation of character as a consequence.

I was doing an almost regular line with my new girlfriend. We went out over Easter, and in a dancehall in Kilburn: I was picked on: boxing skills again. I had been putting more effort into the boxing: even sparring at a proper boxing club with proper amateur boxers, with whom I was generally able to hold my own, if not better. I won the fight, and found out later this man had a bit of a reputation as a hard man. My girlfriend consented to come home with me that night for the first time, despite the display of violence. I done my best but failed to complete my education, this I put down to the fight not inexperience. The next night we tried again and I succeeded: at almost twenty four, my education was complete. The next night there was a knock on my window; the red haired man who I now knew went by the name Nicky was below hitting it with a long thin stick; he beckoned to me to come down. I had to go to the yard replace the number plates on the van and pick up him and the other fellow I now knew by the name Cahal, there would be a third man in the back whom I would not see; my job was simply to drive and pay no attention to anything I saw; they felt I had let them down the night they'd beaten up the fair-haired man in front of his family: this was something I better not let happen again. Obviously something serious was up. I did as I was told. There was a wooden partition between the front and back seats with a hole cut into it: to allow the driver to look into the back and utilise the mirror: this was boarded up. I picked up the boys as instructed and an individual was let into the back whom I couldn't see, and followed their directions; we eventually stopped on a back street in Colindale; before long a man came along and the boys got out and seized him and brought into the back of the van; I could make out the sounds of a brief struggle which soon ended. I was directed to go to Luton, on the turn off the motorway, there was an accident and the traffic was directed into one lane; I somehow got the idea of taking the exact time, the number of police cars there, and further details. I was then directed to a large site in its early stages on the outskirts of Luton; I was further directed to pull up very close to a gate in the fence on the side away from the streetlights, and remain in the van; they appeared to carry the man in the gate; they reappeared about half an hour later: one man in the back, Nicky and Cahal in the front. The two boys appeared shaken: their hands shook, while they chain smoked all the way back to London; they were not so moved the night they beat the man in front of his wife and child. The third man was let out a little before the pub, I dropped the two boys at the pub, and brought the van to the yard and removed the false number plates. What the bloody hell had I got myself into?

The next day: the earliest that I was able to analysis with any degree of composure, the events of that night, I came to the conclusion that in all likelihood a man was murdered that night, and I was an accessory to murder.

My first instincts were to run. I lived in their house with two other men that worked for them; older men with the habit of heavy drinking, but they might well have the task of keeping an eye on me: certainly at this time, doing what I was doing for them; I'd have to flee a long distance, out of London for sure: well I had a few pounds so why not. Reality then asserted itself: these were killers, they would think nothing of killing me. They also had so much information on me: they knew for instance that I boxed; what else did they know.

Luckily I was off for the rest of that week, and had time to think. The first realisation: that over time I couldn't but, be considered a threat to them, and they would seek to eliminate that threat. I had to get a hold on them, as they had on me. Bookkeeping gave me a couple of ideas: the proper way to record things, and a certain familiarity with legalistics; I rented a type writer, printed everything out, was scrupulous with times, dates etc.

I bought a small camera and learned to use it. I made contact with a notary; an Indian with a tiny office in Camden town, and got these records notarised and gave instructions they were to be passed to the authorities if I failed to make weekly contact with him; this cost me the surprising amount of one hundred pounds.

I went back to work the next week to what I now knew were dangerous criminals. I knew that it would be seen as strange if I didn't express some concern: it would conflict with my reaction to the beating the fair haired man got in front of his family. I was told the man got a good beating, which he deserved. I pretended to accept this. I got five hundred pounds for my trouble. It took every inch of effort I had to concentrate on work and pretend everything was normal. After a few days, when I had retained my balance, I brought in the camera to work and surreptitiously took photographs of the fore man and Nicky and of other men of note on the site, and Cahal from the pub; I took several photographs and the best I had enlarged and copied several times: these I then included in the documents left with the notary. The fact they knew about the boxing gave me another avenue of inquiry; I showed the photos around in the regular boxing club, and eventually elicited the information that the red haired man "Nicky" was thought to have had been involved in the bare fist fighting scene. The other identification was "Sid viscous" the foreman, who went under the name "Jim", his real name was thought to be Gerald Howley, and he was described as someone that was into protection racketeering, and was dangerous, as he knew a lot of bad people. This; and I had set out, only with the ambition to earn an honest living, through work.

I avoided further contact with my girlfriend to save her from any danger. Two other "roughing up missions" and then another special; this time I saw some blood on Cahal's cloths. There was a fight on site between Nicky and another man: Nicky hammered into him and clearly was well able to handle himself, he bettered the other man, but kept on beating him until he was unable to move, well beyond what was necessary; the man's inert body was slung in a van, and brought off to God knows where. I did manage to take some photographs from a hidden vantage point, which I had enlarged and copied. There was another couple of roughing up missions and then another "special".

My girlfriend now commenced to pursue me; a woman pursuing John Harn: truly surreal, however I could not bring her back to where I lived for her own safety, and then I found out she shared a room with another girl. I eventually told her a bit about my predicament: and stated that it was my intention to try to buy a house in Ireland, which it was: I seriously had enough of London. "Jack I promise you if you buy a house in Ireland, I'll move in with you and have a hard go at making a life with you"; it shows the obscurification the Irish lived under that even to my girlfriend I changed my name somewhat: John to Jack an appellation that I was never known by; her name was Louisa Anne though she always went by Anne in my presence. I had about eleven and a half thousand pounds to my name; maybe I could get a few pounds from my father: a house should be available for about thirteen thousand pounds, and if Anne joined me, maybe all would work out well.

In early July, prime holiday season, I headed back to Ireland for a brief period. The people there, would have to take me, whether they liked it or not: I was not prepared to be associated with murder, and in the long run end up murdered myself to please the locals: those who were "on the inside track", and who sought to monopolise everything from "my country" for themselves. I quickly located two likely properties; small semidetached properties, not in the best of nick but with all the basics: they were located in a small town between where I came from and Anne came from, and were a little cheaper than in either of our home towns, also an element of apartness from "home" suited me. The price all told would be somewhat over thirteen and a half thousand: I would need a little over two thousand pounds. I had no time to truck around with banks, and the only approach I made was met by, "ah well now, you know, if England is involved it gets very complicated, like", to a request for a ten per cent mortgage on a house. I approached my father, who surprisingly, looked frightened, he hummed and hawed and told me Emanon was getting married, and he didn't know if he could get such money; after two day's consideration he told me nervously he "couldn't rightly at this time with Emanon getting married and everything, but next year it might be better": useless. I returned to England in defeat.

My girlfriend was seriously disappointed: she was thoroughly fed up of London.

My immediate concern was to get out of the mess I was in. The new idea: I leave them safely by showing them my notarised evidence; go back to bookkeeping, and as soon as was feasible, go at least to some other English city; never to stand on a building site again.

I planned and schemed, but did nothing: I was too cowardly. Two other roughing up missions took place; I brought my camera and a copy of the notarised notes to produce as some sort of protection if things boomeranged onto me. Then another special was scheduled, the forth: I began to consider myself a serial killer. I set off, changed number plates, picked up the boys, picked up the unseen one, and I followed their directions obediently. Suddenly I found I was driving in familiar streets, and we parked down from my old place of residence. I seen ould navvy leave the house to go to the pub, already staggering a bit from loading up on the scrumpy as per usual; I was about to say that this man knew me and that I would bend down under the dash board when suddenly the boys leapt from the van; then they had ould navvy: they quickly grabbed him, bundled him up: he could give no resistance, and hauled him into the back of the van. I tried to shout back that they had got the wrong man; but this was answered by frenzied shouts of "move" "move to fuck". I moved thinking, I would talk to them along the way: tell them they had the wrong man, and that this one could be let out along the road, as he was completely unlikely and probably incapable of going to the police; I told myself that I moved because the abduction might be witnessed and the boys would not like to be caught in the act: the truth was I was cowardly. Along the road I did attempt to explain, while following their instructions to drive to a site on the outskirts of Guildford, but anything I said was met by shouts, near screams, of "move" and "shut up and fucking drive". We arrived at the site, and following a now almost habitual practice drove to an unlit side of the site. I tried to shout to the boys; to make one last effort to intervene from the van, as I was told never to leave the van while the "job" was on: presumably so as not to see the third individual, but this was met by the threat to "do me" if I didn't shut up. I could see them lug ould navvy roughly into the site in the mirror. Then it was all too much for me: alright ould navvy might be a thoroughly ignorant and malicious old fool, who did in fact hate my guts, but I had lived in the same house as him for years, and I could not just see him murdered like that and do nothing; not for one minute did I believe that all that was doled out was a bad beating. I left the van in pursuit of them: armed with my camera, a copy of the notarised documents and photos in an envelope, and a three foot nail bar. I sought around the site in which the foundations were going in, and then heard hushed voices and some sort of squawked entreaties'; "get two sheets of the plastic over those bags", "Jesus naw boys, sure t'wasnt like I was serious atoll". I followed these sounds and found ould navvy laid on a bier height, plastic covered, stack of cement bags; his feet and hands were tied together by rope and Nicky and Cahal were holding him down, a large surprisingly good looking fair haired man, with some resemblance to the film star Robert Redford held ould navvy's head back with a gloved hand with the other hand he was drawing a large butcher's knife over ould navvy's neck, already cutting the skin: so this was the "good beating" that was being handed out. "Stop" I roared and took a photograph: all three leapt back letting ould navvy fall of his "bier". "Jesus John have you made a complete, thundering bollix out of yourself", said Nicky as all three approached me. "Hold it" I roared and threw the envelope to Nicky; "inspect those documents first: they are all notarised which means if anything happens to me an Indian lawyer goes to the police, within two days with them: as written in the first document". Nicky read the documents passing them to Cahal and looked at the photographs; the fair haired man withdrew to the shadows and covered his face. I really wanted to murder the fair-haired man there and then; but knew I was likely to have little chance, even if Nicky and Cahal stayed back: this man was clearly something else. "Boys this man is a complete idiot, a drunken dissipated moron, and isn't able to be a danger to anyone, even if he wanted to be"; "every word that man said is true" said ould navvy from the ground. "It's one thing " doing" a bad bastard, but this worthless mindless ignoramus: it's like killing a child that bumped into you"; "that's what I am" shouted ould navvy, inadvertently using words that might disprove what I was saying; "shut up" I roared at him; " yes indeed John" he replied addressing me by my first name, for the first time ever. I couldn't see my argument working, so I gave a speech that I had prepared for similar circumstances after deep and lengthy thought: " you may consider that you can clear this up here and now by doing me in and taking your chances"; I saw the boys looking at each other: this was indeed what was going through their minds, I continued " but consider it also names Gerald Howley; how is he going to take such trouble at his door"; I seen the boys looking at each other with wary expressions especially when I used "Sid Viscouss" real name: they were wary of him, but not the police. "Yea but if we let him go he'll go straight to the police": "the police; that drink ridden buck ass: do you really see the police taking any heed of him"; "that's right' sure I t'wouldn't know what a police station was; sure t'wasn't I only having the crack when I said I'd sue" ould navvy interrupted giving me the first hint of what was going on; "shut up" I roared at him again. This statement about "only having the crack" finally convinced them of ould navvy's total idiocy. "How do we know you won't go to the police" Cahal asked; "who drove the van" I answered. Cahal and Nicky gagged ould navvy's, carried him up the stairs and dumped him the van, I sat in to the driver's seat, the murderer went into the back, still shielding his face, the two boys in the front with me. We drove back to London; the only statement made was: "you'll be a very lucky man to get away with this John my lad": I didn't answer as I knew that to be the truth.

I stopped as per usual before we got to the pub, and Nicky let the monster in the back out, they told me to continue past the pub to a rough estate which had a dilapidated pub on it, one where you could enter with blood on you as ould navvy had, go into the toilets and wash it off, without the police being called: certainly the excuse of a fall would suffice. Nicky cut ould navvy's bonds, and let him out and gave him instructions about the pub; I saw ould navvy still able to stand searching in his pockets in the wing mirror as Nicky got into the van; then ould navvy came up to the window and touching his cap which somehow he retained, as he did to the landlady said; "sorry gents but I wonder if any of you would like have the sub of a small pound, or even fifteen schillings: it's not that I want a loan like, but it'll seem strange to go into a pub and not buy some pint". Nicky and Chahal: murderous thugs though they were just stared at him speechless with shock; I pulled away quickly nearly side swiping a car; "that man is stone mad" said Nicky, "exactly" I replied. I dropped the van and the boys at the yard and told them I'd see Sid Viscous tomorrow at ten.

I packed and left that house within an hour; I went to my aunt Nula's house for refuge, and spent the night on the couch. I rang the notary at nine the next morning telling him to give a copy of my document to a man befitting Sid Viscous in appearance, and going by the name Jim, if he asked for it that day, if not he was to bring it to the police. I was on site at ten; Sid nodded to me as though greeting me, and I went up to him; "you let us down last night" he said; I told him I wasn't going to partake in the murder of someone who was a near mindless moron on a good day; he told me that ould navvy should watch who he's suing; I laughed "ould navvy is no more capable of suing anyone than he is of flying; surely the boys must have reported his behaviour to you: he'd be laughed out of a court or locked up"; "maybe so, but sometimes a statement has to be made" he replied. I told him of the arrangements with the notary: he went off and seen a copy of my material and learned of my arrangement with him. I pretended to work away. When he returned I told him I'd work out the week to put off any suspicions of what had happened, I'd leave and he'd never see me again; he just nodded in agreement. The key was the Indian notary: Sid Viscous, aka Jim, aka Gerald Howley was typical of other Irish bullies and tyrants: no matter how great the depredations, they were capable of against their own people: they were utterly useless against even the most feeble of foreigners: the words bully and coward never went so well together. As I didn't want to bring any trouble onto my aunt; I moved after three days to a tiny room in Southall in west London; it made the room in the house I lived in with ould navvy seem luxurious, again a mattress on the floor, which smelt as though the previous owner was incontinent, and nothing else. I left the job after that week; everybody pretended that nothing happened.

I found out, by making very cautious, indirect enquiries, what exactly the attempt to murder ould navvy was all about. Apparently ould navvy was hired as a day labourer on a site by a big subcontractor; he performed some idiocy with a skill saw and the subcontractor, on seeing this, threw the saw at him while the blade was still moving and cut ould navvy on the face; this was witnessed by some visitors to the site and ould navvy was brought to the hospital; the damage was relatively slight, but it would leave a scar; something which would be hard to discern among ould navvy's other scars; but apparently ould navvy was put in contact with some shyster lawyer by an Irish nurse, who probably felt the general contempt the Irish had with good reason of Irish subcontractors. The lawyer seeing that the boss was the offender sued for twenty thousand pounds. No lawyer however greedy or unscrupulous would attempt to put the likes of ould navvy up in front of a judge: so the object was to try to wring a couple of thousand from the subcontractor of which the lawyer would get a good cut. However avoidance of this bill was not the reason for trying to murder ould navvy; at worst the subcontractors insurance company would lose a couple of thousand and probably not that; even if the subcontractor hadn't proper insurance the loss could not be that big: a few thousand at most. The reason for trying to murder ould navvy was to make a statement: this subcontractor is the "power" and you never fuck with him.

The cost of doing ould navvy in clearly outweighed any losses over the incident: I would get five hundred, the two boys had to get several times that, the murderer many times that, also Sid needed to be weighed-in; in all likelihood heavier than anyone else, and there had to be someone to manage things at the scene of the dump. Twenty thousand the full amount that they were suing for, would never cover it. He was paying to have men work for him that didn't want to work for him, to underpay, to deprive of proper facilities , to drive men, to include among a work teams his own worthless mates and make others overwork to pay for them, and for his own shortcomings in running a business in construction; he was paying to degrade, belittle and enshackle men; men who in the main wanted nothing other, than to get a decent days pay for a decent day's work and a modicum of respect. He wanted a tyranny not a business, because that was all he was capable of running. Ould navvy made the ideal example: no one would take trouble with him; they would know he was missing but no one would go to any authorities; he had no known family: for this purpose he was expendable. The thin faired man who was beaten up in front of his wife and family was not expendable: someone would go to the authorities, uncaring as those authorities were towards the Irish; he had a family: someone would push the issue, or even take the law into their own hands over the murder of a father of a family. And as for my glittering career: I had now participated in "enforcing" at the extreme end of enforcing in the Irish construction industry.

I sought and at the beginning of August found a job in book-keeping; I was determined to stick with this for good, if at all possible. The facilities in my new house were primitive: sheets of newspaper on the ground were my wardrobe, upon which I laid my suit every evening when I came in; the rest of the room was a tip of tools, working clothes and odds and ends; books, a transistor; in the rest of the house, a gas hob with three working rings, and a sink that blocked regularly and which only I would unblock were the only other facilities available. I shared this house with three old Irishmen who were drunkards and gone to seed: not that far removed from ould navvy in truth; I avoided them. I could have got better of course, but considered I didn't deserve it, what I deserved was a jail cell. I ventured out, only to the boxing club: being afraid not to go there, as I was afraid to go anyplace else. For the month of August all went reasonably, but at the end of the month the northern troubles intervened when the I R A murdered lord Mountbatten a member of the royal family; the English tolerant in the main to losses of ordinary men reacted with fury to a member of the royal family being murdered and the ordinary Irish in their country bore the brunt of it. I got no work in September, and the agency I worked for let me go, telling me to give it the winter for things to cool down.

I worked as a day labourer in October: lining out on Southall Broadway to get a day's work for cash. In late November I got a job form working again: from tattle I picked up in the house. In early December the foreman told me he wasn't impressed with my work rate and he might have to let me go: the usual impresurisation. That evening when it was dark, I was crossing the street to the site, when no less a person that Sid Viscous came up to me, he shook hands with me, and asked how I was getting on; I replied I was fine and asked how the boys were for want of something better to say; first class, I was answered, then he asked me how long I would hold the sword over their heads: "forever" I replied. I bid him goodbye and crossed the street. The foreman on the job was nervously observing this; did I know that man across the street well he asked: "Sid a mate of mine ", I replied: he told me not to heed about what he said earlier about letting me go. I looked back at Sid who was observing this; Sid pulled the cap down over his face and turned away walking down the street with a swinging gait: recognition struck me like a belt in the face, that was the reason I had thought I recognised him: he was the individual who stood across the road watching, the night I gave Hughie his comeuppance. I had been hired because of the potential for violence he thought I had, from my actions that evil night.

Chapter 9

Ould navvy's reprieve was brief: in mid-December he dropped dead coming home from the pub. I went to his funeral, because I was afraid that no one would be there, and also to try and check if there was activity following my departure. I also wanted to allay any suspicion surrounding my departure, by doing what would be expected of one; if Sid and co, found talk going about: I was dead.

I needn't have worried about no one turning up: the church was packed. I went into the club attached to the church afterwards where a great crowd had gathered to eulogise ould navvy; "you wouldn't find that man lying in bed in the morning", "sure he used love the crack and to out and mix with people" , " that man never skipped out on work: he was as solid as a rock ", "there is a lot of young people around who could take a lesson from him, ". I knew with Irish people to praise the dead, but a great worker, a fixture of the social scene, an example to the young; I felt an overwhelming desire to go into the church and open up the box to see if it was old James Ignorance that was there atoll. Even the old landlady came up to me, and told me that a few weeks before he died, he told her he thought I was "alright of a sort after all": I was enraptured: I only had to save his life, by risking my own, and indeed such a risk still remained, to gain his approval.

At first the hypocrisy repelled me; but then I realised that was not what I was witnessing: I was witnessing a parody. They were overplaying the part in an effort to recreate what they had known, and seeking the comfort and reassurance of there being still some values present from that time and country. The facts were stark: ould navvy could have been murdered and nothing would be done

113

about it, especially when it became known that he had displeased a particular man; but when he died in a regular manner; they were prepared to give him the heartiest of Irish send offs : they weren't really living in a place such evils could occur. There were many facets to this self-delusion practiced by the Irish in London, such as the exaggerated socialising and merrymaking: having the crack, practised in pubs to hide away from the fact there were in that pub to pay obsequiousness' to a boss who used and abused them.

Christmas and New Year's passed, I ventured no place other than church; this unusual occurrence, due to the fact I was now desperate for a change in the karma from any angle. I went out once in February to meet Paddy O Donaghue. I went home in April to Emanon's wedding; I kept in the background, and nothing much occurred. I noticed my mother looked a bit thin and listless, but put this down to the preparations for the wedding, and the fact that Nuala was pregnant and soon due to have a baby. Uncle Bat avoided me. I also heard that Emanon was due for promotion to sergeant in the guards; one generally got prompted after eight or nine or thirty years depending on whether they were looked upon with potential for a higher rank or just rewarded for good service. It was a nice, no hassle break.

The job finished in June: with the rarest of exceptions I had kept to my room, if it could be so described, listened to the transistor, attended the boxing club, read the paper or a book usually about bookkeeping. It was a drab boring lifestyle: but I felt I deserved it for the actions I had been involved in. I did manage to save money; I was on over two hundred and fifty pounds a week, and my rent and living expenses were below fifty pounds: I had just short of eighteen thousand pounds.

I pulled myself together to a degree; I got a room further out, in a place called Hayes End, which had the luxury of a bed and a wardrobe. This room was in a house that I shared with three other Irishmen: a nurse, a barman and a crane driver: about as far from the building trade as you could get with the Irish, which was what I wanted. I got a job for the third time as a bookkeeper. I resolved, once again never to enter a building site.

All went swimmingly for a time; though I worked with an agency and that meant working short term, I was employed most of the time; I got paid less than half what I used to make with the subcontractor, but with my frugal lifestyle, it was plenty to keep me going, and even to save a bit. I even went out a bit, but with great caution and little ambition.

The old saying "he who plays with fire shall get burnt"; similarly with evil: those who associate with it, are permeated by it, despite what precautions they take to keep it at bay. This I didn't understand until I found that I had some unfilled time in September and decided to take a few days and go home; I had in fact, been getting an unusual amount of correspondence from home asking when I was going back, so I decided to utilise the few days and for a novelty fly home. I noticed my mother was noticeably thinner and seemed very lethargic and depressed; but she said she was fine, when I asked how she was getting on, and nobody else said anything. The next day, the second of the four days I was at home, Bill asked me if I'd like to help him for an hour while he put up a few paling posts along the side of the road; I assented and as I was helping Bill, load the posts in the wheelbarrow, he told me in a furtive manner that, Emanon was coming down this evening and they had to have a chat with me; when I enquired further he said he was leaving matters until Emanon came. This job entailed, I held the posts for Bill to hit them with a sledge hammer, while keeping an eye out for any passing neighbour to have a chat with; Bill moved into the hedge to dig a hole for another post, when a car drew up; Paddy Maher was in it, with his wife a small, dark, ill looking woman who seemed to be pregnant: "well if it isn't the hard man of the Harns" said Paddy, his wife sniggering. "How would you like a rematch, but on your own, this time"; I swung the paling post which was four feet long and three inches in diameter with every bit of force I could muster, and hit him on the cheek: his head flew back and a gout of blood splashed over his wife who let out an unearthly scream; somehow despite her condition she pushed her unconscious husband back and juggled with the peddle and gear stick and got the car moving; I went to go after them when Bill leapt on me, from the hedge which had shielded him from view, and wrestled me to the ground. I nearly turned on Bill, who I would have been able to manage at this stage, due to my English experiences, despite the fact Bill was bigger than me, and strong from physical work, but reality asserted itself. Where had such a reaction come from; if I had thought about it I wouldn't have reacted in such a way: it was a subconscious reaction: so much had the violence and indeed evil, with which I had associated myself, entrenched itself into my very being, that my nature was malformed: I was unable under a certain level of provocations to control myself. Bill pulled my two arms behind my back, and more or less dragged me up into the house; this I resisted less and less as the realisation of what I had done sunk in properly; people didn't act like that around here; yes they fought and hurt each other even breaking bones, this was something Paddy Maher had done, but they didn't use weapons, at least not in offence. Bill sat me in the kitchen and looked at me, as though I had gone mad, and stated he wasn't moving until Emanon came, as he considered me unfit to remain unguarded. He wouldn't even go out to bring the wheelbarrow and the posts into the house, leaving then on the side of the road. I tried to explain myself, but Bill would engage me in no conversation, saying he needed Emanon's advice on how to deal with this. This state of affairs continued for four hours; my mother came in and my father came in from the post round, and we all had tea which Bill helped to prepare; an unusual departure, which under more normal circumstances I'd have noticed, my mother went upstairs for a rest; something else that I'd usually have noticed as, out of the ordinary; my father went out to the fields. Emanon arrived and Bill went out to meet him, and signalled him to go into the barn. I could see an animated, gesture heavy conversation taking between them; Emanon went to come into the house when Bill stopped him and after a brief conversation, Emanon headed out in his car, Bill came in, saying he had to milk the cows, but should I stir and he would check often, then the other man would use his "official authority" to deal with me: brother or no brother. After about a half hour Emanon returned and joined Bill; though I knew I was well out of turn, their theatrics was getting to me. About a further quarter of an hour later, two very grim men entered the house and stood there looking at me, hands on hips, saying nothing, not even answering me, when spoken to. Finally Emanon spoke; "have you gone clean out of your fucking mind", "look I know that what I did was over the top, but that man is in good part the reason I went to England: I did have the offer of a council job" I responded a bit lamely; "I'm just after phoning around and Paddy Maher is in hospital and his condition is so bad they're thinking of moving him to Dublin: you are liable to have done serious damage at best, maybe even murdered him at worst" roared Emanon "and your excuse a fight you won, years ago", "you don't know what I went through since then" I answered lamely; "no " roared Emanon , " I know you were nearly two years out of work around here, I know ,many promised jobs never materialised and now I'm wondering did they see something in you the rest of us didn't, but should have"; "do you still know that murder is wrong" came in Bill, tapping the table with his finger to emphasis the point. I didn't give any further answers; the lecture continued: "do you know that at best you're looking at two years in jail, if he presses charges; and this time I won't stand up for you" shouted Emanon: "I never asked or expected you to stand up for me Emanon" I shouted back. "You got into a fight with Maher by going into a pub you should never have gone into; you struck sergeant Peader Mulvey, driving him across a chair and marking him, you have now possibly murdered Paddy Maher, certainly you have hurt him severely" said Bill counting out my offences on his fingers; "yes; if you were prosecuted for all three: you would now be looking at ten years in jail" said Emanon, and on it went; after a half hour they ran out of steam. I got and said I was taking a walk; someone had mentioned P J Mohan was at home and I thought I'd see him: I needed to see some friendly face. P J was at home and going back the next day; he offered me a lift which I accepted though I had a return air ticket; I'd let things cool down at home. I spent an hour that evening chatting to my parents, went to bed, got up, had breakfast and went out for P J to pick me up. Bill and Emanon asked where I was going: back, not to trouble them any further, I replied; they stood there with my parents, looking at each other and sort of mouthing and shuffling back and forth: itching to have another go at me, or so I thought. Paddy Maher suffered a cracked cheek bone and displaced orbit, he also lost six teeth from his upper jaw and his eye never quite regained the same shape: I never heard anything from Paddy Maher ever again.

P J Mohan was bringing his oldest child: a daughter, over to England to start training as a nurse: how little did that family get out of Ireland. We caught up on all the happenings: the main one being the Paddy O Donaghue had got into a serious brawl over an opened pay packet, and though he managed the foreman, he had failed against the foreman's mates and ended up with a broken hand; I had to force myself to show the appropriate concerned response, though Paddy was a good mate, so immured had I got to violence.

I settled back into my job, and seemed to be doing well: I even got a pay rise. I ventured out cautiously with the other lads in the house; they seemed to attend pubs whose patronage were more Irish descent than Irish in nature, and here one found Irish people who did something other than construction: train and bus drivers, teachers , nurses and office workers like what I now was. These people were very cautious and thought they would have a laugh and the crack as good as any, when you veered on to serious subjects the shutters came down: one man who lived near where I lived was married and appeared to have his own house, yet when I enquired into his affairs he told me that he was single and rented a room nearby. I could appreciate their reserve, due to my education with Sid Viscous. Throughout this time my mind returned again and again to Ireland; how could I've been so stupid, tell Paddy Maher to fuck off or my brother Emanon a sergeant in the guards would deal with him: what would he have done, what could he have done: leave a pregnant wife to fight with a man who nearly managed him, when he was still young and was likely through work and his "English experiences" to be far harder now, and Bill was near at hand: he'd simply been trying to wind me up. I was also getting more con-cerned about my mother; her appearance was definitely off, and

Bill making the tea and her going for a rest after tea was just not her usual form; but I thought if there was anything seriously wrong I'd been told, but it nagged at me; finally I decided to go home over the Christmas break which was only three months away, I'd check things out and try and repair some fences.

Things went along well enough in October and most of November; the past returned with a bang in late November; I was going into Marble Arch tube station after work dressed in a suit not the smart casual look I normally wore to work, and maybe that is what triggered the jealous vibe in one of the men from Sid's site in Sutton, but who didn't work for Sid, that happened to cross my path; he also had drink taken and the hard man, which by virtue of being a member of Sid's inner circle I was, is always resented. He shoved into me, and asked me if I thought I was a "subbie" now, or had I risen to full scale gangster. I pushed him off: once or twice and the affair became prolonged, then he took a swing at me: he missed but I struck back and drove him down the steps of the station. I turned to make my escape and strode full tilt into two metropolitan policemen; they were always some police present at that corner of Hyde Park; immediately afterwards a police car drove up with another two policemen in it: I was nabbed. There came an ambulance for the "victim" of the assault and a paddy wagon to pick up the "offender", who had remained handcuffed and surrounded by police, but in full view of the public. I was taken to Charing Cross police station, down the other side of Hyde Park and beaten up; I was then humiliatingly strip searched, and beaten up again, before being questioned. The questioning tended to veer off, more into whether I was an IRA man, and how did an "Oirish" like me have a white collar job, than about the incident. Finally I got to make a phone call to the Indian notary, and he sent me a criminal lawyer. The "victim" had sustained a fractured skull, and three broken teeth and originally I was to be charged with grievous bodily harm and sent for trial to the crown court; I could expect a sentence of up to two years; but the lawyer successfully interceded for me: he got the charge reduced to actual bodily harm, and managed to find a witness, that seen me being provoked, so it was scheduled for the magistrates court just before Christmas. I got out on bail of a thousand pounds after three days; I also had to pay the lawyer fifteen hundred pounds. I returned to work: it was brief periods in different places, so missing a few days didn't matter. I attended the boxing club with renewed zeal, knowing that once again a scenario was about to present itself where I would need such abilities. On Monday the twenty second of December nineteen eighty, I stood trial at the city of Westminster magistrate's court on the charge of causing actual bodily harm to a Mr Roderick O Rourke: a labourer on the twenty third of November. My biggest aid was that Mr O Rourke never appeared; indeed he had disappeared once he left the hospital. I knew that the possibility of the subject of the row coming out, was not a chance he could take. Upon the lawyer's advice I plead guilty with extreme provocation, a witness was produced who truthfully told of Mr O Rourke provoking me. Tests from the hospital prove, that he was intoxicated. The police testified that they seen me hit the blow, but also had seen Mr O Rourke approach and push me, a couple of times first. He had suffered a fractured skull from his fall down the stairs, and injuries to his mouth, principally three broken teeth: this was a serious assault. Against that was the fact that I pled guilty, and as to my claims of provocation, well the injured party didn't bother appearing to contradict them, so they would have to be accepted. I got sentenced to two months in prison starting at once, and was told by the magistrate I was very lucky to get such a sentence: this I knew by my own research to be true.

I resented my sentence in the respect that if it wasn't for O Rourke I wouldn't be going to jail, and also because that jail sentence would serve no purpose; but in another way: morally I accepted it: it had occurred albeit indirectly because of the outrageous activities I had been involved in with "Sid's gang"; I knew that what was going on was wrong and though I didn't partake enthusiastically, or volunteer, I had partook and knew what was going on; I could have got out of it: I did eventually, but cowardice, greed, machismo, and self-pity reinforcing itself by the acceptance of a harsher arena of life: "look what the bastards rejection of me has led to", had caused me to go along with the most heinous of crimes. That some payment was to be made was not unfair.

Eight weeks in jail or six with good behaviour; and I had no intention of behaving badly. Maybe just maybe, I could hold on to the room, and prevent word getting to my family at least for some time; when the memories of Paddy Maher would have declined somewhat .

I gave the landlady three weeks rent and told her I going home for Christmas and was unsure of the date of my return, but if it was longer I would get someone to go as far as her with rent. I intended using the Indian lawyer as I didn't want my mates to find out about my imprisonment as word of it, would spread home. I had been home in September so would not be expected to go home again for a while, and I was never a very regular correspondent at any rate.

I was taken to Pentonville in a prison van with other prisoners; I was stripped searched, and forced to take a shower with disinfectant, all the while getting occasional slaps from the prison officers and forced into an ill-fitting suit. I was then interviewed by the governor, who told me he considered the sentence I got totally inadequate. I was given a cell with a fellow that appeared brain damaged, and was introduced to the pleasures of prison cuisine and using the "potty" or chamber pot and slopping out. I told myself throughout this time to keep calm and be realistic of the fact that I deserved a lot worse.

Things started off reasonably enough: it was Christmas time, there were some distractions; I could imitate, to some degree an English accent: a sentence or two, but enough to pass under the radar in a casual contact; then it was New Year: more distractions.

However during the third week I was there it was found out that I was Irish: this pretty much had to come from the staff. The others started to harass me: from verbal: "Paddy bastard: I'll fucking kill you", spitting in my food, the odd jab or kick as they passed me, one particularly severe jab in the kidneys resulted in me passing blood. I attempted to ignore this because half my sentence was almost served, and also I felt I deserved punishment. My good intentions came apart during the weekly shower. I was unused of and disliked being naked in front of others, but put up with it and when there concentrated on getting things over as quickly as possible. I was standing under a shower head, when I found myself surrounded by four men and someone attempted to put their hands between my legs: I stepped forward towards the wall as though assenting to this, then pushed back with all my strength, shoving them back, I then quickly turned and using once again my boxing skills landed four of the hardest blows I ever hit; one on each man; if a man however strong and though he may be, is hit hard enough, he will unbalance and fall: this the four of them did; I then jumped on the private parts of the biggest a large shaven headed tattooed thug, giving him a very strong sensation in those parts, just not the type he had been expecting; I then jumped on his ribs and I did hear one crack. This granted me some respite. I had no fear of official consequences due to the "code" the prisoners adhered to of not "ratting" on other prisoners' iniquities. However a low level of hassle continued, and it was only common sense to expect something a lot worse down the line, from what I heard this sort of thing generally occurred just before release. I ascertained what to do from a strange angle: prisoners were encouraged to pursue some sort of education while inside. One of these courses was about computers, and there was a lot of talk about computers coming into bookkeeping; I sought to join this course which was to familiarise one with basic computer operation; I was informed there was no place for Irish on this course, but if the was a course about digging holes I would be put on the top of the list; however as things transpired they couldn't get enough applicants to fill the positions available: thus I got on. There another inmate, an older man who I was able to assist, told me how to sort out the problem of hassle from the other prisoners; he also was of the opinion that they would attack just before I left; this would minimise the possibility of repercussions for them as the victim would not want to ruin his chances of parole; he also claimed this was covertly encouraged by the guards. He told me to look for a weakness in some of the hardest men like after he had a fight, then attack him: if I done a "hard man" the rest would leave

122

me alone. I didn't like it, but didn't see I had much choice, and I had long known, that offence is often, the best form of defence.

During the beginning of the second last week, the hassle stepped up a peg, and I noticed one offender was favouring his right side; I knew enough of people at this stage to find out what happened: he had been hurt in a fight to decide who would be the top man on this wing; he'd won but been injured. His offences on me were not great: spitting in my food the food the main one; but he was an ideal victim for me. He was a big, well built, but wiry man with black coloured eyes, his face was widest at the jaw: he looked viscous. He spat in my food the next day: I said nothing then, but met him in the conjunction of two passageways, an unobserved area very popular for fights: I demanded to know why he spat in my food: "I'd spit in any Irish bastard's food" he sneered. I walloped him as hard as I could: he didn't go down; I then belted into him again and again always moving to the right as he couldn't use his left hand: he seemed to have a cracked rib that side; I kept landing and easily blocked his left but he would not go down; I managed to kick him between the legs and still he fought back, he even got one or two in which had effect, and I was beginning to think I had made a big mistake, when I struck him a heavy blow to the right of his ribcage: this put him down; I just stood over him: I wasn't fit to do anything else, and challenged him several times to get up: he failed. That was it, but I well realised if he had been at full strength he'd have handled me with ease, boxing experience notwithstanding. I was left alone from that on.

On the following Wednesday:, five days before I was scheduled for release, which was on the following Monday, I was summoned to the deputy governor's office: I went puzzled at what this was about. The deputy governor was a smallish hard faced balding man, with a distinctly curt and harsh attitude. "Ah prisoner Harn; we have a communication here from the, I think, the police in the Irish republic: the gurdy shitini; ahem, is my pronunciation correct": "whatever" I answered. "Do you know a Mrs Maryann Harn of", and he went on to name my mother: "that's my mother", I replied: totally bewildered at this stage. "Aha some bad news then

I fear: the gurdy shitini informs us of the death of the said Mrs Maryann Harn, last Friday the second of February. It appears the delay in contacting you was due to the fact that you didn't bother informing your family of your present status": I was unfit to speak: my mother was dead. "There is some further information; the cause of death is thought to be cancer, and the funeral is on tomorrow the eight of February". "Well" I stuttered finally "could I get out, to go to the funeral: I'm due out Monday any ways": "you are in prison Harn, you can't just waltz in and out like that" shouted the deputy governor starring hard at me. "Well I could come back later and serve the last few days" I stammered; this was met by a burst of laughter from the deputy governor and the guard; the deputy governor coughed and said, "Laughter is perhaps not appropriate at this time; but you must realise how ridiculous your suggestion is. You're in prison Harn and you get out when you have served your time and not before; er condolences etc. Take him back to the cells". I was stunned; my cell mate spent most of the day staring at the wall nodding back and forth, he even forgot to go for meals: I became the same, at least for that day. There was grief, vain hopes: a mistake could have been made. During the last few days I constantly went over the events of the past month in my mind; I had noticed that my mother had lost weight and lacked vigour even at Emanon's wedding in April, and certainly she had declined when I saw her in September, an awful suspicion came into my mind; Bill had said something about him and Emanon having a word, then Paddy Maher happened along; was it my mother they were going to talk about, but the row over Maher put them off. I spent the last few days there not all that far removed from my cellmate: not fully with it. I was released on Monday, a day I had been looking forward to but now was dreading. I returned to my room in Hayes End and was told to remove my gear pronto: there were no criminals allowed there; I returned to Southall to my old room, where I found out that one of the old drunkards I had shared the house with, had never realised I had left: theirs might be a life without gain, but they were spared a lot of pain too; was that why so much heavy drinking took place among the Irish. I met my parole officer the next day: I would be on licence for a month, and until that month was up I couldn't leave Britain. I wrote home at once asking what had happened and why I had not being told. I visited my sister and her husband in South Norwood and could find no body at home, even after trying four times over three hours. I visited my aunt Nuala and found she was still in Ireland, her husband Steve told me he didn't want to get involved in any arguments concerning another family; it was a fair and understandable position, and he did offer to loan me a couple of quid. I went out as a day labourer again, signing on twice a week at a police station, with other criminals, I thought.

I dreamt of my mother every night, at some point in the dream, I would realise she was dead and wake up. I got no reply to my letters except a brief note from my father giving the time of the month's mime mass; it was later than an exact month and I would be able to make it. Their attitude to me would be expressed there.

The month passed and free of licence; I flew home and rented a car and drove home early on the morning of the months mine mass, arriving about an hour before the mass. The door was answered by my sister Nuala; who stood there with a grim thick looking scowl on her face; "who are you" she asked me; I didn't respond and she turned and left the door open for me to come in or not: I had to expect some of this, I thought. I went in; everybody was inside; "come in John " my father said; nobody else did anything, but stare belligerently at me, even little, or now not so little Muriel starred at me in that intensely offended manner that only teenage girls can. "Well people, I can see that I'm not meeting with much welcome here, and I don't blame you in some respects. You know why I couldn't see mammy before her death and I regret that"; "shockingly generous of you" Nuala said; "in jail" said Emanon. "Yes it wasn't my fault", "you were wrongfully convicted", interrupted Emanon. "I was assaulted for no reason: he lost and was injured and the police got me" I responded: "another Paddy Maher affair" said Bill; "no Bill I was attacked and assaulted for no reason and had to defend myself: these sort of things happen in London"; "tell us all about it" chimed in Nuala. "But on the other hand: thanks for telling me about mammy's condition"; "we were going to tell you that evening you were home, but you went ape and tried to kill one of the neighbours" roared Bill "Emanon was coming down especially to join with me in telling you"; "that's right" roared Emanon "like fools we were going to trouble to break it to you in as easy manner as possible". "And you couldn't have done this the next day, or wrote" I responded: "you took off unannounced the next day, and we didn't get the chance" said Emanon. "How long would it have taken to tell me, and could you not write, what about all the people who live up the road from me" I answered indicating Nuala. "Who the fuck do you think made contact with you, or tried to, only to find out you were in jail" shouted Nuala. "Stop" my father interrupted "this is doing no good and it's time for mass. We stood outside the church to wait for the family to gather in full and proceed into church in a group which was the usual way of doing it at a family ceremonial. A big car drove past and parked nearby: uncle Bat whom I had forgot about; it would be interesting to see if Bat would do much to avoid me today. " Aheak, aheak" roared Bat shying back as though frightened, "tis a ghost"; "what are you on about Bat" asked my aunt Brigit my mother's younger sister who lived in Nottingham: "tis the ghost of John Harn", "what rubbish are you on with Bat" asked Brigit: "what other reason for a man not attending his mother's funeral could there be, other than he's dead" roared Bat, " I've known scum and thrash and men that not I, nor any other decent man would design to spit on the side of the road that they walked on, yet they managed to attend their mother's funeral" said Bat now in a low breathless type voice as though totally taken aback. "Well John Wille you have a fair one here, and I could see that years ago" he said to my father, "it's time to go into mass" answered my father. The mass was held with a distinct lack of Christian fellowship among the congregation.

We returned to the house afterwards as was usual: where a powerful row was in prospect.

My mother was the eldest of a family of six; next to her was Nuala then Bridgit that were both in England, them Imelda who was married in Dublin, after that the two brothers John and last but far from least; Bat. Bat was about eleven years younger than my mother.

From the start Bat decided to hold court; he told me to sit down in front of him but I ignored him, which was easy to do as people were moving about. I heard my Aunt Nuala say to Bat that he'd had his say and to leave it at that; "I have not" replied Bat adamantly.

The avoidance strategy could only last so long, but had a perverse effect as Bat had the opportunity to have a few brandies. Finally he got going: "right John Harn kindly explain to me how come you failed to visit your mother on her death bed, or attend her funeral" ; "now Bat you know he was in jail" answered Nuala on my behalf; I could also see her husband Steve wasn't enjoying this; everybody else was silent. " In jail" roared Bat, "in jail; do you know that some of the rest of us also went to England in our day, and somehow managed to avoid jail, indeed we managed to bring back the price of the best farm in the parish, and the pub, and do both up and get them up and running, and even buy a shop later on; now I have long given up on any such progress here, but I would ask that a man manage his affairs so he could avoid the likes of jail and visit his poor mother in her last hours": "right Bat you said your piece" said Nuala: " I have not" roared Bat, " you have the same attitude as his mother: leave it go, don't take him to task, and look at the thanks she got; I wouldn't be doing it if I thought anyone else would take the responsibility"; "but is it your responsibility Bat" asked Steve Nuala's husband ; "call me particular if you like Stevie but I object to a man failing to attend his mother's deathbed and funeral. Therefore I will speak if others whose duty it is fail to": this a stab at my father. "Once again John Harn explain to me how a man ends up in jail, when he should be visiting his mother in her last hours" asked Bat; "Emanon we'll have to get you to arrest Bat to silence him" said Nuala with a laugh. "It's very difficult to arrest a man for telling the truth", responded good old Emanon. Newly invigorated with this support Bat stepped up a gear: "now Nuala I'm the only one of this family that has done any good: what did any of the rest of you do; but barely keep a roof over your heads?; Well what did you do?" roared Bat looking around belligerently, getting no response he said: " Thank you; now I consider that when no one else will open their mouths: the "herd bull" so to speak must"; "ya you tell us Vinne Mc Daid" came in Steve out of no place. I didn't know what this was about, but the effects were dramatic: Bat blanched and looked frightened and fell silent: a most surprising transformation. Nuala immediately interjected: "all stop: things are getting too worked up" Bridgit and Imelda spoke up to support her. Shortly afterwards Bat summoned his family to leave. He recovered somewhat and spoke to my father: "some of us tried any ways John Willie, remember that" and he left; I didn't know what had occurred and neither by their blank looks did most of the family. After a time the others left.

Nobody was saying anything much to each other and nothing to me; so I decided to take a walk out the fields: as a break, to let the atmosphere cool and to do some thinking.

Initially I looked with some interest at the fields I had been so used of; but inevitably scenes of the past and of my mother evolved. There was one place: an old path we used to walk along to the hayfield, and an abundance of wildflowers in great variety grew along the ditches that bordered it; as a small child I would pick different sorts of flowers there, and present them to her, she would pretend to be excited and claim that she never saw such a flower before: only a mother can grant happiness from such little inconsequential things to a child. Yet I was not present in her last hours; did she ask for me: it was unthinkable that she did not. I was not part of the family mourning at her graveside: how could this not but induce the censure of neighbours. How wrong in the final analysis was Bat. I walked up to the highest field on the farm on a low hill which was called the high field in the tradition of Irish farming of naming every field; there was a good view of the surrounding countryside; as a teenager , these views of distance, used to stimulate me to daydream of the future. I seen myself as an adult: I was either in collage, or in a good office job like my performance at school led me to expect. It was September, always September: the start of the new school year, the start of the collage year, the date of the new intake of office jobs; the leaves would be beginning to change colour, there would be a slight bite in the wind, and I would be an independent, successful young man, I would be walking on my way from work through a park where the leaves were beginning to fall; later I would be meeting my good looking girlfriend, and I would drive her to a trendy nightclub, in my car, a red Opel manta sports model with twin headlights; there I would meet all my mates and I would be the life and soul of the party, afterwards home to my luxurious flat for romance and sex: no!, no! no!, NO!: I wandered the roads as the leaves were all colours and not there atoll, jobless: the village idiot, the dosser of the "Harns"; I worked as a navvy and lived in a room without a bed, I shared a house with drunkards and thugs; I drove men to their deaths in a red mark 1 transit van; my romantic life was rough Irish dives and Hughie and Cherie, and poor Anne: a thirty year old woman, who still shared a room and was desperate to go home: desperate enough to look at me; I failed to make it to my mother's funeral or to see her before she died, due to being in jail, which was where I deserved to be, but for a lot longer, in fact forever.

The evening was coming in by this time, and there was rain on the wind and the grass was damp; typical March weather for the west of Ireland. The sinking sun gave the damp grass a metallic silver hue; which made everything seem very cold. I was approaching the end of the high field where a sycamore tree stood, leafless yet, its branches were stark and black against the darkening sky. Then the whole scene metallicised and everything was harsh and sere and desolate: what hope could there be for me. There was some smooth strong "bull wire" in the hedge near the sycamore tree. I could easily climb the tree, bend the wire into a noose, a jump: that would be it. What was ahead, if it was like the past: picking flowers for my mother, to transporting men to their deaths; wasn't hanging considered the correct punishment for murder; as for a judge what better informed judge could I have of myself, than myself. I circled the tree and circled it again; was such a life not better ended. "John, John" I heard my father shout: it broke the spell: he couldn't be expected to take my death; "come in for the tea". I followed him not speaking for a while, until I had sort of recovered myself. I asked the question I was bound to ask: "did mammy ask for me, or want to pass something on"; "we'll talk about these things later" he answered. "I suppose I'll never be forgiven for not being there" I ventured. "Look I've never been to England and I don't know what happens there" he replied: a neutral response. I remembered his brother George had been in England and to fill the silence mentioned it: "your oldest brother George was there for years, wasn't he" I asked; my father turned to me with a wary expression and asked me; "what about George", "I just mentioned he was in England" I said, puzzled at his reaction, "yes" said my father and we arrived at the house.

My father pointed out a place at the table, but Nuala who had cooked a fry up for the tea would give me nothing; my father objected to this, so she produced a cup of tea and left a loaf and some ham in front of me, to serve myself. I was not welcome in that house any longer. The next morning I was going through some of my mother's things, and I came across some photographs of Bat when he was younger: these I decided to keep and get them blown up and carry out an investigation into Bat stroke Vinnie Mc Daid .

Later that day my aunts arrived and I began to elicit what had occurred. In August or September of nineteen seventy nine, about eighteen months ago my mother began getting sick for no particular reason: she went to the doctor who prescribed anti acids: these helped for a short time, but the symptoms returned and in November she returned to the doctor who scheduled tests at the hospital in January; it was only then that she told anyone; these tests were delayed until February: the doctors there recommended she go to Dublin for more tests; she got Emanon to bring her to Dublin, and cancer was diagnosed, but Emanon was told first and he asked for her not to be told at that time; why: possibly Emanon wanted to tell others in the family first, but it was also a possibly he didn't want his forthcoming wedding ruined. In June my father heard of it, but was not told it was incurable, instead that the radiation treatment that she was then taking would cure her, or certainly give her about ten more years; when I arrived home in September it was clear to Emanon and Bill that there was little enough time left.

The events that occurred then and the following events in London prevented me from being told: well according to my family they did. Aunt Nuala attempted to defend me: stating I should have been told earlier by some means, my other two aunts backed her, and a very uneasy peace descended.

Before they left I asked my aunt Imelda who lived in Dublin and apart to a degree from the rest of the McNamara family where in London Bat had being based. She told me she thought it was around Canning Town in east London.

Two days later: I was getting ready to go back to England and was taking my leave in front of the house: my father, sister Nuala and Bill and Emanon were there.

The row resumed. "One way or another I should have been told a lot earlier. Emanon you especially are a bollix: it's hard for me to believe you knew since last March" I said "I didn't know the full details, and wasn't sure what I was hearing" he replied: "and it would have ruined your wedding" I said: Emanon came for me; my father got in his way. "You Bill and Nuala why did you not tell me, or even you father" : "we were going to, and were taking pains to do it right: when you attempted to murder Paddy Maher", "if you hadn't not attacked Peader Mulvey I could have sorted it out for you like that" said Emanon, clicking his fingers "Paddy Maher was on thin ice with the guards": "if the "gurdy shitini" were anything in the near region of a police force Maher would have been in jail long before the row in Scully's pub years ago ," I responded: Emanon went purple with temper, but knowing this to be right, said nothing. I turned to Nuala;" well I spent nearly two weeks running after you like a dog chasing his tail: you didn't tell me or anyone else where you were; and you always were very secretive about where you working and kept little contact with any of the family": this was I reflected true and for very good reasons which I couldn't go into. "I wrote you a Christmas card which told you to return at once, because your mother was sick. I didn't think things would progress half as fast as they did" said my father. "We all wrote": a chorus. "This was known since last March, and you failed to tell me: that's the bottom line" I said. "In jail, attempted murder, attacking the guards, half saved", were a variety of the chorus of comments that came my way. "Shut up to fuck: the whole fucking lot of you" roared my father: this silenced everybody as my father very rarely shouted or used bad language. "This argument is at an end. Come back after a few months John when people have cooled down" said my father to me: "come back to what" I asked: "your family" answered my father; "I don't consider I have any family but you and Muriel" I said. "But I hate you too" screeched Muriel from the window out of which she had been observing the entire affair after being confined to the house, to keep her out of the row. This hurt more than anything else: Muriel was the youngest and somewhat of the pet: untouched by the tribulations of the rest of the family; uninvolved in such disputes. I got into my hired car and went back once again to England.

Chapter 10

I set out again as a day labourer. This entailed that one lined out each day along a given street or part of a street; subcontractors or their ganger men would come along and pick out a man of interest, this man would step forward and be offered some money for certain work, which he would accept or not: "you here", "ten pounds concrete breaking ", "no fuck off", "and fuck you too", or alternatively: "right", "get in the fucking van". This was the lowest form of construction work. Along Southall Broadway this took place about six o clock in the morning where the day labourers were joined by street men: tramps and homeless men who had no place else to go and might cadge some money from the day labourers; virtually all were alcoholics and Irish. It was not infrequent that brawling broke between the drunken street men and often not so sober day labourers.

Indians from Africa and India and the Caribbean had been moving into the area in the last few years and not a few of them, with reason, considered the Irish stone mad.

I stuck this for a month, and then decided that if one was to be in construction one might as well try and make money: I would return to formwork; once again in another circle of my life, I intended to just get the summer out of it. I sought about and being somewhat wiser than I once was, I had now had formulated a method: pass a site twice, and disregard the one you could see progress being made on; I eventually got a job on a site for a subcontractor I had worked for before, as they were stuck; the usual welcome: "I'll give you a chance but I don't think you are worth it", "I doubt you were only a bollix when you were here before" etc, I simply ignored; after a week and seeing they were stuck, I managed to get a pay rise from them; "fuck ye any ways ye bastard, ye bastards would thieve the very balls from between me legs if ye could" was the gracious statement with which the subcontractor acceded to my request for more money.

I stayed in the same dive, and every night sleeping and waking, my mother, Sid, ould navvy, Hughie and Paddy Maher vied for my time. I even tried drinking to escape them and would likely have broken my neck down the stairs if it weren't for one of the old drunkards in the house; that at least ended the attempt to hide in a bottle, a method that was tried unsuccessfully by all too many Irish.

Finally in April I pulled myself together somewhat: I got a room in Hayes End again, I also followed up on my experience of computers, by taking up a course on computer operating in a nearby collage. This time I intended to break with the buildings for good.

I shared a house with two crane drivers and a postman all Irish. We lived separate anonymous lives: after I was a month there one of the crane drivers spoke to me in the street and I had trouble recognising him. This was fairly typical of Irish people on the fringe' and outside the building trade: they didn't need to "flock together" to survive, and were wary with good reason of those who did. This however did not help people to communicate or assimilate with those outside Irish circles: they tended to overplay the part: too jokey and voluble: acting the stage Irishman, or totally withdrawn: living at work, the life they lived in general.

I went out infrequently; initially to the Irish descent places I had gone to when I had lived there before, but word spread in that close settings of the fact that one was a criminal, and I was avoided.

I got to some degree wiser in the way of work as well: if one had a tough guy patina one was less likely to get hassled: one quick slap earlier on was better than a battle later on. Patinas can permeate however, and this was something I should have known. There was an accident on the job near me: a man cut himself with a skill saw; it looked very bad: a rip across the belly; I initially turned away shrugging aside any responsibility in an though unperturbed manner, then caught myself on: had I not seen enough of uncivilised behaviour; I went to help the man, as it turned out it looked a lot worse than it was, the cut was broad and would leave a scar but was shallow. But once again it emphasised I was in the wrong place. The summer passed; hard work, inept bullying overseeing, surreal interactions with workmates: same old same old. I attended the boxing club out of fear, tried with no success the odd dance, went to see Paddy' and some of my very few other mates every so often. I had no communication with my family. I passed my computer course.

I took up a hobby; I decided to look up my favourite relative: one Vinnie Mc Daid. This should show one how to succeed: I thought. I went to Canning Town which was on the far side of London, and in the course of a few visits ascertained the likely hangouts of Irishmen who would be contemporary to when Bat was operating, around about twenty years ago. At first I got no place: the natural wariness and caution of the Irish towards any investigation from any source, and even more so from any Irish source was a difficult barrier to overcome. Pubs were generally aligned with one particular subcontractor or another, and acted like self-contained hostile ghettos towards each other: the keeps of the fiefdom. Various activities that did not bear the light of day regularly took place, and to protect these ventures from scrutiny of either the authority's or more so from their peers, it was not unknown for "agent provocateurs" to enter a rival pub and bad mouth or "investigate" a subcontractor, to provoke a response so as to identify an individual hostile to that subcontractor. I could see I was getting some reaction; one man even told me I looked a bit like him, around the eyes: not impossible, but I could get nothing concrete, however by the coldness and reserve of their initial reaction, I could gauge that Bat had got up to nothing good.

Drink answered this problem: after being seen in the pub a couple of times and not linked to anybody or pub associated with "some other crowd", I managed to worm my way into their company; then with a few drinks too many, at my expense: the tongues loosened. "He was an evil bastard of a gang master, who screwed men from here to Timbuktu and back again. Time and again he screwed men: getting them to work for him paying them initially, then in part, and finally not at all"; "Vinnie operated several such cons here(Canning Town) and in Mile End and in Hynes Park"; "Vinnie done serious damage in Hynes park"; "there was a man who Vinnie caught at the wrong time; bill's wife, children, who knows, and the man ended putting up the rope because of it": what the hell did Bat get up to. Drink promotes loquacity, but also unreliability and from what I was eliciting, things were far more serious, than I thought, so I needed reliability.

The Irish in London as in Ireland used the salve of religion to compensate for a hard existence; and churches provided a venue to meet people in their soberer hours, and to meet more reliable people. Starting with those I met in the pub I expanded the scope of my search; eventually more respectable sources were found to qualify the gossip from the pubs. I was expecting an attenuation of the reports from the pubs: which would be the usual thing; instead I got augmentation. I also got directions as to who to speak to in Mile End and Hynes Park.

The whole sordid miserable tale emerged. My uncle Bartholomew Mc Namara had emigrated to London in fifty seven at the age of twenty two: latish by the norms of the time. He was apparently no good of a worker: I had heard whispers like this before, and nowadays, at home he did little, but give orders, so this computed. Around that time there was a lot of construction work: slum clearance and rebuilding after war damage; the hard graft: the demolition, groundworks and structure erection was performed by the Irish; finishing and services: gas, electric mainly by the English. The big construction firms found the supervision of large numbers of Irishmen who were in general very poorly educated and sometimes from dubious backgrounds, thus using false names, and having no fixed address very tedious; these Irish, were however good manual workers, and essential to the post war rebuilding and redevelopment; the answer they got was to "sub out" work, initially to gang masters, then when the Irish became capable of better organisation, subcontractors proper.

In its initial stages this "scheme" was makeshift and crude ; anyone: qualifications not needed or considered who could gather a gang of men and afford to pay them for eight or even six weeks was granted a contract: which would pay them back the wages plus ten per cent extra or so. The work was generally simple digging or demolition, and was overseen by the firm's management and if a certain amount of work was done the "gang master" was paid. The "gang master" benefited by a wage plus ten percent of the wages of ten men: commonly double wages; with more work or by paying the men less: they benefited more. The key to this was the fact that Irishmen of the period had an extremely poor basic education: they were educated to the age of twelve; a great part of their time was spent learning a dead language and topics like religious education, also other subjects like history and geography, had a very narrow nationalistic base. This entailed that they were very ill prepared to operate in a foreign or strange environment, indeed they were ill prepared to make even the first moves: like learning about the society they were in, and how to assimilate themselves , or advance in that society. These men almost required an environment that in some ways resembled home. Thus when a gang master offered a job at a initially a little less money but in straight cash: no stamps, no union dues and no cheques, men accepted it; other factors were that you were usually with old neighbours, and you were working for one of "your own", in short: in an understandable environment. It was a charter for abuse. Any crook, chancer or person unwilling to do a proper day's work, that could find the initial lump sum could get in on it, if they knew who they were dealing with they could usually wrangle an early payment for a consideration. Somehow Bat got in on this, probably due to the fact he was too lazy to do a day's work; from investigations made much later, the initial money appeared to come from an aunt in law who was a slum land lady. He gave himself a false name Vinnie Mc Daid(taken from a young child who went to school with Bat and was killed by a horse and cart), set himself up with some sort of van and started picking up men around Canning Town an east end slum where he lived. He concentrated on those that came from one pub: thus were sort of isolated from other Irish people around the area, and hiring men from only that pub, would allow him to move operations later. He pay cash the first couple of weeks alright, then find out the bank wouldn't accommodate him, so he would pay the men a "sub": enough to keep going on, with the balance promised when the contractor paid him; this sub would decrease with time, and at the eight week period he'd pay a part of the money, but not all, entailing men were tied to him fearing if they left "let him down" they would not get all their money, he'd continue giving an ever decreasing "sub" until the last two weeks when he wouldn't pay atoll; then he would scarpper. Cliques and gangs based in pubs were encouraged to foster control and tie men to one subcontractor; resentment and vying between these gangs were encouraged as it isolated men and enhanced control. This isolation allowed Bat to move only a small distance away and repeat his scheme. The final toll appeared to be sixteen such cons over a period of about five years; nineteen sixty to sixty five. He "employed" about twelve to eighteen men per job, and paid them overall less than half what they were owed; a typical scheme in sixty three was fifteen men employed at twenty pounds a week for sixteen weeks: Bat paid them about one hundred and forty pounds keeping one eighty plus the bonus payment (about sixty extra) for himself: a total of about thirty six hundred pounds, less perhaps a hundred or so in backhanders to the site management for early payments, and blind eyes turned to safety, and the dissatisfaction over wage payments. He pulled this stunt three times in nineteen sixty three, probably getting over ten thousand pounds. A house in a town in Ireland was about fifteen hundred pounds in nineteen sixty three; nine thousand pounds would buy you a farm of seventy acres of average land in the west of Ireland: a decent farm at that time. In nineteen sixty five he operated two such schemes with a new alias, Charley Reynolds, and did destruction. I got talking to an old Irishman who knew of Bat's operations around Heynes Park after mass in Corpus Christi catholic church in Brixton; he depicted the effect of one of Bat scheme on one man, a James Davern: "I went to school with Jimmy Davern and he was bright, I suppose too bright for the buildings, but there was nothing else for him, no more than any of us, but to come to England to the buildings. He was a bit sensitive and highly strung and the rough life on the buildings didn't really suit him. Eventually though he seemed to settle, and he got married to a nurse, but she was a bit of a nag: hard to satisfy. They had three kids and had bought a house by the time he hit into Reynolds. He hadn't been doing so well: you know the ups and downs in the buildings, and I doubt the wife was getting on his case. Reynolds offered him more money, about twenty five pounds a week I think instead of twenty odd, so he went with him. That scumbag Reynolds started his games: "the bank wouldn't give him enough money, would they take a cheque: one man did but was sacked the next week. The shortfall rose but Reynolds got a general foreman to assure them he would be paid: then they would be paid, at eight weeks he owed something over five weeks: he came up with two; what could men do, leave and maybe never get it; Reynold' kept on about "not letting him down": he knew how to play the game; the same the second eight weeks; and the third eight weeks; he wasn't seen after the fifth week; if the job wasn't finished he wouldn't get paid then neither would the men: they had to stick at it. He paid less than one hundred and fifty out of six hundred owed; twenty men were done. Jimmy was supporting a wife and family, and the story goes that the wife was overheard screeching at him and berating him as a useless husband and father a couple of nights, after it became clear he had been done. Jimmy Davern went up to Clapham Common that same night and hung himself from a tree". I showed him Bat's picture that I had had blown up and expensively touched up and refurbished; "you're certain this is the man" "absolutely" he answered; "you knew him under both names": "I heard him described under both name. I was apart from all that: I was a plasterer, and you didn't get yourself involved in what was none of your business; indeed it was only later that I found out what was actually going on". I pressed him further: "this man is suspected of similar offences and this would back that up strongly. It's thought he may be "settled with", so I must ask for certainty"; "that's him for sure", "it may cost this man dear, do you want that on your conscience"; "I'm sixty four, that's old for an Irishman in the building trade in this country": it was; "what is on my conscience is that I let such men go by me, without the slightest opposition". I decided to be thorough: I asked him if he could get another person to verify that this was Charley Reynolds or Vinnie Mc Daid; he led me into an Irish pub nearby where a lot of the mass crowd had gone and in the space of an hour, I talked to four other witnesses who identified Bat: all doubt was banished.

September came and I applied for and got a job bookkeeping once again: they seemed particularly interested in my experience with computers. I lumped in the form working job a week before I had to start on the bookkeeping job, and "borrowed" or subbed near a week's wages from the subcontractor, who being dependent on me to do the stairs had to give it to me. I didn't return to him, leaving him stuck: what goes around comes around. I went to Ireland to pay my respects to uncle Bat.

The old Chinese saying that when a man seeks revenge, he needs to dig two graves, has a lot to it. But sometimes one's passions has to be in some part assuaged. More than revenge however, I sought reason: why had he turned on me; he gave me a hard time when I was out of work, after leaving school, when he could actually have helped me: he could have given me experience behind the bar for instance, he was a sort of figure in the county and a known business man, he could have wielded influence to get me in to some sort of job, even on a temporary basis, so one could get some sort of work experience; instead he chose to goad me and demoralise me at a very low and vulnerable period of my life. When I was doing alright, he ignored me for all the attention that he was paid me when I was down; when I fell again: he lay into me at once with determined ferocity: why.

I flew to Dublin and hired a car and caught a red eyed Bat, clearly not long up, opening his pub at twelve o clock. I entered as he was returning to the bar; "well what in the name of, fuck has some stray dog dragged in now", he said in welcome. "Give us a pint" I said sitting at the bar. "You are the filthy useless bastard that failed to make it to your mother's death bed and funeral and you think you're welcome here" roared Bat. "Well it's like this much Vinnie, I was thinking of becoming a gang master, and leaving the men without their wages: so I could make enough money to buy a big farm and a pub and a shop: in the family tradition like, and I believe I couldn't

get better advice anyplace else" I said. Bat had alternatively gone
red and white while I said this, finally he more stammered than said:
"what has that jealous little man Stevie Brennan being on about;
that little failure, that chance your arm bricklayer has resented me
for years: I went over to England and in eight years of hard graft
and enterprise, made the price of a farm of one hundred and sixty
acres: the finest in this parish and the local pub and got both up
and running. I bought the local shop and a further sixty acres of
land since. I employ three people fulltime: your uncle John, and a
barmaid in the pub and a woman who works some of the time in
the shop and some of the time in the bar, and I employ up to three
people part time. These people would never get jobs around here
without me", his voice had speeded up and had risen to a roar "and
what has Stevie got after forty years in England: five times as long:
a little kennel of a house, a son that just a tradesman like himself,
a daughter a bank cashier, sure he's jealous, so he magnifies and
exaggerates every rumour, and slander and adds to it as soon as he
can get another failure like yourself to give him an ear". I digressed
to lull him a bit; "you pay your employees highly, I believe that you
pay John the same as he would get on the dole" I said; "and where
else would the fucker get a job that would still allow him to farm
his little place, and give him the free use of machinery, etc etc;
him and his family would be on the breadline if it wasn't for me.
Now fuck off out that door and never return" roared Bat. "No
Charley Reynolds I will not: I want to discuss a Westmeath man
called Jimmy Davern who hung himself due to your hard graft and
enterprise": Bat went white and lost the talk.

I continued: "for the record I never got one word of this from
Steve", I went on then to name my sources, and give details of his
operations, that Steve could never have given me.

Finally he recovered a bit; "what are these lies and slurs all about:
because I expected you to attend your mother's death bed, because
I wanted to wake you up years ago when I seen you going to the
dogs, and how right I was: a common jailbird and your poor mother
crying out for you, from her death bed. Is this your answer: throw
shit back, instead of accepting I was right and sorting yourself out

": it was no bad defence. "First of all Bat there are no lies; believe me when I say I did not want to be related to anybody that screwed his own royally and caused at least one man to destroy himself, leaving three young kids without a father: I checked everything out to the last: the very last. There are rumours about at least two other men who did the same thing, but since they couldn't be proven I disregarded them" I answered. "Proven, proof: what proof can you have" shouted Bat his energy back. I struck: "Bat you screwed in the region of three hundred men, twenty years ago, do you not realise that many are still alive and ready to kick; do you really think that none can be brought here if necessary, if you continue to deny it, then that is exactly what I will do". This took Bat's defence away for a few minutes he just stood there mouthing but not finding words; eventually he spoke; "all I did was to take advantage of the situation I found there, as did many others, and many did far worse than I ever did". "No good Bat: how many of us went to England and never had to screw anybody" I replied. "And end up in a kennel in a London slum like Stevie Brennan", "yes Bat, better that than a thieved farm upon which I enslave my brother, a thieved pub and shop that a man hung himself for, and hundreds went without their dues for". Bat was visibly shaken at this stage: he could hardly deny it anymore, "you don't understand: the Irish gangers of the fifties: there were barely sane. I took the only path out I could, and I wasn't alone "replied Bat weakly. "Bat the Irish gangers of today wouldn't be what you'd call rightly sane either, but to cause men to commit suicide", "that wasn't meant to happen", "maybe not Bat, but you surely weren't there for his good. Why the attacks on me?"; "why? why?, is it not obvious I didn't want you to have to do the same, or something similar, and later I felt sorry for my sister: were you not a younger son like me going no place; I thought to stop the rot earlier"; this had a basis of veracity: Bat would have left school at thirteen, and been idle until he went to England at twenty two; practically the only work around was farm work and Bat was no farmer. Did this arouse resentment and jealousy; resentment and jealousy that was reinforced in England when Bat presumably, proved no worker, and did all this "baggage" get an outlet when men were in his power, and get another, albeit indirect outlet, when twisted into an altruistic gesture of helping an errant nephew by waking him up. "How was it your place to act in such a manner" I asked. "Other's trough lack of experience or soft heartedness wouldn't, and how wrong was I: did you really go to jail because of a totally unprovoked attack", "and it would make you the big man: which is just what drove you to do what you did in England and here"; I turned to leave having scored as well as I thought I could; a final thought occurred to me; "did it ever cross your mind that you left three hundred Irishmen distrusting of their own. Did you ever consider the divisiveness you sowed in your own people, and its effect: a people always pulling against each other; you could have pulled the scam for one year and had a pub or a shop or even a farm you were fit for; why didn't that do you". I left and went to drive home to see my father. I had torn a right strip off Bat, but I hadn't got away unscathed: why had I been in jail. If Bat through greed and jealousy had caused a man to die, had I not myself facilitated the deaths of men. How unalike were we: I was an able worker but I had been prepared at the very least to have ensured my own skin was safe, by staying longer than I had too with a pack of murderers; I could have left earlier but with risk; Bat probably didn't want a man to die because of his actions no more than I did. There were two losers in the encounter. My father was unspecific about what my mother said of me in her last days, saying she went downhill very fast at the end, and was taking strong painkillers which confused her: most obviously he was sparing me. I bought Muriel a Walkman; very new and very expensive in late eighty one; thus I sort of wormed my way into her good graces again.

I returned and ascertained by chance that the subcontractor had called on my old house in Southall with a couple of heavies. I went to his office that Saturday morning, and got him alone: " aha me boy: I want you" he said when he saw me, and all five foot four of him came at me: he must have thought he was as big a man physically as he imagined himself; I hit him and drove him across the chair he had got up from; I then booted him in the guts three times leaving him retching and half-conscious on the floor;

I then raided the office and his person finding about four hundred pounds: this I kept. There was little doubt in my mind that if he caught me in Southall, I'd have ended up a lot worse: no one needed to tell me about the capabilities of subcontractors. I knew he wouldn't go to the police: he was probably dodging the law in several areas, and he would lose face. If I left him alone he'd try to follow me; but if I showed him that I was capable of violence, then he'd wouldn't chance it. Once I conned him I had little choice but to follow through. In early September for an unbelievable forth time, I started work as a bookkeeper determined never to go back on a building site again.

Chapter 11

I had feelings of hope, tinged with wariness, when I began my new bookkeeping job. I had dreamt and looked forward to starting my adult life in either a job or collage in September: it was the month of beginnings, so things seemed apt, but experience had wiped away any youthful earnest: if I did O K I would be satisfied.

I started off on the tedious job of sorting out incomplete accounts and finding the source of the discrepancies; this I did well, and found myself in the companies "good books".

This and my ability to use the computer entailed that my position was reasonably secure by November. I worked throughout Christmas booking a few days off in early February to return to Ireland for my mother's anniversary.

The only regular extra work activity I attended was the boxing club: bookkeeper or not I didn't know who I might hit into and my past was not bland nor benign. I went out to meet Paddy after he returned after Christmas. He confirmed my strong suspicion that the opinion held of me about the locality was dim: very dim. A jailbird that failed to make it to his mother's funeral: "now it wasn't for no reason that that man was without a job for two years", said Dermott Mullen, the man with the pull; "and that so and so wanted to come back here, only we dissuaded him ", said the lads in general. I had the very occasional drink in local pubs just to see what they were like. That was it. I spent the rest of my time looking at a television I bought or revising my work. It was boring, but I needed to experience a boring life to regain some sense of equilibrium in my life.

I returned for three days in February for the anniversary. Uncle Bat couldn't make it; that very morning in front of his brother

John he took a toss in the fields and so badly twisted his ankle that John nearly had to carry him into the house; I commented, "poor uncle Bat should take better care of himself; he's working too hard, what with his big farm, his pub and shop"; this comment got no response whatsoever.

Life improved; bookkeeping was monotonous, but there was no hassle, if you did your job correctly you got credit for it; it didn't matter who you were related to, connected to, in with: it was straightforward. You got co-operation not condemnation if you hit a snag: things got worked out, not torn apart. You didn't need to maintain some form, of social cum manipulative, aspect to the job. You didn't need to watch your back. The boss was the boss and you knew him; there wasn't someone else in with the right people, nor some informer unfit or too lazy, to work himself who covered himself by bringing tales to the boss, and when tales didn't suffice: lies. All was not perfect; being Irish there came a few belittlements my way, but I was now mature enough to accept this: in the end of the day, I had come here with my hand out, the English had not sent for me.

Life started to speed up: time was not so long, and I was not so young. I met my mates a few times; ventured to the rare dance; push and shove and wary of whom I might hit into: I made no progress there. I had a drink with one girl from the office that year: nothing came of it. I attended the boxing club, completed a short computer course, went for the occasional drink with my housemates, went to the occasional football match and a little sightseeing. Nula and Emanon's wife both had babies; I sent a card and a present in both cases: neither was acknowledged. I could scarcely believe when late August came around and I realised that a year had passed since I done the subcontractor and I hadn't had to hit anyone else in that year: times were seriously on the up. The rest of the year also passed peacefully. In January of eighty three I was doing the books of an important client, and noticed that the value added tax was seriously underpaid; I brought this to the attention of a senior accountant with the firm, and he took over the case: this ended up saving the client a criminal conviction, and they were very grateful to the firm and sent them more business, thus the firm was grateful to me. It was proposed that I add to my bookkeeping qualification with a short course in accountancy to get a certificate in accountancy, then possibly follow through and become an accountant; if my progress was good enough the firm might just sponsor me. John Harn accountant: things were indeed looking up.

The second anniversary of my mother's death arrived with bewildering speed. I went home for it. I enquired with Nula and Emanon if they received the cards I sent: both had, but didn't return any acknowledgment, as they considered me no credit to the family. Uncle Bat again failed to appear, this time poor Bat hurt his back. I brought Muriel who had left school and was doing a secretarial course, a portable television: this pleased her greatly. I then made some enquiries with concerning my mother's last days: did she say anything. Muriel thought money was mentioned concerning myself; this puzzled me completely, but in some further very tentative enquiries, I could get nothing further from anyone.

I returned and all went very well on the job. I started doing a certificate in accountancy; this would take six months and leave open the option of doing a two year course to become a certified accountant: this I found very easy as the only new parts were aspect of law and a little on business patterns; the rest: making up, balancing and presenting accounts I already was able for. There was no hassle in the house. I never crossed paths with anyone I didn't want to. My social life was barren, but then again it always had been.

I should have been happy, but some contrary feelings were niggling at me: I didn't feel I should be there doing a job I liked; this was not a sense of non-entitlement: but a perverse sense that I should be suffering, should have a hard life. This did not spring from a logical basis such as atonement for the acts I had been involved in, but illogically: that the life I should live because of who I was, a navvy, should be a hard one. This was a sort of self-pity, which sought to reinforce itself, by inducing more self-pity through hard living. Our identify was that of the wrongly banished the unjustly punished, and when life went well: it just wasn't in sync with this. I had to genuinely work hard to assuage such feelings.

I attended Paddy O Donaghue's marriage in Ireland in June, called to see my father for a few hours, again failed to find out if my mother had said anything about me, before she died. I gained my certificate in accounting. I took the first steps towards buying a house, upon the advice of senior personal in my firm. I had been thinking about going for an accountancy degree that autumn, but put it off for a year: one, to buy a house, and also to fill more holes in my knowledge, as I would be entering after certificate level. This relaxed time line was in sharp contrast to the urgency I felt was appropriate when I came to England first; feeling as I did then, that I had missed out on life.

I bought a small three bed roomed terrace house on the out-skirts of Uxbridge for thirty five thousand pounds in December. I borrowed twenty, and the firm helping to arrange the mortgage. After everything was finished with I still had over ten thousand left; once again there was no denying it: England was good for money. I met Paddy O Donaghue after Christmas . My stock was still rock bottom at home. Paddy told them I was an office worker and had bought my own house; "it just goes to show you: bad bas-tards always get on" was the comment of Dermott Mullen of the "pull"; "the devil takes care of his own": the general consensus. Paddy's wife introduced me to a girl who seemed interested in me; "we met up for a drink together at a later date; she seemed particu-larly interested in my house, so I invited her over one Saturday"; she inspected it carefully, but didn't seem impressed; anytime I rang her after that she was doing something else; my allures for her appeared to be my possession of real estate. I found a serious discrepancy in a client's book' pointing to fraud; I brought this to the attention of a senior accountant, who informed the client leading to unveiling of a fraudster, and gratitude towards the accountant and firm; I didn't seek any credit, and the accountant became my backer. I returned for the third anniversary of my mother's death, scarcely believing it had come around so fast. Poor uncle Bat had a heavy cold and yet again failed to attend. My father and to some degree Muriel welcomed me; the rest were cold and formal: answering if spoken to but otherwise remaining silent. The only thing they conversed about was the state of the country; it appeared to be dire; references were made to the palmy days of plenty ten years ago, and how hard it was to get on today in comparison to then; this appeared to be a slight dig at myself, or so I registered it to be, in my heightened state of sensitivity. However on further investigation, it became apparent Ireland had indeed fallen off the horse again. Muriel was talking of coming to England; I invited her to stay with me; Nuala immediately vetoed this; the rest agreed with her; I wanted no arguments so accepted this. I returned to England. I picked up a tenant; one of the crane drivers I used to live with. I strove ahead at my work.

Even the dance halls and pubs were somewhat more restrained: the same faces often enough, but now a bit older and quieter. I managed even to get a few dates; nothing came of them but I appeared to be playing the game at last, at least to some degree. Nothing was without hitchs in this life, or at least my version of it: I ventured to the "grab a granny" and scored; a good looking woman in her mid-thirties; we came back to my place and she went to the toilet; unusually for a woman she didn't lock the door, and I could overhear snorting noises inside; when she returned she appeared to fall asleep, and then she wet herself; I, afraid she was seriously ill called an ambulance: it was too much cocaine and she was a regular at the hospital. Organs spelt with a "b" other than the brain are simply no good for thinking with.

But generally the year was excellent: I did well at my job and entered Birbeck collage off Tottenham Court Road to study for a degree in accountancy in late September. In October I paid off over half my mortgage: reducing it from nineteen to eight thousand pounds; the rent from the crane driver easily covered the repayments. Some of the time I almost had to pinch myself: was I only dreaming things could work out so well; other times I had to discipline myself against the self-pity, which sought to direct me perversely back into a life of hardship.

I spent a bit more time in the Irish dance halls: there were really the only place an Irishman was welcome, now they were quieter. This however changed towards the end of the year as a mass of new arrivals attempted to compete with those that preceded them in disorder, drunkenness and debauchery. Twice at the end of that year, I barely escaped injury as some fool fell down the same stairs in the same Irish dancehall in Cricklewood and almost landed on me. The cycle was beginning again: the exiles in disarray as they were forced to become adventurers. There were reams of destitute Irish on the streets. The sight of a bearded, bedraggled Irish beggar became common place, once again.

Christmas exams results: excellent. I experienced a new environment, met different people, had my mind opened to new concepts. The majority of people there were English and as in the night school they kept a cool reserved distance from one, but there was other foreign people there particularly Indian and a informal grouping of all foreign people took place. I helped one Indian with an awkward point on probabilities and he became friendly with me; he told me that he figured the place to aim for was the city; that the financial sector was about to expand; I then read various financial articles that seemed to agree with this analysis. The wind seemed set fair for a brighter future: John Harn, city gent.

I met Paddy O Donaghue after he returned from Ireland after the Christmas. I was still considered the spawn of Satan over there; I couldn't have cared less. I went home on the fourth anniversary of my mother's death, reflecting on the ever accelerating passage of time. Muriel had been in England four months working as a cashier in an Argos store; this was the first I'd heard of it. I offered to visit her: Nula vetoed this: I was only trouble and should at least keep my distance. Poor uncle Bat had yet another fall; "that man will kill himself yet, with the dint of hard work" I said to a totally silent response.

I returned and was told by the boss of a short contract that was coming up, but with the right client: the treasury; "some civil service staffing kerfuffle"; it was not a valuable contract in itself, but a valuable recommendation. Would I be interested: "of course", "carry out this successfully and it will enhance your career. I think you are well fit for it. I don't think the work is in itself anything out of the ordinary, but be as thorough and pains taking as you can" replied the boss. He then checked a few points: particulars of my qualifications, age, the work record with them; then he asked me if I had a criminal record; "what, how do you mean", I asked taken unawares; "oh you know fraud, cooking the books" he answered: "no, no fraud nothing like that" I answered hastily and unthinkingly; "of course not. It's just we have to ask these questions" he responded. I knew that I had likely enough blundered, but felt I could only stick with the story, and hope for the best.

Of all the circles in a life, which constantly appeared to fashion itself into circles: the most constant one was of an over the top payment, being paid for the lack of a little common intelligence, at particular times in my life: why did I go into Scully's bar where no sensible person went, thus meet with Paddy Maher; why did I not move away with that woman when I saw Hughie acting suspiciously that dammed new year's night, or say something: even a loud remark; "I don't know what this individual is up to, but it isn't any good": it might have dissuaded him; left Sid's gang immediately, when I saw the first roughing up mission, I could have easily have afforded to; ignored Paddy Maher. I could and should have gone in the next day and explained myself : I was in construction, a business which allows people of a type: criminal, uncivilised , within it's precincts that no other business would tolerate, and I was attacked; defending myself I procured a criminal record. What would have happened: probably nothing, and even if I was let go, I could have got another job: I hadn't been asked if I had a criminal record when I signed on there, would I be asked elsewhere; I could hardly be blamed for not answering a question that wasn't asked.

I didn't tell the boss; why; a part of it was because of what I was: a foreign supplicant, a man who arrived with his hand out: I couldn't disappoint; a part of it was the self-pitying sense of inferiority, I felt perversely that such work was above me, and I couldn't justify this by showing myself to be a criminal; a part of it was the mode of behaviour and manners involved, when contrasted with what I had experienced in the past: "Harn ya stupid lazy cunt, get to fuck up there and put those acrows (supports) up for the fucking deck"; "John if you wouldn't just mind doing this balance sheet please, of course that is if you are at nothing else"; the balm and comfort of such intercourse compared with what I was used to just didn't allow for crudities like criminal records. I felt I was unworthy: thus was undermined and failed at the first challenge.

In late March I dressed up in a suit, complete with borrowed briefcase; met the boss outside Westminster tube station, and we proceeded to the treasury; we were both finger printed and photographed; the boss had a brief conference and left, and I got down to work. The job itself was pretty straightforward, my use of the computers seemed to impress; my work colleagues were co-operative and courteous if a little cool and formal. I remember distinctly that there was a woman who travelled the same route: Uxbridge to Westminster every day, and she seen me go into the treasury; towards the end of the job I was going down in to Uxbridge station and I could overhear from my position above her on the stairs mention to her friend; "see 'im he's a treasury gent , 'e is": her mate tried to smile at me, and attract my attention: nothing could come of it, but it was flattering to have a bit of status. The job ended after a month; I was informed I had pleased the client and my computer skills were praised. I returned to my normal work breathing a huge sigh of relief; maybe everything would work out after all. I was given more prestigious clients and even allowed to assist the accountants some of the time: valuable, considering that I was due to sit exams for a diploma in accountancy. I considered giving up the boxing that had saved me so often; one of these new-fangled gyms seemed more in line with my new way of life. I did the first of three parts of the exam to obtain a diploma in accounting on the Friday being allowed "paid time" off for it. I revised for the exams all the weekend, to work Monday as per normal; on Tuesday morning I was told to go into the bosses office; I demurred saying I in the middle of an awkward calculation, and would later do, no drop everything and go in the office now "Mr. Harn"; no first name; on my way to the office I still felt that it might be something other than my criminal record that was an issue. I was soon corrected; "Mr. Harn did you tell me that you had no criminal record"; "well not for fraud or any financial crimes", "I fucking asked if you had a fucking criminal record Harn" roared the boss: unique behaviour for him in my experience and therefore shocking. "I was in the building trade as you know" I started to give the explanation I should have given at the start; "criminal record or fucking not"; "technically but nothing to do with financial crimes" I started dissembling; "shut up: you're sacked, and both you and I, and I have to attend Charing Cross police station as soon as possible to give a statement to the police explaining how a convicted criminal got to work in the treasury. I will take a loss of tens of thousands if I don't go down altogether. If you had but told me, something could have been done". When I returned to my desk my gear was packed for me. I went to the police station by separate means than the boss and admitted misleading my boss and the treasury. I was bailed on my own recognisances to be tried at Westminster's Magistrate court on the charge of misleading a government department about my criminal status. A month later I took the full blame, and with the intersession of the Indian lawyer I was fined one hundred pounds. The worst part of the whole affair: outside court the boss came up to me; I forestalled him: "look sir I took the full blame; what more could I have done in the circumstances"; "maybe so, but you don't know the trouble I went to employ an Irishman in the first place: I openly defied my partners, and now I'm out thousands at best". Meanwhile I had done the other two parts of the exam, and despite all distractions felt sure of passing; I took the career's advisor into my confidence and asked whether I should now pursue a degree; his advice was " not to": an accountant had a position of trust and a criminal record and any attempt to conceal it mitigated strongly against trust; with a lesser qualification, the standards would not be as high, and I was likelier to fit in someplace, in some occupation where my record would not be as detrimental. That day as I went home on the tube, I knew it was the end of any hope of a career, or even of a reliable civilised existence. I passed my exams and for the sake of it got a diploma in accounting; I picked up bits of work: my record with other firms was good; but as word spread of my shortcomings, these got scarcer, by the end of July I only got what nobody else on the firms was able or wanted to do.

P J Mohan: that solidest of men, was going home for a break in late August; he offered me a lift: I took it. I wasn't busy and the money was getting tight, also I was very unsure about the future. Things at home were prospering: Bill had bought another farm and now had just short of one hundred acres: a respectable farm. I couldn't help but wonder where he got the money, but wasn't going to inquire as feelings in the family were sensitive enough, and poking my nose into other's business would not be helpful. Emanon' wife was pregnant. My father was talking about retirement. The country was banjaxed. Nothing of note. I returned with P J Mohan who was bringing his son over to England to start an apprenticeship as a diesel mechanic with London buses; what earthly advantage did this family have from being Irish, and how many more like them were there.

That September I recorded four years since I had hit anyone, and couldn't but consider that this was highly unlikely to be repeated during the next four. The loss of my bookkeeping job was akin to a bereavement: a fundamental loss of the substance of one's life. If I had been allowed the full expression of my potential from the start, I would be of that grade, of lower professional: accountant, bookkeeper, teacher perhaps a civil engineer. The years that passed from the rightful date of the flowering of that potential; when I left school, to this date, although event filled, with a little success and many dramatic lows, I began to envision as a period past, thus excisable from my life: we had to wait a long time for the train, and got wet waiting, but now we are on board continuing our journey of life. Now I was back to square one.

I got very little work in September: at the end of the month I had to revert to being a day labourer for a week to pay the bills. This was an unwelcome shock to the system. On the third day, two old men started fighting in the canteen; the cause of the fight whether you swam or boated cattle across the Killerary (Killerary harbour) when transporting them to the north in the nineteen thirties: "taa sure didn't I know didn't I swim them across myself many's the time", "if ye were there atall ye'd know they were boated over". Where did those men spend their lives: here in England physically, but where were their minds? I later remarked to one man I thought "Thatcher, the prime minister" was no good for the working man; "tad and twhat would that have to do with me" was my response: they were still crossing the Killerary after fifty years in England. "You're home John Harn" I thought.

After the emergency bills were taken care off. I again sought any sort of bookkeeping work while keeping an open mind towards any other types of non-site work. I eventually got a badly paid job with an agency which served Irish subcontractors; thus I got "up close and personal" with these "captains of Irish industry".

Let me start off by being honest: a high standard of conducting business and general behaviour was not in prospect. My expectations were borne out. The first individual I was sent didn't seem to keep any books atoll, and I ended up searching in the glove compartments and behind the seats of vans to get receipts to make some sense of his accounts. The second something similar, with an added portion of thickness; "an, an, and twhat the fuck is this about accounts anyways; do the fucking work, get the fucking money, pay the fucking wages, and the hire bills, and keep what's left over: if there is any; seeing the fucks I've got working for me" he said staring at me with his mouth open and an amazed expression on his face. "No Mr Carey if you don't keep accounts it's very difficult to keep a proper track of things: you could for instance end up paying more tax than you strictly need to": "oh holy fuck no". The third one I went in to informed me: "now my man the only reason I want you here is to get me out of paying tax"; "such a thing is a criminal offence, Mr Corcoran; to keep your tax as low as legally possible yes, but to avoid paying tax altogether no", "ye're hardly much use to me are ye, ye bastard, then fuck off": this from a sizable subcontractor who, at least at times, employed over one hundred men. A worse case in late November: a heavily built middle aged Donegal man whose mouth was miss aligned, the top and bottom unclenching, whether through nature or "misadventure"; "how can I get out of paying tax" ,"you cannot Mr Mc Carron", "what the fuck do you mean, what sort of bookkeeper are you", "I can't get you out of paying tax "; another tact: "do ye call yerself an Irishman atoll; you have to know some way of doing it", "no Mr Mc Carron I don't", a Donegal man would find a way", "then hire a Donegal bookkeeper sir", "fuck you sir, and fuck and fuck you, find a way", "fuck you just find a way , find a fucking way, find a fucking way," he now almost screeched: this was the brute strength and ignorance approach to fiscal rectitude; apply enough force it'll go: abuse the bookkeeper enough, he'll do it , the legal consequences to himself notwithstanding. I had to leave, he stood in my way; I told him I'd straighten his twisted mouth; he laughed at me: I had a hard go at straightening his mouth for him; it was four years and three months since I last had to hit someone.

Another man did not seem to be able to read and write properly, yet had work and somehow employed men. Christmas came; I couldn't, for the first time in England, really afford to go out. The days of youth no longer stretched endlessly in front of one, and the opportunities of that phase in one's life should have been acted on, whilst one could, but I had trouble covering the bills even with the crane driver's rent, on what I was bringing in. This was accentuated by the fact Paddy O Donaghue and his wife had a son; others were moving on with their lives, leaving me completely behind. I went on a couple of missions; just to see what was going on and to somehow partake of the pretence of the living of a full life. In a lot of ways, my life could be described as: "thirty and out". I went, almost ritually now to see Paddy O Donaghue on his return from Ireland. The news that I was going on to be an accountant was greeted by my fellow professional accountant, but by means of his contacts, Dermott Mullen by , " a bad bastard like that, and I know good men that cannot get into the profession". "Little wonder the Irish have trouble getting on, when that the "sort" that gets on": the rest of the lads.

I met the two brothers for the first time in a long time; both were still form workers, they claimed they could bring in up to four hundred a week; I was lucky to clear seventy.

In January of that I got the task of doing the accounts of a sizable grounds work contractor: P C Hanley, an unusual stipulation of this job was that I work from our firm's offices, he would bring the material to me; it soon transpired the reason for this was the officer had a view of his biggest site, and he wished to avail himself of this opportunity. I was working on his accounts when P C came in, a small balding fat man with a red drink ravaged face, he had an expensive three piece suit on, and flat cap; "don't heed about me atoll now" he said, as he knelt down in front of the window and pulled the blinds: this was totally unnecessary as the site, while in clear view was some distance away; you would need binoculars' to see the details of the men working: these he had; he lifted up the bottom of the blinds a little and from his kneeling position observed his workforce; they would have trouble seeing the window never mind him. After a time he gave me a running commentary of the on goings on site, and incidentally an insight into his management style: " I don't like the walk of that fellow atoll", "that man must be manufacturing the concrete as well as spreading it; the speed he's going at", "I knew that fellow was no good: there is an awful eye in his head"; then as an encore: "is that man pissing again"; some time afterwards; "thisn't he pissing again" pointing at him as though I could see; after another while; " the fucker is pissing yet again; I must be paying that man to make his piss: that's it. There's men all over London making their piss, and sure they don't get paid for it atoll: they should come in to this ould fool, and sure won't they get money for it"; he now shouted clearly worked up; he then left to sort out his workforce. This went on for several days, and I even got extra work out of it. How in the name of hell did the Irish arrange their affairs when such a man could get his hands on a sizable firm.

I went home for the fifth anniversary of my mother's death: shocked once again at the speed this milestone came around with; despite the traumatic year I had spent; I could just about afford it. Neither Nula nor Muriel made it. Uncle Bat was legitimately absent, being up in court over not paying the brewery for beer he claimed had gone off, yet sold to his customers. My father was retiring at the end of that year. Bill was complaining that farming was finished, but when wasn't he? All agreed that the country was destitute.

I returned to little work: I had to live off the crane driver's rent. At the end of the month the mortgage was in arrears. Ireland was kaput according to all accounts even from the media. I could get no job outside construction other than a shelf stacker, which paid very little. Eventually I rang the brothers and got information from them that led to me taking up form working again. Yet again I'd get the summer out of it; I'd get rid of as much of the mortgage as possible and go back to bookkeeping. The same circle once again.

Chapter 12

The summer, the autumn and the winter. The good side of this was that by the time I returned for the sixth anniversary of my mother's death, I had almost all the mortgage paid off; and that was the start, and the finish of the benefits. I had stepped into this world without any conditioning, but in the full flower of my youth, coped with it, in the main; the return was more stressful; added to my waning youth was the competing experiences I had obtained of a logic based more civilized lifestyle. I was physically stronger, I was far better able to stand up for myself: I had even competed in two interclub boxing matches, with scraped success, but against younger taller opponents, I was far abler at my job, I had far more "site smarts", so I managed; but on a foundation of loss, of the reopened wounds of unfairness and injustice: work was at best a burthensome necessity.

Not that an illogical, surreptitious way of working always worked against me; I was a bit rusty and was doing the stairs; managing but slow, when two other chippies were hired to do the other stairs, they totally out worked me, but were sacked after the first two days; the foreman came over to me, with a leering wink and said, "them two men was too good to have them hanging around here": they were sacked because their competence was a threat to others, like the foreman. I was tuned up enough to avoid most hassle; early in the job a young idiot: big, strong and thick, tried to act the bollix with me; a row started; I belted into him and gave him a fairly bad beating: more than was called for, but it made its mark as was its purpose; I was generally left alone after that. This sort of thing though "de rigueur "by now, grated. The modicum of maturity and common sense I had achieved railed against this: I was only trying to make a living. My social life was as bare as ever; I went out a bit more despite the "livening" social scene, I knew that my "dancing days " were numbered so decided to make use of the time left as best I could. I accepted the shove and push and all the other bullshit, as a sort of duty: I had to try while I could.

I picked up a seriously drunk woman one night and brought her home; I probably could have done what I liked but felt like a rapist, and let her sleep on the settee; the next day I felt doubly like a rapist and wondered if the subject of sex, was twisting my mind. I had a couple of dates with a couple of other women. I could have done more and knew it, but the morale was low on a good day, and that was always an undermining factor; add that to an ever mediocre unlearned performance, and there was just no results.

Christmas came and I went and pulled someone like myself: running low on time; I updated my education but little else: desperation is a poor aphrodisiac.

I ritually met Paddy after the Christmas. On hearing of my demotion to site work, my stock among my former neighbours had risen: "well maybe he might make something of himself at that": Dermot of the pull; "that's a bit more in his line": the lads in general. It was my success, not my failure to attend my mother's deathbed, or the disgrace of my jailing that offended them most.

I went home for my mother's sixth anniversary. Nuala and Muriel failed to make it; neither did Emanon. I had sent a present to Emanon and his wife upon the birth of the baby, a first granddaughter to my father, but as expected received no acknowledgement.

None of the Mc Namaras made it: my mother was passing from the realm of relevancy.

My father and Bill talked of nothing else, but the dire state of the country, and the hard time they had getting on. This despite a clearly expanded operation with new machinery and more stock. I ended up telling if they were trying to put me off coming home they were wasting their time; I wasn't contemplating coming back. They denied any such motives. I returned to the same job that soon ended. The subcontractor offered me a job a long way out of town; I could think of doing nothing else, but to accept it.

I was now fully emplaced in that position of most Irish in England ; in a place that I didn't want to be, not knowing where I was going to, thus not knowing what corrective actions I could take to achieve my unformed ambitions, in a word: astray. I in common with so many lived for that day, doing what I was doing because I could think of nothing better to do. We were in a state of abeyance as far as the living of a full accomplished satisfying life went. Often the minds of the Irish were in both England and Ireland at the same time. Unusually a geographic metaphor describes this best: we were mentally orientated between two islands: at sea, giving us that most unsatisfactory of foundations: water.

Nineteen eighty seven was in most ways a copy of the year before. It had its moments; in April the thick young man I fought the year before and his brother attacked me; I used a particular kick I had picked up from a martial arts video which I studied to augment my boxing, to unbalance him and bring his jaw within range, I then levelled him; I did the same to his brother. They were both sacked and the subcontractor designed to complement me; "ye're not a big one but ye're a hardy enough of one: ye might make a charge hand yet"; the work, general behaviour, intelligence all were as naught in this firm, but being able to fight was laudable. How did they get away with such activities; how did they conduct a business with such methods. The best answer I had is that, those without direction were easy to lead, those without a base were easy to sway and those who were impermanent, easy to impose upon: it was all short term, sure weren't they all going home someday. They could ask, and get of such men, whatever was needed above the normal expectations of work to make up for their many deficiencies. I was made acting charge hand late in that year: acting meant no extra pay. I went out fairly regularly: the Irish dancehalls and pubs had regained their old levels of disorder; indeed in some cases a new level was reached, but time was not on my side so I endured it, and anyways I didn't know where else I would be welcome. Successes the same: the desperate and the drunk; one woman who came home with me, must have been near or even over forty; she lay there beside me in the bed gripping the bedclothes and pulling them up to her neck and said "well": clearly she thought this was something that was expected, and that she had to endure. I thought about it and could not do a thing, I said I never did anything the first night, she breathed a clear sigh of relief. We remained in bed, but in conversation: she was here over twenty years; she never had much luck with work; cleaning and packing in the main, she stayed with a crotchety old unmarried aunt, for whom she was now a skivvy, she wanted to go home to Ireland, even to stay with her widowed mother; it all had the ring of truth about it: I gave her two hundred pounds the next morning to do just that.

The year passed rapidly. I paid off my mortgage, saved some money, a tenant, the crane driver left, I replaced him with an electrician who disappeared just before Christmas; he had left without notice or his deposit or even all his belongings; I didn't like the look of it, but didn't know anyone to contact, to inquire with to see all was alright. London was like that some of the time: too anonymous by far. Christmas came I got a report from Paddy on my status among the "folks": still bad but interest in me was waning. I returned for my mother's seventh anniversary, shocked at the speed it came round with; depressed with the amount of progress I had made in any part of my life since in the year that had passed. My father, Bill and myself attended. The conversation: the hard times they were enduring and the debacle that was the country. Bill and my father were more like brothers now than father and son; two dried up old men, though Bill was yet in his thirties. Bill was the heir; not for him the stravalling of seeking work and eventually the emigrant boat to make a living; but the restricted life he lived had its downsides: he didn't develop, being in a lot of ways the child who ever followed the parent and didn't mature.

Another circle in my life formed: I returned to the same job because I could think of nothing better to do. I was thirty three that year and well realised that the time to get hitched was passing; I went on a rather frantic hunt. "You cannot fatten the pig the day of the fair" goes the old Irish saying: I was trying to. I attended the dances, all the "trendy" places as much as any Irish venue could bear the title trendy. The dregs; those who like me were coming to the end of their "courting" days and were anxious to make the most of the short time left; those who for one reason or another work simply didn't work out for, and sought marriage as a necessity; those who had some shortcoming: drink, drugs or psychiatric problems, were about all that was available now. I done my best with this material, and had a few "successes", but nothing that was ever going to run. I even got going with a free spirited younger woman in her early twenties later in the year; she seemed to value me because she held me as "experienced". She even moved in with me for three weeks, and I was getting ideas of permanency. She abruptly moved out saying I was just too old; all she was after, was the novelty of trying something new. Unfortunately I developed an element of infatuation, and went around to places I knew she frequented to "bump into her accidently", and see if there was any "spark" left. Some of these places were definitely not suited to my patronage; one was a rare joint with mixed English and Irish clientele, average age no more than twenty situated the London side of Southall at the junction of the Uxbridge and Greenford roads called Barbarella's; on the night of Saturday the 26th of November I went in on my stupid quest; the mother and father of all rows broke out, which in common with a youngsters row quickly spread to involve everybody including me; indeed I was probably specially picked on due to my incongruity; I was well fit for the competition and dispatched a couple of opponents quickly; the police arrived, and the combatants all turned on the police; I made a hasty getaway not wanting anything whatsoever to do with the police; I climbed across a chain link fence on the opposite side of the road and almost drowned in an artificial pond there; choking and gasping I pulled myself out, and being covered in slime had to walk home to Uxbridge a distance of about four miles: this cooled my ardour. I read scathing's reports of the brawl in the local newspaper the week after: "when the police arrived, the brawlers stopped fighting each other and started fighting the police": funny if you were eighteen, not funny at thirty three. The thought then occurred to me that if I was involved in the same sort of thing, at a different location of course, when I was eighteen not thirty three I could have laughed:

it would have been apt for that age, and if I had lived my life to a more standard timeline, I might well not be what I was: the round peg in the square hole once again.

The overall image of London for the Irish I had known for some time: we done what others wouldn't, and for that we were allowed a constrained life: it was that compared to nothing. The fault of our bleak existence lay elsewhere; we had been driven to this, and it suited the people here to accept us in our unbalanced depleted form; as well as doing what they would not, we troubled each other, achieved relatively little: less of us moved from lowest rung, less of us married, thus less housing, schooling, health, and eventually pension costs. I was a case in point in relationship to women; alright I was no Adonis, or genius or tycoon; a little above average intellect, but middle of the road for the rest: the physical and social; I was never the life and soul of the party; but I was middle of the road, yet I never even came near a genuine bond with a woman. If I had left school, got a lower professional job like a teacher on accountant; got out at eighteen made my mistakes and learned from them progressed akin to what my abilities would indicate, would I then not then had got married and had a family. No certain answer exists, but the odds favour things being different. I had the worst of starts; I had spent as much time thinking about women, as the dark side of the moon: lack of progress in every other part of my life ordained this; I had come into an alien environments with its many obstacles: some of which downed me heavily; by the time I started trying in earnest, the field was reduced in quantity, but more so in quality. The very able performer would manage, the chiseller and chancer would get in there: an unstable situation allowed such men opportunity; the ordinary man, all to often would not. From eighty eight onwards, I was only going through the motions, for the sake of form, and I knew it.

Work changed; a new development, which shockingly brought about a disimprovement in working conditions and standards was the arrival of labour agencies; the subcontractors had in general required and thus had to maintain a certain level of ability among the men, and they did pay better than with these labour agencies.

I tried one in late eighty eight, sick of the subcontractors and anxious to try something different; it was scarcely within the region of belief; men who no subcontractor would employ were hired in every trade there was, men who were clearly disturbed, men who had served hard time in prison: I couldn't even imagine how they were entertained as workers. You could come from Ireland with no experience or background in the buildings, never mind training and go straight into a tradesman's job, with its higher money and generally lighter work. I, though not formally trained came from a farm, where repair work was always being done, and handyman skills essential ; I had spent over two years labouring, picking up bits and pieces of knowledge from the job as best I could, before I went out working as a tradesman. There was also an economic disaster in Ireland and a building boom in England: it had the ingredients for graft and opportunism: desperation and greed. There was always a fair amount of shenanigans going on; an unnecessary alteration would be charged for at a premium rate, a backhander going to the architect and contractor's management; men would be hired on a "day work or short term" basis to do the snagging, and more men would be on the books than actually employed, their wages going to the site management and subcontractor. Now with the labour agencies, the method was a straight forward bribe: he who paid the biggest bribe got the job. One thing, probably the only fundamental thing that always stood to the Irishman: he was a good and able worker, and managed despite all the guntherings of the subcontractors to produce a good quality of job; with the labour agencies this vital attribute began to slip away.

I returned to the subcontractors in nineteen eighty nine; working long hours for an Irish fronted company with Indian shareholders, as it was later found out to be. It was a great year to make money: I cleared over forty thousand that year. I went home. I made a fool of myself going to dances, attempting to gather up spilt milk; the song "the oldest swinger in town came to mind". Paddy O Donaghue and his wife had a second son and I attended the christening.

The nineties arrived and the official end of my youth. I was unmarried and most likely to remain so. I had money enough, but was dissatisfied with the buildings; mainly the company which was ever dodgy; also you never knew when an old friend reappeared; there was a bridge or overpass going up between Hayes and Southall which was near where I lived, and though I was employed, I knew that the only honest way to remain constantly so, was to keep one's ear to the ground even when working, so one Saturday I ventured in to the site see what was going on, as I approached the site offices a familiar figure emerged: Sid Vicious. I evaded him and retreated, but you just never knew. In the early part of that year my last approach to a fulltime relationship finished; she was about my age and similarly desperate; it was now or never for both of us; we both gave it a hard go, I think, but it just wouldn't suit: we had nothing in common, after just short of a month living together, we parted; as she left she looked wistfully around the house and not at me atoll, sighing: "I suppose some things are not meant to happen"; clearly referring to her ambition to be a married and live in her own house, just not to me. That was that: I was permanently established as a singleton.

That year was also a good year for money though there was signs of a down turn; house prices falling, unemployment going up. I went home for the tenth anniversary of my mother's death in February of ninety one; everybody with the exception of uncle Bat made it; it was the first time I seen most of them in years, and that I ever saw Emanon's daughter. Cold politeness was the order of the day: some things just didn't change. Ten years which I couldn't believe had passed had in fact passed, but what changes; my father and Bill were like two seedy old bachelor brothers; Nuala and Emanon were two distant strangers and Muriel was talking about getting engaged. I was a man with greatly narrowed horizons even if ten years ago I was leaving jail. Work, the addition of an unneeded extension and the odd foray to dances and pubs as a matter of form was the content of the rest of that year.

Ninety two was basically the same. Muriel got married; I attended and kept as always a low profile, but not low enough, I could see some of the neighbours pointing me out in a furtive manner to their mates, "that's the quare one there: the jailbird" or some such; I was glad when that day was over. There was talk of Ireland coming up, but despite the fact Bill had bought twenty more acres giving him a very decent farm, he in common with my father, still claimed poverty. I got screwed by another subcontractor that year. The vast majority of workers were now self-employed, this was supposed to give a worker more disposable income: less national insurance, tax back for costs : clothing, tools etc. It also done away with contributory pensions, proper insurance and weighed against unions: it reduced the value of work considerably, seriously so in the long run; the government and employers would get a little less in the immediate future, but would gain over time; massively so in the long run: no pensions, cheaper and reduced insurance cover, no redundancy etc. When you worked for someone; they were supposed to give you a certificate proving payment of that tax. This subcontractor hadn't paid the tax and couldn't give us any certificates; his excuse: "tad and twhat thid I do, but thidn't I go back to "Kerrai" with all me paperwork to do it all in the peace and quiet, and thad thid I do then?" smiling at us with a wide astounded type smile as though ready to announce to us we'd won the lottery; "thidn't I come back and leave the whole lot behind me" : it was the purest bullshit poured over us in an openly contemptuous manner; but he had the power and we simply had to put up with it. It was quite simply the wrong game to be in. My social life more or less ground to a halt.

Ninety three arrived and Muriel had a baby girl; when I returned for my mother's anniversary Bill informed me that the baby was early: it was a full term child and less than eight months had elapsed since the marriage, and that there would be no luck upon the house because of it; my father a generation older was too enlightened to agree. Bill was heading towards the nineteenth century, not the twenty first. Nuala and her husband moved back to Ireland that year, just as their oldest boy was going into secondary school; both got jobs, albeit not as good as the ones they had in England. I attempted to stop a fight that broke out on site, and as result got involved; I won but with trouble as my opponent was bigger and far younger; not for the first time I reflected that the singularly best move I had made since I came to England: that which had benefitted me most was to take up and preserve with the boxing: time, other and again it had saved me. I was proffered the promotion to charge hand on the strength of my performance; this I accepted, not so much for the pay rise as for the fact it would grant one a greater chance of continued employment in the relatively bare times that were the early nineties. I got two years with that employer; the odd bit of hassle came my way but I handled it alright, though it was becoming increasingly apparent that, even with boxing taken into consideration, I was not as handy as I used to be, I was simply not getting any younger. Ninety four and five passed in this manner; work, the boxing club where I was now a seasoned veteran, but still afraid to give it up; home for my mother's anniversary, now to the new and primitive but handier Knock airport; the odd visit to the pub; a trip to New York for Paddy's day, where I rapidly wondered why I had spent money to see such a children's parade; a trip to Spain: a boring life of limited activity and experience. Ninety six was enlivened by the breakup of Muriel's marriage: some sort of physical alteration took place and Muriel spent a night in hospital; I went to see her ex or otherwise husband and using my most valuable attribute, my boxing, put him in hospital for near a week. Emanon rang me concerning this; the first time he rang me in many years, and said he was glad that I was good for something; I replied that if I seen him at our mother's anniversary I might oblige him with a better demonstration of how good I was at that something; he informed me he had made it to the rank of inspector and he'd sort me out anytime, and in any way, I liked; I changed my offer to a challenge: same old, same old. He didn't turn up; tempted though I was, I didn't ring him to ask where he was. Bill informed me given that given the circumstances of the child's birth, this sort of thing was only to be expected; I began to wonder if the seedy Ryanair plane I had come over in was in fact a time machine and I had been transported back to some century past.

I began to see a new phenomenon on the sites that year; eastern Europeans. I had seen some probing excursions by these people back in the early nineties; their lack of any building skills and the danger they posed in a building environment due to their lack of English, resulted in their not being entertained; however over the early nineties the building scene changed: the rise of the labour agencies and the pre-eminence of graft and the backhander took prominence over the subcontractors who despite their incompetence and shenanigans had preserved the core sustenance of the Irish effort in England: the quality of workman and workmanship: thus the bar was lowered and the eastern Europeans, mainly people from the old communist security forces, people who had done God knows what in the Balkan wars, common criminals, and others that were not wanted where they came from, could make the grade. If they failed initially, then they worked cheaper, so a larger backhander could be afforded to pay for this.

The Irish emigrant of the eighties was somewhat better educated and were not as tied to the fiefdoms of pub, old neighbours and a singular subcontractor as the old Irish emigrants of the fifties; they had a greater ability to move about in, and explore, this society; they could assimilate new ideas and were more adventurous, and they had the bleak example of the broken old navvies of the fifties to show them the fallacy of that way. They were more independent of the subcontractors, moved into other fields , bought houses here and in Ireland which given the price rises of property in both countries often meant that workmen ended up quite well to do by the late nineties. This aroused the envy of the subcontractors who often, despite an abundance of opportunity, were often not so wealthy, either through lack of business acumen or frittering their wealth away through daft spendthrift habits: gambling and booze in the main; far worse it sapped their control: if a man owned a house in Ireland and in England, that man would not have to except the nonsense nearly always doled out by subcontractors: the good workman having to carry himself and also the subcontractor's creatures, and cover for the mistakes of incompetent management (subcontractor) and supervision(foreman), as well as rubber cheques, opened pay packets, tax certificates left "in Ireland" and a plethora of other bullshit; nor could such men be bullied; if Sid Vicious took up his old ways, the authorities would be involved and if it took it, be forced to act: without control the subcontractor was dead in the water. Their answer was the eastern Europeans: firstly to put the wind up the boys and show then who had the work, " tad and the bouys mightn't understand just exactly who has the work around here: well then I'll show the bouys who exactly does have it, and that I can give it to anybody I like" were the words of one subcontractor to me when I questioned his hiring of obviously useless and probably dangerous eastern Europeans; secondly and probably equally it was an opportunity to sap the "bouy's" progress by cutting wages: "do ye not see that fine big strong man over there, I pay that man forty pounds a day, why am I paying you one hundred and ten". Ireland was at long last taking up and initially the best of the " bouys" left the subcontractors to hire the "fine strong men" from the east; over time others followed, and this started a trend: in the end of the day only so much bullshit could be swallowed.

I was offered the job of a foreman by the subcontractor in mid ninety six; this I refused shocking the subcontractor speechless (a unique occurrence in my experience) at the refusal of such munificence. I was sacked: obviously I was mad. I made a final attempt at the bookkeeping. I had sort of kept up over the years: reading books and going into the new internet cafes. But my computer skills were not good enough, once the best computer operator in any company, I was not now up to it with the new windows type computers; after the first couple of weeks I was sent only to clients who used and understood only the old systems; a half a day here, a half a day there. After a month I had to resign myself to the fact that, that door was closed forever.

I returned to the buildings, for a time as a fixing carpenter with an agency; despite my lack of experience, I was the best man on site, but a number of thefts including of my boots irked me; there was no effort by anyone to redress wrongs of this nature; also the sheer incompetence of some of my eastern European co-workers and the dangers entailed in working with such people simply bettered me; by the end of the year I was back form working.

Ninety seven I spent the year form working. I got promoted to charge hand under a useless, brutal driver of a foreman. I ended having to figure every problem out, and finished the job as acting foreman when the foreman went to jail for assaulting a site manager; as acting foreman I got paid at the lower charge hands rate; I did manage to keep the eastern Europeans off site, but that was all I accomplished that year.

Ninety eight a similar year, but I failed to keep the eastern Europeans off the site. I sacked one for incompetence and he attacked me in Hayes town as I left church; with a great effort I managed to better him, but it took everything I had and I didn't get away unscathed; upon hearing about this the subcontractor promised vengeance; this apparently took the form of hiring the same man on another site: working for him though was perhaps vengeance of a sort.

I had started going back to church because it was something to do, and I always had some shadow of belief, but in the main it was the desperate hope, that in all existence something better than doing a dangerous job, to make an inept criminal a fortune, had to somehow exist, however little proof there was for it. This in ninety eight extended to partaking with some charity work: distributing food to down and outs; a shocking proportion whom were Irish. Muriel and her husband made up and had another baby at the end of that year. I got a phone call from Muriel telling me I was unwelcome at the christening; it was indeed hard to please the other members of the Harn family.

Ninety nine: I got tried. The constant stream of hassle, aggression, lies, ineptitude and corruption was getting to me; it seemed to have the same effect on many of the Irish who were leaving for home; going back to an Ireland that seemed to be booming. The buss words of the year were the "Celtic tiger": the new booming Ireland; and the millennium when a wild party to beat all parties was supposed to take place. I lacked the energy to contemplate either. I was a forty four year old Irish navvy, I was single and not even thinking of trying to change that anymore; I had a poor relationship with my family; I had enough of money; sometimes I wondered if I should buy another house and rent it out, or buy a house in Ireland; I could almost do so without a mortgage: then I though why should

I, and found no good reason to do so; I barely socialised; I had less and less patience with the pubs and the carry on that went on in them; the boxing club I was still afraid to leave; the occasional bit of charity work, and a computer I bought with some idea of exploring the bookkeeping for the last time, but ended up playing with, were my entertainments. A lonely anonymous man in an anonymous area in an anonymous job. I was not alone; my rare visits to the pubs showed there were many more Irishmen like myself: they went to the pub because they were wanted no place else; it was easy to see , why so many fell prey to the drink later in life even if they evaded it in youth. At the end of that year I sought a job as a directly employed carpenter with some big firm: this would grant me some sort of pension. I found such jobs practically didn't exist any longer; the only directly employment type jobs that did exist were in welfare: toilet cleaning. A general foreman (site manager) I asked about this told me they weren't all that badly paid, and in the long term I'd probably be better off than if I remain a form working carpenter: I demurred, but only for the present. I stayed in the wonderful millennium night: and found out later everybody else I knew did the same, for all the enthusiastic promotion it received beforehand.

In the new year/centaury/millennium, I got more and more fed up with the formwork: wages were going down, the work was far more dangerous due to the numbers of eastern European now in the game; they had no reflexive use of the English language and couldn't even shout a warning if they let something fall: a constant possibility with formwork. I had a number of close shaves, despite being constantly on my guard, and began to suspect that these accidents might not be accidents atoll: I easily showed them up for the bodgers they were. I constantly had to carry more than my own weight; getting all the awkward and dangerous jobs. The trend of the Irish departing the bullshit and chicanery to partake of the economic wonders of the Celtic tiger accelerated, and exacerbated this problem. In February of that year I took a welfare job with an agency and found I could handle it. After a month I went back to the formwork and the same problems. It came down to what I wanted from a job, and in my position it was to make use of time, I didn't need the money, I certainly didn't need the hassle, as for status: a navvy was a navvy to the ordinary member of the public. Finally I looked at my life; alright there was a number of tough breaks, but I also failed miserably on many occasions: what position on a pedestal did I deserve. I took the job as a welfare operative in May: this would give me twenty years paying into a contributory pension, versus a basic pension: roughly one hundred and thirty versus seventy pounds in two thousand. It was an unpleasant and dirty job, but it wasn't very strenuous or stressful: no one envied you your position. It wasn't as badly paid as I thought: less than one hundred pounds a week as received into your hand, and when you took in the benefits: pension, holiday pay, proper insurance even some travel and clothing allowances, one was probably better off, at least in the long run. I had ended up a toilet cleaner, and I felt alright in the role. Paddy O Donaghue and both brothers, one now married the other not, headed home; I had had little to do with them in years, but it was another link with friends broken: I felt myself more alone than ever.

The twentieth anniversary of my mother's death was attended by all the family. In contrast to the moans and laments of my father and Bill over the past years, now the rest expressed a high degree of approbation about the state of the country: everything was booming mightily; Emanon who was expecting promotion to superintendent, stated that his house was worth seven times what he paid for it; Muriel and her husband who nodded distantly to me, then blanked me, were planning to move home; Nuala stated to me, "sure we're doing better than ye are now": I didn't bite. I remembered the "palmy" days of the seventies, and how things went in the eighties, but diplomacy to the fore, I didn't comment. There was even some talk of foreign people moving to Ireland to work; I didn't believe that this was significant: how could, even Ireland, which somehow managed to fall over every rut in the road, allow foreign people in, after it had spent seven and a half out of the eight decades of its existence, kicking its own people out, to the four corners of the world. Times were puzzling and disturbing.

I gave up the boxing club: too old; but still wary of the fact I worked in a dodgy environment, I set up a sort of gym at home. I took in the odd tenant. In general however I went to work and did not think, I was at work and did not think, and I came from work and did not think: thought and contemplation were simply unaffordable luxuries: rendering unbearable, my type of life.

Instead of my mother's anniversary I came home in April for my father's eightieth birthday reflecting on now rampant pace of time. My sister Nuala's son, for instance was a civil servant aged twenty one; I didn't know how such things happened so fast. At home my father was spritely and in good order. The main talking point was the presence of an unmarried mother in the parish; my father put it down to the changing times; my brother Bill was scandalised and predicted dark times for the entire parish: truly a man of another time.

I was promoted that year to be in charge of basically toilet cleaning on a large site, and I had an assistant under me: first two eastern Europeans who had no grasp of English, then an old paddy who never made it on a Monday; I accepted him as the best of a bad lot, and ensured that he made up for in the rest of the week what he missed every Monday. Surprisingly with the extra hours I put in to cover for my assistant I now brought home in my hand as much as I would have if I was a shuttering chippie(form worker), and in the long run would be a lot better off.

The years that followed were basically the same. I got "promoted "to be in charge of welfare on bigger sites. I still took in the odd tenant, if I knew them well enough: living on your own was not such a good idea. I kept myself fit, although age was clearly taking its toll. I partook of some charity work, just to pass the time as much as anything else.

I returned to Ireland every year, usually in the summertime, becoming more and more confused at what was going on there. There was indeed a boom; something that was decades and decades overdue, but there seemed to be no end of foreign people going there; I began to wonder if the powers that be knew we existed atoll; alright going back wouldn't be much use to someone like myself, but there were many younger people who could still make a life for themselves there given a chance; and what of the children of emigrants: many Irish people weren't happy with the way their children were growing up in this environment: drugs, loose sexual practices, racial tensions and discrimination because they were Irish; would they not be grateful that their children be given another chance in a country they could call home, and would this not go a long way towards redressing the wrong of emigration their parents had to suffer . Despite these facts all I heard from people who did return was that every attempt possible was made to cheat and con them: prices of houses rose by tens of thousands when it was found out where they came from. Jobs given to people who could hardly speak English or were qualified in any ways, before them. It was like a pig eating her own farrow.

I went home for the twenty fifth anniversary of my mother's death. I drove just to see how the country had changed. It was clearly a lot busier, and there was clearly a lot of foreign people there, involved in every sort of work.

The family had changed; uncle Bat made it, but only to the church, he had aged a bit, but his brother John looked like a walking mummy: the stress and strain of working two farms had worn him to shreds at the age of seventy two. Emanon's son had qualified as a teacher, his daughter was training to be one; Nuala's second son was a mechanical engineer; my father was still fairly spritely, certainly he looked far better than John that who was thirteen years younger than him. I as always put diplomacy to the fore, not even responding to provocative remarks: "so a toilet cleaner is all you ended up in the end of the day", "someone has to do it", "but even a carpenter is at least a trade; how come you didn't hang on to at least that sort of job", "I'm not ambitious inspector, sorry superintendent" I replied knowing Emanon's was sore over his lack of promotion. He took pains to explain that when he signed on for three more years, the job of superintendent was promised; he'd get it by two thousand and nine, and conceivably go even further. I was an unwelcome stranger in that house; all beneficiaries and partakers of the great "Celtic tiger economic boom"; I was an unwanted reminder of other times. Ribbed by this I ventured to question the amount and role of foreigners in the country; "were we forgotten about", "toilet cleaners with criminal records and tendencies, didn't exactly provide much in the line of competition to these foreigners" responded Emanon; my father stood up and told Emanon to leave the house, or shut his mouth; it was a timely and fortunate intervention: determined diplomacy notwithstanding one could only take so much. I drove up to Dunlaoghire docks slowly, stopping to inspect what was going on where ever I could, cafes, supermarkets, buy a small thing in each, have a look, building sites; ascertain the language spoken, see who had the work. There seemed to be every class of foreigner everywhere. The only take I could make on the matter was that when a former Irish president called us the diaspora, she had really meant the defecated: once got rid of from the body or state we were the last thing on earth one wanted anything to do with.

I returned to the same worn life. To pass the time and give some positive inclination to my life I got more involved in charity work: becoming a volunteer at a local hospice; my role was simply to talk to patients particularly Irish ones and see if they had any non-medical wants, to contact relatives for instance , then bring these to the attention of the staff who would deal with them; it merely required one to be a patient listener and spend time with these patients that the staff could ill afford. As time went on I became more committed to this endeavour; these people in extremis needed me as Irish volunteers were extremely thin on the ground, and it was informative, as people at that stage of their lives would expose aspects of their lives normally hidden. If I had a bugbear which I always seemed to come back to, it was the progress of the Irish people in general and in England in particular: despite a river of sweat and a certain amount of blood, we seemed to get nowhere; a great part of this I put down to the users and opportunists and plain criminals that the Irish had allowed to run their affairs; but in was only in the hospice I saw their true effect. As stated people in extremis are unguarded: they show what is really bothering them: time and again the last thoughts of Irishmen were the opened pay packet, when they were picked on in the pub for working for someone else, when they were "let go" before Christmas with a young family on their hands so they would be forced to come back begging in January. The belittlements, the beatings, the bullying; far, far too often these thoughts, and not of wife or family or religion, were what possessed men in their final hours. With such poisoned depths was it that surprising that men struck about them at who they could; that they resented their own; that ambition amongst their own, was viewed in a universally dim light.

From another and most unlikely source came what was in it's own way an even darker aspect of the Irish effort and of Irish affairs in England. The head nurse in the hospice was an Indian woman and over time she picked up the trend of these conversations and she talked with me about them; in the course of a discussion she told me she had a sister who had been a teachers in Dormers Well school in Southall in the seventies and eighties when the two main ethnic groups of pupils were Indian and Irish; her sister had remarked many times that Irish didn't pursue education properly: smart able Irish kids left school at the O levels stage to become plumbers and bank clerks, while not so able Indians stayed on to become professionals. I had a very good idea of the dynamics of this situation, but did a bit of checking to be certain; it was the down to the "manufactured unreliability" of Irish controlled construction work. A scenario: the man has four kids on his hands, he's let go at Christmas, he has his pay packet pilfered, etc; he is totally unsure of the future, and the oldest kid wants to leave school at O levels and get a bank job or an apprenticeship as a plumber, is it not tempting for that man to think; what's wrong with a job in the bank, or a "good" trade such as a plumber, and will it not also lessen the pressure on him to provide for a family on an unstable and uncivilised basis; what kid doesn't want to leave school; what knowledge would the father have all too often of professions; it was easy to see how this outrage came about: the Irish subcontractors and labour agency men not only buggered up their own generation, but stunted the next one as well.

Other facts of which I was aware, but which had been hazy in my mind, were crystallized: there was a far lower age profile among Irishmen than any other patients in the hospice, as a proportion fewer were married, they succumbed to a wider range of diseases than others: one example was a man who died of squamous cell skin cancer which started on his chest; this cancer is very slow growing, and almost everybody that gets it , is cured; he had to have ignored it for a long time, and upon questioning, this was what transpired: he kept putting it off , he just didn't feel comfortable going to a doctor, he'd "have a drink" and try to forget it, etc; basically a very poor education, allowing himself to be tied to the same pub and subcontractor and keeping in only with his old neighbours: thus not develop; he couldn't cope with a new situation, even when, as he must have known in the later stages, that he was in serious bother. If it spreads slowly, it kills cruelly, spreading all over the body and giving months of suffering at the end. I prevailed on him to allow the doctors to examine him, which they were anxious to do, due to the rarity of the case; the most senior doctor asked me if I had any idea how he let it get so far; I knew the answer but as an Irishman was ashamed to give it.

What of the subcontractors and labour agencies? One good thing: the decade brought was their severe diminution, and they brought it about themselves: the ex-policemen, renegades, criminals on the run, people that done God alone knows what, in various wars, whom they hired to screw their own learned; and as they learned they came to the fairly obvious conclusion that their bosses didn't know much: so they started taking over the work themselves. In reality they were up against nothing, but a herd of frauds, and gangsters, and they won. By the end of the decade all that remained of the Irish construction effort in London and to a lesser degree in the rest of England were the biggest firms, and old, long established localised ones: usually consisting of one to a few men in size, and some of the rougher roadwork and ground work firm's; work that the eastern Europeans just didn't find to their taste. Often an Irish firm was bought out by eastern European's interests, but kept the name and sometimes Irish front men. Once on virtually every site the great bulk of the work was done by Irish subcontractors, now this had gone near completely. After thirty and forty and more years of existence, all they knew was how to pull the stunt, screw the men, and crook the client, sometimes descending into pure brutality: J J Corcoran, "eight plus six loads, that a total of seventeen loads"; young site manager, "no Mr. Corcoran, eight and six is fourteen": J J gives the youngster a belt in the mouth which levels him, "now eight and six is seventeen", "no Mr Corcoran it's fourteen" : another levelling belt; the young site manager is now tearing up despite the tough image he wants to portray as a building site manager, "we'll settle on sixteen", "yes Mr Corcoran", "now no Mr. Corcorans, J J: we're very informal around here". When any viable alternative appeared, unsurprisingly it was taken.

All to the good, but for one fact: old Ireland had fallen off the horse yet again!

It was eminently predictable to any logical analysis: houses rising twenty times in price in twenty years; a number of major shopping malls in a town of five hundred, forty miles outside Dublin, built on the premise that people were going to drive those forty miles from Dublin to buy the same items that were available cheaper beside them, and other such like "enterprises. But apparently in Ireland no one expected it. True it was part of a worldwide effect, but the rest of the world did not effect an economic miracle, and where there were problems elsewhere like in Greece, they had been in trouble for a long time. A EEC bailout and a bridging loan from England was all that kept Ireland from probable destitution.

Family life continued with less and less participation from me; in twenty ten Nuala's oldest son got married and had a daughter; a first great grandchild for my father; he was the only one I mentioned it to: I was simply out of the picture. I was promoted to a regional welfare supervisor; an equivalent position to a general foreman or site manager. I had a company car and was on line for an executive type pension: so some things did work out.

A new entry was made into the lexicon of Irish occupations in England in twenty ten: whore. The Irish had been builders and bus drivers and dustmen and dossers and nurses and navvies and soldiers and sailors even, and near about everything else one could think of, but never did they resort to whoring or at least not to any appreciable degree; until they had to take refuge from the implosion of the Celtic tiger. This came as a severe shock to the mostly oldish Irish people who ran and worked for the charity that I volunteered for, and an effort was made to ascertain the truth of the matter, three men, myself included were to enter suspected premises, acting as punters and verify this once and for all; I dressed up as some old roué and for the second time in my life entered a whorehouse; I requested and was granted an Irish girl; I of course did nothing, but enquire of her how this situation had occurred; she pointed to the ceiling and mined that we were being bugged; I paid the charge, fifty quid, and gave her the address of the charity.

There was nothing else I could do.

In the past when the republic got into trouble: the thirties, forties, especially the fifties, to a lesser degree the sixties and seventies, to a far greater degree the eighties and early nineties, the first port of call was England; it was near, the same language and suitable to long and short term stays; the core venture was construction and on it depended the pubs, the shops and other sources of Irish employment. Without construction there was nothing: this time the Irish would have to stay inactive.

Time as always passed; my father went into a home that Autumn; he was getting frail, but conditions at home were also declining as Bill was turning into a seedy miserly old man, when I visited him on the thirtieth anniversary of my mother death, he treated me to a cup of tea without sugar and a margarine sandwich: he said he couldn't run to much more due to the times; there was no fire in the house, a constant in the experience of my entire life, and patches of damp were seen on the walls where I never seen damp before. The family was continuing but it had its discards: me disreputable, my father old age, and Bill who somehow had overcome the normal flow of time and was travelling the opposite way to all others. Whenever I went home after that I stayed in a boarding house near my father's nursing home and avoided the rest of them.

In twenty thirteen I was promoted to area welfare supervisor with an executive style car and the salary of a senior site manager, I even had a desk at the head office and had access to a sectary. I was thinking that I hadn't done so bad, when I came across an article in a financial magazine which I sometimes still read, though now just for sentimental reasons which mentioned a major city hotshot , who was none other than the Indian I had helped out with probability calculations years ago as we both trained to be accountants:

he now made more money in a year than I would in three life times.

That June I was called back home as my father was failing.

Chapter 13

Over the few days after the reunion, I pondered my life and visited my father, I also reacquainted myself with the rest of the family; a distant politeness was the order of the day. The sole topic that was discussed was the dire state of the country. Laments and gripes about every aspect of the state of the country were the order of the day amongst the family, and also among the neighbours. Tax, pensions, unemployment, emigration the entire shebang, were discussed in great detail. Nuala's son had emigrated to Australia. Emanon's pension was well below what he had expected; he claimed if he left at thirty three years' service in two thousand and six, he be getting a quarter more, and he had been denied his promised promotion. Muriel and her husband could only pay the interest on the mortgage, and that with a struggle. Bill added to these economic woes by complaining about the weather which was the worst in living memory, but unlike the others he made some stab at an explanation: "there are three unmarried mothers in the parish and at least ten couples living in sin, and God knows how many in that state in the town: did anyone ever consider, that that sort of thing was hardly going to bring good luck".

I had booked two weeks off, something that was easy to do when you had a bit of rank. I moved the second week to a bed and breakfast: tired of the cold attitude of my sister, and spent more time with my father who was having good days and bad days. I noticed as time went by he appeared to be more troubled. In the beginning of the second week I met an old mate of mine who had joined the guards years ago and was like Emanon retired, but unlike Emanon he was visibly scarred: quite noticeably so in fact. I asked him if he was glad to be retired; he said, considering his service, that he was, and he appeared bitter. Over a drink he began to talk; he figured he been used: "there were only two other men taller than me in a class of forty, this is the guards remember, two out of forty; my role was simple: I was there to do the rough work; that's why that little scumbag Peader Mulvey advised me to go into the army: they needed a quota of tough able men to take care of the bad areas, to provide backbone and ultimately to cover for all the boys with the pull; I had to do the worst of work: drugs, gangs, fiercesome violence, while the favoured ones spent their time looking for someone's straying heifer", "well you got promoted to inspector" I replied uncertain of where I was going; "so did those with the pull: look at your Emanon", Emanon didn't have the pull" I protested; "John Willie er sorry Thomas, I be forever grateful to you for what you did to that scumbag Mulvey, but I'm telling you Emanon had the pull; in over thirty plus years: it does come out", "nonsense the Harns are connected to nobody" I replied now somewhat indignant; "a bribe is also a likely enactor of the pull, in fact in my experience more likely; look into it" he said. I left him thinking he'd taken a few too many to the head.

The evening following I came to see my father and Emanon was with him; my father appeared upset. Emanon started back as though guilty of something; I asked if I was interrupting; my father said no, and that he wanted to talk to me. Emanon came to me and took me by the arm and smiling at me, whispered that he wanted to tell me something; I was totally stunned at this approach from a man who barely nodded to me, or threw barbed comments my way for nearly thirty years. "The mind is failing" he whispered to me.

I went past him and sat by my father, thinking that I saw no sign of this, but I couldn't rule it out, as he was ninety one and failing. Emanon sat across the bed from me; my father's eyes were going from one to the other: something was seriously disturbing him: "John I'm going to die soon: and I want to come clean; I have something to tell you"; Emanon leaned across him and said "daddy no, there is no point in rising a row now," "he's entitled to know"; "know what" I asked; suspicion now stirring: my father didn't sound in any way unsound of mind, and Emanon's Damascene turn in manner towards me definitely smelt fishy. My father was tearing up now; a most unusual event: obviously something was affecting him strongly: "I'm not going to my grave, with this on my conscience"; "let him speak if he's you know, er, mistaken: we'll know it" I said to Emanon who now looked desperate. "Daddy listen if there is something to be said at least consult the rest of the family first" said Emanon; my father looked uncertain and seemed to be unsure of what to say,"when will they here," asked my father, "tonight" I answered; "I'm not entirely sure" said Emanon, "I spoke to them on the telephone earlier today" I answered, "oh right" said Emanon woodenly. "Look let him rest and we have a cup of tea" he said. My suspicion was rising all the time; over a cup of tea a transformed friendly Emanon told me the end was near and the mind was going fast: he hadn't wanted me to find out this way, particularly after the debacle, he had made over telling me about my mother's death; this was some admission, after over thirty years of disclaiming any fault in his actions of that time: it informed me there was something very potent being kept hidden. I pretended to accept this and agreed to meet up that evening between half seven and eight with the others. After we left and parted I doubled back, but seen Emanon sitting in his car with the nursing home in view. I withdrew, but rang the doctor later and asked him if he seen any signs of mental deterioration in my father's mental state; none, indeed it was in fact remarkable how alert and with it he was, the doctor told me; he was suffering from progressive heart failure and his kidney and liver function was compromised, but his mind was fine. I was now sure something dubious was afoot. I returned to the nursing by a back route before seven; and soon, over a half an hour early, I saw the family drive up in their cars, and stand in the vestibule having an obviously heavy discussion. I joined them.

Talk about a spectre at a feast: there was shock and perturbation when I walked in; "oh hello" I said pretending to be surprised, "I was doing nothing and thought I'd call a bit early": this got no response bar wary glances between Emanon, Bill and Nuala. I led the way in, checking with the nurse to see if all my father was all right; she said he was. "Right father what did you want to tell me,"

I asked. "Hold it," said Nuala swinging her arms over the bed like a swimmer doing the breaststroke," daddy, nothing you say, can undo the past, and it can only lead to more strife and trouble, where there has already been too much"; "I'll not meet my maker with this on my conscience," said my father tearing up again. "Daddy", now shouted Nuala, "you cannot undo any harm done, all you can do is rise trouble"; "let him speak "I said; Bill stepped forward and brought his arm palm outstretched down between the me and the bed like a referee parting two boxers; "the mind is going: "non compos mentis" I think is the term"; "that's the opinion of someone that blames the unmarried mothers for the bad weather" I responded: becoming angered at these theatrics', " let him speak and we'll judge the sanity of what he says". "We've told you plainly that no good can come out of it; what do you want: more trouble" said Nuala to me Bill and Emanon nodding strongly in agreement. "I want no trouble but he appears troubled, and it's not fair doing this to him at this stage" I replied. "Your uncle George" my father began when he was drowned out in a chorus of shouts; "stop", "hold it" "have a word with the three of us and Muriel alone first". I had had enough: "hold it" I said, "if this continues, I'll call in the staff and then he'll get to speak". "John your uncle George left you money"; I had to think for a minute exactly who Uncle George was: "who" I said; Nuala was grasping her hair as though ready to pull it out; "my brother", "oh right " I said "but he died over forty years ago: didn't he", "that's right and what happened then, can't matter now" jumped in Emanon; "if it can't matter: what's the problem" I asked, now completely at a loss; I used to visit uncle George when I was a child, doing errands and chores for him; he had a house in the town and with two bigger brothers breathing down my neck, I often took refuge there; after a time I found him quite entertaining and interesting: he'd spent his life in England and had travelled a lot, and had many stories about trains and ships and travelling that as a boy I found entertaining. Indeed even when he became sick, the rest of the family seemed to have little to do with him. I thought he left his house to his sister. "He left you twenty five thousand pounds" said my father; "good God" I replied, "and how much was it originally" I asked: completely missing the point. "It was twenty five thousand pounds originally"; then it struck me; the only way I had of computing its current value was my knowledge that a house in London cost five thousand in nineteen seventy: that would make it worth about two million pounds today or nearly three million euro. I was astounded; then I started thinking; what had happened to it, why did the rest wish it to remain unknown; the conclusion wasn't hard to reach. "I take the reason for the secrecy is that my dear brothers and sisters had the benefit of it" I ventured, "yes" answered my father. The cat was among the pigeons. I sat down, "you may as well continue" I told my father. "And what good will it do" said Bill. "We've already discussed that " I said ," if he wants to unburden himself: why shouldn't he". "I was the executor of the will and the money was left in my hands until you were twenty one," went on my father, "I invested it in high yield accounts and you know that interest rates were very high back then. After a couple of years it had accumulated interest and I decided to take a bit out", my father hesitated and I could see Emanon looking daggers at him; "why " I asked, "I went to see Roger Mac Sharry and paid him to get Emanon the pull into the guards"; this was unexpected, "how much" I asked: "two thousand pounds"; this was really unexpected and I took a moment to recover myself; then I had a thought; "how much did you get paid in nineteen seventy two or three when you done this" I asked him: "about twenty five pounds a week", "you gave near two years wages to Mac Sharry, to get a man a job he didn't deserve", "that's how things are done here, I wanted him to stay at home and he was failing at the plastering": Emanon had done a plastering course before going into the police. I was silent for a moment," and what else I prompted" , "and later when he was getting married; I went to the next constituency to Sean Doherty and gave him eight thousand so he'd be made a sergeant", " and how much did you pay to get him promoted to inspector" I asked; "I got that on merit", shouted Emanon. "You got that on merit Emanon, you didn't deserve the two lower, less responsible positions but you think, you did deserve the higher one. That explains to me a lot of what is wrong with this country": silence. A thought occurred to me; "in the same year Emanon got married I asked you for a loan of two thousand pounds, even after paying for Emanon's promotion there must have been money left over", " well there was land for sale, and the farm was too small. The Harns have been on this place since the early nineteenth century; my great grandfather married into it in about eighteen thirty, and the family he married into the Cawleys were there for at least two generations before that; I didn't want to see it all go"; "I take it I paid for the land bought in eighty five" ," yes", "and the other land later" ", yes"; "what did Nuala get", "she got nine thousand when she came home"; "that can be returned" said Nuala sharply; "do you also have a time machine to return me to that time, when it would be some good to me", I asked: silence.

Over the next few days the whole story came out in full. George was the oldest and my father the youngest of a family of five, there were three sisters in between them. George was born about nineteen ten; he was good at school and he got an appointment to train with the post office, which meant in the twenties going to England even with the advent of independence. He qualified as a clerk and did well, becoming a postmaster in London by the end of his twentys; but the war came along and he got conscripted, he managed to put this off for a time, but eventually had to go to war. Starting in the desert, he went to Italy and the south of France, eventually getting decorated, wounded and promoted and ending the war as an acting officer. Upon reflection when put in a position like that: your life relying on other men and theirs relying on you: he probably had little choice but to partake: Irishman though he may have been. He returned to London where he got a management job with the post office, and he bought a couple of properties which were cheap after the war. Which he made a handsome profit on by the sixties. He didn't marry and returned to Ireland in the early sixties. He bought my father some land. He appeared to settle down, and had a job as a truck driver, but with the advent of the troubles in Northern Ireland, his past as an officer came against him; my father apparently had as little to do with him as possible, the rest of the family followed suit with the exception of myself. He had died of cancer in early nineteen seventy, leaving his house to his sister, and his money to me, in the stewardship of my father until I was twenty one. My father, to some degree on the advice of my late uncle who had experience of investments from his work in England, invested this money in long term saver accounts and government bonds which in the seventies and early eighties gave a very good rate of return, almost always in excess of ten percent with little risk; by nineteen seventy three the amount was over thirty thousand; two thousand was taken out to fund Emanon's transition into a policeman, by seventy nine due to the high inflation of the seventies the amount stood over fifty thousand Irish pounds as they then were; eight thousand was taken out to pay for Emanon's promotion, also of interest was a adjoining farm of fifty acres which at that time would transform our barely adequate farm in to a fine farm; in view also here, was that such a farm would facilitate the capacity of Bill to marry and thus continue the line: therefore even though well over forty thousand was available it was reserved for the propagation of the line. I couldn't help but consider if my father had given me that two thousand odd: then there was a solid possibility I'd be married in the locality and conceivably able to produce an heir; something that hayseed Billy was never all that likely to do. Certainly Emanon's son, a teacher in Wexford the other side of the country, or Nuala's sons were not going to provide such a continuance: after Bill, the place would go. By eighty six this money had risen to over eighty thousand in value: seventy was spent on just short of forty acres and some went towards refurbishing the farm: new machinery, land reclamation and such like. The ten odd remaining was invested in government bonds and by the early nineties had doubled: this allowed Nuala to move home without a mortgage: they had sold their house in London on a downturn in the market, and bought a fine house in Ireland on an upturn in the market; a bit of common sense would have avoided all of this: a smaller house here; waiting a while in England. The rest was spent on Bill's last purchase of land. My father had given any other spare cash he had to Muriel. Finally the big one, why: "well, t'was ,like you had a good education, and the times were on the up; I was afraid Emanon would have to go to England; I was the only member of my family not to go; in your mother's family half had to go; and I'm not at all sure what Bat got up to": so Bat's secret wasn't so secret;" I thought them days were passing; Nuala went, but I thought that would be it; you'd have an education; I thought the place would do Bill, and Muriel was a child, so I thought Emanon, the guards, and then Emanon was getting married and needed promotion and well the place wasn't near big enough; and well then you went to England and well, I thought to take care of what was here: that you'd be alright ." "I became ye not us", I said, "I suppose" was my answer.

That was it: I was in the end of the day a discard. He's gone, he's different, he's one of them, not us any longer. My father acted no different than anybody else in Ireland.

"So that shows who's what they should be, and who isn't" I said to no response atoll when it was all over. After a time Nuala spoke "I suppose you'll be bitter and resentful now" ; I thought about that for a while and the thought of what could have transpired if he had given me that two thousand pounds especially bothered me: I'd have got together with Anne; whether it would have worked out or not was another question: her motive was to get finished with London, more than attraction to my charms; but certainly I'd have avoided further involvement with Sid Viscous and co; I'd have avoided jail and many a rough encounter. But in the end of the day what was the point: for one what was done was done, but more significantly my father and siblings were only doing what everybody else was doing in Ireland: you simply didn't get on by playing the straight game; the big question was why did they and others have to; of what value was the Irish state when it continually operated like this, and why could there be no change. I forgave my father.

I returned to England and was recalled at the end of August as my father was at his end; he had picked up after my visit in June, but it was as expected, a temporary reprieve. I attended the funeral and played my expected part in the formalities. The next day I was walking through the town when a wizened old man came up to me; it took me a bit of time to recognise that it was Paddy O Donaghue. The past near fourteen years since he left England had not been good to him or his family; all had gone alright in the beginning, he bought a house without having to rise a mortgage due to the sale of his house in England; he got work and generally it was fairly good, if not as good as was touted; but after two thousand and eight there was nothing: he was virtually fulltime out of work in nearly six years; his wife was now the main support of the family and she was only a waitress. I knew this would get to Paddy. I offered him a place to stay if he came back and the promise that I'd try and get him work, but I told him things had changed drastically for the Irish: those that profiteered among the Irish had killed the goose that laid the golden egg and opportunity for the Irish was limited. He said he just wasn't up to it and I could believe him: the strong, hard man of years ago had departed. He wanted me to help his son; he was twenty seven years old and had done nothing for the last five years. I explained to him what I did: indeed he already knew, the failure of others is music to the ears of the Irish, and spreads like the plague: people that could barely recognise me in the streets could tell one that fellow of the Harns cleans toilets; I said I'd do what I could. His son had gone training at seventeen to be an electrician despite Paddy trying to point him away from the buildings, due to his own experiences. The boom was in full swing, and his mates started to leave after two years when they got a junior certificate as employers were willing to hire them as electricians with this qualification, again despite Paddy's protests he followed his mate's lead. The boom ended and he lost work, and he couldn't even get back into training to finish his course. He was now over five years without work. I told Paddy that without a full qualification it'd be hard to get an electrician's job however able you were: thanks to all the crookedness that had gone on, there had been a major tightening up of the rules. He said he knew this already and all he wanted was any job for him even cleaning toilets. "An electrician cleaning toilets" I said somewhat taken aback. "He's twenty seven, he gets up in the morning about eleven when his mother gets up: she's a waitress and works late; he has the breakfast and sits down all day looking at the television, or playing computer games or with his x-box, some evenings he goes out, and I don't know what he gets up to, but it's not just taking a drink. If he doesn't get off his arse soon he will never be fit to work; so a job as a toilet cleaner is acceptable, indeed as it's fairly light and there is no real pressure, it might be just the ticket for him to start in such a job". I agreed to give him a place to stay and get him a job as a toilet cleaner. I drove up to Dun Laoghire docks with Paddy's son two days later, and headed once again for England.

Chapter 14

Arachnophobia or fear of spiders is a common phobia affecting a very large proportion of people; yet who ever heard of someone being killed or injured by a spider: it is extraordinarily rare even in countries with dangerous spiders and unknown in Ireland; buses often cause death, yet there is no phobia to buses. The genetists explain this by saying that in man's evolutionary past, spiders were a danger for so long that fear of them got hardwired into the genes. Could this be taken as a template for the Irish attitude to those in power or positions of influence? For centuries the Irish were ruled by a foreign power; generally in an abysmal manner. This had led them to have a critical view of those in power, and had this then established itself as a mind-set. Nothing of the good was expected from the boss; competence, honesty and fairness were just not available from that source. All things in nature abhors a vacuum; was the truth any different: an incompetent, dishonest, opportunist was expected in such a position: was it that surprising when one came along to fill it. Decent able men viewing the opprobrium men in the position of power were viewed with would hardly be encouraged to pursue such a position: thus it was left to those who deserved such scorn. A viscous circle was then formed, which constantly renewed itself.

The efforts of the Irish were for naught in such hands: a loser can only succeed by making bigger losers out of everybody else.

I talked a bit to Paddy's son on the way up; he seemed level headed enough of a lad and was willing to accept the meagre position going as necessary to rescue him from a life of uselessness. He went up on the deck to survey his new surroundings. I followed up later as the ship was pulling out of harbour and as the lights of Dublin became more distant, I could not but think of what the purpose of the state was. What other could it have been than to replace the incompetent, unfair foreign power which negated the abilities and efforts of the people with the opposite: a fair competent and honest power which would allow the efforts and abilities of the people to flourish and bear fruit: to see they were granted their due reward. Instead they done the same as the foreigners and worse: they had replaced an unfair oppressive system that was at least recognisable as a foreign tyranny and could be faced, by an unfair oppressive system that was unrecognisable and hidden thus could not be faced. An open tyranny that oppressed, to a criminality that undermined.

I walked up on the deck above the main deck where I saw Paddy's son standing near a door in the shade trying to pick up on the conversations of those nearby as I had done myself, many years ago. From my position above them I could hear their conversation better than someone on the same level as them. Three small men came out shoulders up to make them seem bigger: they sounded as though they were from Athlone. "I'm not doing twelve months in Castlerea ", "I had to give him the knife", "it wasn't meant as rape: I thought the bitch wanted it, I had GBH and meow meow on me, and was off my head, but it wasn't meant as rape": were some of the snatches of conversation I overheard. I remembered three other such men having a similar conversation, the first time I came over to England. I remembered the women talking about the cattle boat. They of the fifties; me of the seventies and Paddy's son of the tens. I looked back at the fading lights of Dublin and for the first time put into words that, about the Irish state that I had always known, but never enunciated. We had been betrayed.